WOOD You Be Mine?

Lovewell Lumberjacks Book 1

Daphne Elliot

Published by Melody Publishing, LLC

Editing by Beth Lawton at VB Edits

Cover design by Enchanting Romance Design

Photography by J. Ashley Converse Photography

Cover Models: Cody Varano and Jordan Bucholz

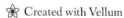 Created with Vellum

This book is dedicated to my husband Craig.
The original lumbersnack and the person who inspires me to
push harder and dig deeper every single day. Thanks for twenty
years, two kids and endless adventures.

Foreword

This book contains a brief description of child neglect and abuse as well as death of a parent (occurs off page). Please be advised.

Chapter 1
Henri

I had a new neighbor.

I had planned to meet her this afternoon, but the day had gotten away from me. According to my mother, who had come by to give her the keys, she arrived late in the afternoon and seemed happy with the place. I should go over and say hello, but it was already after nine, and at the moment, the thought of having to be social made me want to vomit. We had texted a few times, so she had my phone number. If there was something wrong, I'm sure I'd hear about it.

Bobby Redmond had talked me into renting to her at a discounted rate, and since tourist season was wrapping up, it would have likely been empty for a while anyway. And a school principal was an ideal tenant, right? She was probably a sweet older woman who would join my mother's weekly bridge game. Nothing to worry about.

I had built the cabin, and it had been my home for years, so the idea of renting it to strangers always made me cringe. But it was necessary. Money didn't grow on trees. I knew that for a fact, since trees were my livelihood. And my rental properties were an important source of extra income these days.

Paz and I were still trying to get out of some of Dad's more generous contracts—just a few of the messes we were cleaning up—so I wasn't in the position to turn down the money.

My house and the cabin sat on a little more than ten acres and weren't all that close. From what I'd heard, I doubt I'd see her much anyway, especially with the hours I was currently working.

I stretched out on my leather chair—a gift from my mother after I built this house. I had been up since four a.m., when I got a call that there was an issue with one of the trucks up at camp, and every muscle in my body ached.

A steak, a glass of scotch, and a long, hot shower—preferably in that order—were on the agenda tonight. But right now, Rochester was not having it. Instead of curling up beside me, he was whining and pacing in front of my feet. So much for a break. All I wanted was to play today's Wordle and zone out in front of ESPN for a while.

But he would not be denied, so, grumbling, I grabbed a coat and stuffed my bare feet into my boots. I flicked on the floodlights and opened the back door, cursing the damn dog for needing to pee.

Soon, Heathcliff joined him, running in circles and barking. I stepped off the porch so I could holler at them if they went too far. But when I looked down the hill toward the cabin, my heart nearly stopped.

All the lights were on, and the door stood open, smoke billowing out into the cold night.

I didn't think. I just ran. *Fuck, please don't let there be a fire.* My phone was on the kitchen counter, but I didn't turn back for it. Response time up here on the mountain was shit anyway. I needed to get there.

WOOD You Be Mine?

My dogs passed me, sprinting toward the cabin and jumping all over the poor woman on the porch, who was bent over coughing.

"What happened?" I yelled while running full speed down the hill.

Her eyes widened as I skidded to a stop just inches in front of her, nearly taking her out.

I grabbed her by the shoulders. "Are you okay? What's going on? There's a fire extinguisher under the kitchen sink."

She looked at me in a daze and coughed into her elbow. "Calm down, flannel fireman. It's just smoke."

"What the hell is going on?"

"I lit the wood stove, and the cabin filled with smoke."

I heaved a deep breath, peering around her at the cabin. "There isn't a fire?" I was still gripping her shoulders.

"No. Just a lot of smoke. I know it's August, but it's chilly tonight, so I tried to start a fire in the wood stove."

I leaned against the door frame and braced myself, my head spinning and a stitch in my side. *Note to self: run more.*

"You're not in danger?"

She shrugged. "Only of smoke inhalation. And getting tackled by you." She seemed pretty unbothered for someone who'd almost burned to death in my cabin. It was only then that I noticed she was wearing a threadbare T-shirt and no bra. And she was a far cry from the dowdy older woman I'd expected. She was young. And pretty. And thoroughly unimpressed by my attempted heroics.

"Who are you?" she asked.

I stuttered, too transfixed by her very prominent nipples.

"Eyes up here," she said firmly, pointing to her eyes with two fingers and frowning.

"Sorry," I mumbled, staring at my feet. I was absolutely making this worse.

3

She sighed. "I keep making bad first impressions. I'm Alice Watson. And I assume you're my landlord?"

I nodded, still unable to look her in the eye.

"Hmm." She tilted her head and gave me a once-over. "I thought you'd be, you know, old and stuff. Bobby Redmond said you've been around forever and know everything about the town, and I guess I thought you'd be a kindly elderly man."

She took a deep breath, but before I could respond, she kept going.

"Like the kind who keeps Werther's on him at all times and carries a handkerchief? Not, you know." She waved her hands up and down the length of my body wildly, making her breasts jiggle and my pants tighten. "This. Whatever you are."

My brain reeled with her chatter. *Would she ever stop talking?*

"I'm Henri," I said, hand outstretched. "That's Heathcliff over there." I pointed. "And this guy," I scratched at the ears of the dog who was always parked by my right kneecap, "is Rochester."

A smile spread across her face. "Brontë fan?"

I shrugged. "Who isn't? Now let me see what's going on."

I pushed past her into the cabin with my dogs on my heels.

I headed to the corner of the open plan living space and toward the stove. It looked like she'd piled a bunch of newspaper on top of one log. The newspaper was charred but only smoldering, and the log hadn't caught. She clearly had no idea how to build a proper fire.

"Are you out of your fucking mind?" I shouted as I tipped at the waist and ducked my head low to inspect it. "You didn't open the flue."

She looked at me blankly. "I put a log and some newspaper in and lit a match."

I winced, rubbing my temples to keep from tearing her

head off. She could have died of carbon monoxide poisoning. Idiot.

"The flue," I said slowly. "The little hatch that opens the chimney to the world. It's how the smoke gets out. The stove pulls oxygen in from the room to fuel the fire, and then the carbon dioxide is released through the flue up the chimney and outside."

She stared at me with wide, confused eyes, mouth agape, but for once, she was silent.

"When you *don't* open it, the smoke goes back into the house, putting you at risk."

I expected her to apologize. Or at least seem upset. Instead, the most confusing thing happened.

She laughed.

And not a dainty, cute laugh. A full-on leg-slapping, face-splitting belly laugh.

"Of course I almost burn the house down on my first day," she said, wiping tears out of her eyes. She continued to giggle. "God, that is so Alice."

She walked over to the coffee table and pulled out a bright pink Post-it note from the box on top. On it, she scribbled *open flue,* and she then stuck it on the wall next to the woodpile.

"You need a Post-it for that?" I asked, still confused by the woman standing inside my house.

"It never hurts to have a reminder!" she said brightly, hands on her hips. "I didn't realize. It's just so like me to almost burn the place down."

"You didn't burn it down. You just almost caused smoke damage."

"But still. Fuck, I have so much to learn if I'm going to survive winter in Maine."

She was not wrong. And all my protective instincts heated

to a simmer beneath. She was pretty and helpless, and that T-shirt was really thin.

I put a hand on her shoulder but stayed an arm's length away. "How about I teach you how to pack and light the stove and how to adjust it? If you want, I'll write you notes." I chuckled.

"I know you're making fun of me, Brawny Man, but at this point, I'll take all the help I can get." She looked up at me, those hazel eyes tear-filled from her hit of laughter.

My stomach clenched at the vulnerability laced with the good humor in her expression. This woman did something to me that I really did not have the time or energy to unpack.

After I showed her how to stack and manage the wood stove twice, she took a video of me doing it a third time for future reference. By the time I finished, the wall was covered with neatly arranged Post-it notes, detailing the step-by-step process.

We aired the place out and got the stove roaring. She was eyeing me suspiciously as I finished up, adjusting the opening to increase the heat and scratching Heathcliff behind his left ear while he kept his attention locked on our new tenant. The damn dog looked smitten. Bastard. "You are such good boys," she cooed. "I wish I had cute furry buddies to snuggle with and keep me warm."

That statement sent my mind reeling. I was cute and furry; I could keep her very warm. But I said nothing. Just shook the thought from my head and stacked another armload of firewood next to the hearth.

She was right, of course. She probably would not survive the winter here. As much as I didn't want to get involved, my protective instincts were already kicking in. I'd have to keep a close eye on my distracting new tenant.

Chapter 2
Alice

I spent the morning unpacking and making a trip to the hardware store to fix up my new home. The cabin was clean, spacious, and charming. It was so much more than I could have hoped for. The log style home had a green metal roof and a beautiful porch occupied by two rocking chairs. Not to mention windows and rustic charm for miles. Massive mountains surrounded by dense pine forest provided the perfect backdrop for my next chapter.

The interior was open plan, with a large bedroom and a small study. The main area had a wall of windows that faced the mountains. Granted, it was a bit spartan, with simple furniture and a masculine leather sofa, but I could work with that.

Leaving my little bungalow in Havenport behind had been heartbreaking. I'd spent years scraping and saving and painting and scouring all the local antique markets for the perfect finds and making it mine.

But Havenport real estate was in demand, and I had several offers within a day of listing it. And after putting my furniture into storage and packing up what was left in the back of my

Subaru, I was ready to start fresh. Even if I had spent a good part of the drive north yesterday crying.

If things went well, I'd be looking for a cozy house of my own up here soon. I hadn't seen much of the town, but the scenery I had seen so far was beautiful and peaceful. So different from what I was used to, but I craved something new. And Lovewell, Maine, would be the perfect place to start again.

After heaving a load of my new purchases from my trunk, I turned and started for the door, but a few steps in, my heart stopped.

I was face to face with a moose. And not just any moose, but the largest moose to ever walk the earth. A *Guinness Book of World Records* moose. The moosiest moose to ever grow antlers and stroll lazily across my path.

Because this was one big fucking moose. Granted, this was my first moose sighting, but I'd never been so close to a creature of this size in my life. And it was terrifying.

I stood perfectly still, gripping the purple storage tote of throw pillows in my hands tightly. While I had spent the past few minutes admiring the simple beauty of my new home, I had failed to anticipate that it came with killer wildlife. In Havenport, the most dangerous creatures around were the harbor seals that sat on the docks in summertime, looking for snacks from gullible tourists.

I took a breath and tried not to scream. The moose was nonplussed, walking right across my path to the house. Hopefully it would keep moving before it noticed me. Then I could run inside and scream out the terror currently choking me without startling any wildlife and getting myself trampled.

But then it turned its head and snorted, condensation flying out of its massive nostrils. *Gross.* And it made eye contact.

My heart stopped. Its antlers were wider than my car.

Speaking of antlers. Could this giant animal impale me on

WOOD You Be Mine?

them? It would be just my luck if this moose hated teachers. Or yellow, which was the color of my dress. What if yellow was to moose what red was to bulls?

I had spent too much time reading about the history of Maine and not enough time googling safe moose interactions.

I took a small step backward, catching sight of my car in my periphery. If I could just scoot back and get inside, I'd have a small amount of protection. But the trunk was closed, and I had already locked the door. And, of course, my purse was in the house with my keys and phone.

The moose kept me in its sights as I took another gentle step back. My legs shook with the need to flee, but I fought the urge. I had to stay in control.

Breathe. Step. Breathe. Step. When I got close enough to the hood, I slowly lowered the storage tote onto it and climbed up. I backed up against the windshield, wondering whether I'd break my neck if I tried to get on the roof. The moose took a step toward me, snorting like it was going to charge. I reached into the tote in search of a weapon, anything I could use to protect myself, and grabbed the first thing I could find, which happened to be an economy-size box of super tampons. I ripped it open and threw them at the moose one by one, shouting as loud as I could.

The first plastic-wrapped projectile flew into the air and landed two feet from his long, brown, bony legs. Undeterred, I grabbed a handful and threw them as hard as I could. Most missed, but a few bounced off his car-sized antlers, and one hit the top of his head. "Go away, you monster," I shrieked while raining Tampax down on him.

To my horror, he didn't seem fazed. Instead, he regarded me with more interest—if that was interest in his eyes. I'd never studied the expressions of moose before—as I continued to throw Tampax with all my might.

9

"Have you developed a taste for human flesh? I will not be your next victim," I yelled. He ignored my verbal and physical assault, leaning down to munch on long strands of grass as I berated him. When he was satisfied with his snack, he lifted that thick neck and examined me again.

Could he smell my fear? I launched another plastic missile in his direction. This time, I hit his large, wet nose and made him snort. *Oh shit. Now I'd made him mad.*

I'd closed my eyes, praying he wouldn't attack my car, when laughter echoed from nearby.

"What are you doing?"

I slowly opened my eyes and caught sight of something even worse than a moose.

My hot landlord. The grumpy lumberjack with the superiority complex.

He was standing on the road, laughing at me.

"Laugh it up, Brawny Man," I shouted, turning my attention back to the massive beast, only to realize he had lost interest in me. He was meandering back toward the woods as I stood on the hood of my car, clutching an empty cardboard box of feminine hygiene products, still throwing tampons. *Success! I had vanquished my enemy. Take that Maine!*

But now I had to deal with a grumpier and more challenging adversary. Henri.

He wandered closer, hands in his pockets, inspecting the scene unfolding in front of him. My earthly possessions were littering the ground, along with a few dozen feminine hygiene products. Most of which had missed my target, as I had terrible aim, and tampons were not super aerodynamic. And he wasn't alone. His dogs were now sniffing around my winter sweaters, which were also on the ground. "Are you okay?" he asked, his brow furrowed in confusion, but a hint of an amused smile playing on his lips.

"I won! I scared him away," I yelled, pumping my fist. I was panting and sweating, and I didn't even care. Scanning the horizon, I could see his enormous brown body walking toward the forest.

"Clive?"

"That monster has a name?"

He shrugged. "Yeah. He's ancient, by moose standards, and there are a lot of birch trees on this property. They're his favorite snack."

I put my hand over my racing heart, working to slow my breathing.

"He usually takes off when he sees the dogs. And he's not dangerous. Just make loud noises, and he'll go elsewhere."

I swallowed, trying to square my near-death experience with his casual response.

"If anything, climbing on top of your car is probably more dangerous."

I fought the urge to roll my eyes. It wasn't his fault I always managed to look like an idiot in front of him.

He offered me a large hand. "Let me help you down."

I took it, and before I could step off the hood, Henri had effortlessly lifted me up by my waist and gently placed me on the ground. I was not tiny by any stretch of the imagination, so it felt strange to be so effortlessly manhandled.

I stood almost pressed against his chest for a moment while my pulse raced and my cheeks burned. Why did he have to be handsome? And why was he constantly coming to my rescue? After an awkward minute, he took a step back.

"What were you throwing?" he asked, crouching and picking one up off the dirt. "Is this..."

"A tampon," I said coolly, lifting my chin. "Super plus absorbency."

He looked at the object in his hand with disgust. "Probably not an adequate defense in the event of a wildlife attack."

"I improvised." Shrugging, I grabbed it out of his hand. "Thanks for the help."

"My pleasure. Do you want a hand cleaning this up?" He waved an arm at the carnage around us. Even Rochester had a tampon hanging out of his mouth.

"No, thank you," I replied. "I really am a functional adult, I promise." It was bad enough that I was always making a fool of myself in front of this guy. I didn't need his help cleaning up my mess.

He continued to scowl at me, clearly thinking I was some kind of silly damsel in distress. And I certainly was not, thank you very much. Alice Watson could take care of herself. And I would show him and this entire town that very soon.

It had been a crazy first two days, but it would get better. I knew it in my bones. I was on the precipice of some exciting things. This was just the bumpy start.

After staring at me for a few uncomfortable minutes, Henri gave me a small wave and turned in the direction of his house. He whistled, and his dogs followed, leaving me sweaty, confused, and with a huge mess to deal with.

So I did what I always did. I squared my shoulders. Today was a new day, and I was a new Alice. From now on, things would be amazing. So I had a few hiccups. They just helped pave the way for the awesomeness yet to come.

And it was coming. It had to. Before now, I had been stuck —stuck in a job that no longer challenged me, stuck in a town that underestimated me, and stuck in habits and patterns that no longer served me.

It was time to get unstuck. To find myself and get out of the rut that had consumed the last decade of my life. It was a whimsical rut, yes, filled with fresh baked goods and antique furniture and exotic tea I bought on the internet, but a rut, nonetheless.

My sisters, Maeve the driven one and Sylvie the bohemian musician, not only knew who they were and what they wanted to do, but they had met amazing people to share their lives with. They inspired me to get unstuck. So when I was contacted about an opening in Lovewell, Maine, I jumped on it.

Because I may have narrowly escaped death by moose today, and I may have had another run-in with the hot grump, but at least I wasn't stuck anymore.

Chapter 3
Alice

An d things did improve. I got unpacked, did several loads of laundry, organized my closet, and put on my favorite pump-up playlist.

After changing into a fresh dress and swiping on deodorant and lip gloss, I headed into town.

As I made my way through the small, picturesque downtown, I didn't exactly feel like a leader. I needed to get my head on right. Today, I was meeting Superintendent Redmond for the first time and needed to be on my A game. He hired me, sight unseen, two weeks ago, when I decided to completely blow up my life.

As I parked my car and looked at the diner where he had asked me to meet, my stomach sank.

I grabbed my phone and dialed Maeve.

"How was day one?" she asked before I even got a word in.

"Full of excitement. I met a massive beast of a moose. An actual moose, Maeve. It was the size of an elephant with legs taller than my car. It stared me down and snorted gooey moose boogers in my direction. I thought it was going to charge me."

"Holy shit. Where are you? Should I call 911?"

"No. I'm fine now. I chased him off," I chirped.

"How did you get rid of it?"

I twirled a lock of hair, embarrassed by my answer. "Um. I stood on the hood of my car and threw tampons at it."

She guffawed. "Did that actually work?"

"He wandered off, didn't he? And he didn't gore me with his giant antlers. I'm putting this one in the win column."

Maeve giggled on the other end of the phone. "I swear to God, only you, Alice. Jesus."

"Laugh it up. But I can now add *threw tampons at a bull moose named Clive* to my list of life experiences. Can you?"

"Sadly, no. I probably would have run and gotten trampled. You have good instincts."

I opened my mouth to mention Henri—how amused he had been, how sexy he was, and how he had come to my rescue the night before—but clamped it shut before I let any of that slip. Maeve would pounce on those details, and I'd have to spend even more time thinking about him.

"Are you okay?"

"Yup," I said, affecting a chipper tone. "Amazing." I wasn't going to voice my doubts out loud. I was New Alice, who wasn't fighting imposter syndrome—the faceless, nameless enemy that sometimes reared up and threatened to swallow me whole.

"I wish I could be more like you," Maeve said. "Always smiling, always kind. Everyone loves you, where they just tolerate me. You are an optimist and a dreamer, and people like you are rare in this world."

"Yeah. Because we're dumb."

"Not true. For years, I watched as you wasted your potential. As you fought your instincts to dream big and take risks. But now you're out there doing what you want to do. And I

15

miss the shit out of you, but I'm so proud."

I nodded and gulped past the lump in my throat. We had grown really close over the last year. After her fiancé cheated on her three weeks before their wedding, she moved in with me, and we worked through so much of our childhood baggage. We spent so many nights curled up on my couch, watching Hallmark movies and drinking. She was my sister, my best friend, and the person who inspired me to do all of this in the first place.

"I love you."

"I love you too. Now go be your amazing, positive self and rock this meeting. It's day one, and if I know you, you've got a notebook bursting with ideas and endless energy to get started. Don't let anything hold you back."

I hung up and flipped down my visor to check my makeup, feeling more alive than I had in a long time. I had spent my thirty-four years on this planet on autopilot. Waking up every day to do what others wanted while ignoring myself and my needs. Living in a perpetually numb state while I lived the life others expected of me. Day by day, I smiled and nodded and behaved, paralyzed by the need to please those around me.

So I worked my perfectly good job and lived in my perfectly good house and resigned myself to a future where I kept myself wrapped in a protective shell.

But one day, before I could stop myself, I was talking to Superintendent Redmond, accepting the position, and googling Lovewell, Maine.

Because I deserved risks and failure and experiences and a full fucking life.

Why couldn't I be a principal? Why not me?

More and more, I'd realized that being quiet and polite and playing by the rules and waiting my turn like my parents had drilled into me wouldn't get me where I needed to go.

I went to my principal, who had been my mentor for more than ten years, and gave my notice. And to my absolute astonishment, she laughed. Told me I didn't have what it took to be a principal, especially in a struggling school. And that if I quit, I'd never be welcomed back. It had completely rocked my confidence.

But a pep talk from my sister and a very generous offer on my house helped me push through. Despite the response from my principal, I was lucky, and I was grateful. And I would conquer any challenge I found here in Lovewell.

Since I had already humiliated myself twice in front of my hot neighbor, I figured I was due a win. The worst had already happened, so things could only get better from here, right? Outside my car, I squared my shoulders, hitched up my tote bag filled with notes, questions and plans, and headed inside, taking in the small-town Americana spread out in front of me.

I'd come from a small town, but this was a *small* town.

One long Main Street, dotted with pretty trees and people strolling the sidewalks. A lovely park along the river.

The hardware store, a market, and what looked like a bakery and the post office.

A tiny little haven surrounded by forests and bisected by the Pemigewasset River.

"Call me Bobby," Superintendent Redmond, dressed in shorts and a hat covered in fishing flies, insisted as we grabbed a booth in a small but charming diner.

"I'm a river guide in the summer," he explained when I stared. "We have some of the finest fly-fishing in North America here. I'd be happy to take you out sometime."

"Thanks." I fought the urge to cringe. This was certainly the strangest meeting I'd been to in recent memory. But I was saved from voicing an awkward response when we were interrupted by an older waitress wearing a plaid shirt and a scowl.

"Coffee," she barked. Not a question; more of a command.

I flipped over the mug on my paper placemat, and she filled it up, barely acknowledging my existence.

Turning on the charm, I gave her my warmest smile. "Could I trouble you for some almond milk?" I asked.

"No," she replied, turning to give Bobby a big smile and inquiring after his mother's recent hip surgery.

"Don't mind Bernice," Bobby said, flicking three sugar packets and tearing them open in one go. "You're from away." He bit back a smile when he dumped the sugar into his mug and stirred.

I sipped my burned black coffee, pondering what the hell that even meant, then pulled out the binder I'd filled with the faculty assignments and notes.

Bobby's eyes were wide as I started with my list of questions, pausing to take notes and ask follow-ups.

Lovewell Community School was located in a converted mill building across town. It was a K-8 school with about two hundred students. Since I'd taken the position, my inbox had been flooded with emails and spreadsheets regarding budgeting, improvements to the facility, and faculty retention.

"You've done a lot in a short time," Bobby said, taking a bite of what looked to be truly excellent blueberry pie—one that had appeared without being ordered as I went through my list of considerations. Sadly, Bernice hadn't found me deserving of pie, so I just watched as Bobby enjoyed his, which only made me more determined to win her over. "But don't burn out too quickly. This isn't an easy job. And don't get your hopes up. We gave you a one-year contract for a reason."

I chafed at his pessimism. The school had had a difficult time with principals recently, but I was here and ready to give it my all. I intended to succeed. I wasn't yet sure what that looked like, but I wouldn't rest until I'd tackled the long list of issues.

"This is about getting in there and building up morale. The last few years have been difficult. Principal Heron was beloved. When she passed, the entire community was lost. And the string of failed replacements certainly didn't help."

I nodded. Bobby had been very honest on the phone.

"Which is why this is a one-year trial," he said. "To be sure this is the right fit for you and for our faculty and students before we look at a long-term contract. People used to move to our town because the schools were some of the best in the region, but since the mill closed and folks had to move to find jobs, we've lost some excellent teachers. Our statewide test scores have plummeted, too, and we've had to cut the art and music programs down to almost nothing."

I took a long sip of coffee to give myself a moment to think. I knew this was a big job. He hadn't glossed over anything during our phone interviews. This place needed a principal, and I needed a challenge. So here I was, ready to work and terrified of letting everyone, including myself, down.

A woman wandered over, a baby on her hip and a small child playing a game on a tablet.

"Layla," Bobby said, getting up and giving her a kiss on the cheek. "Come meet Alice. She's the new principal at LCS."

The woman, who looked to be in her late twenties, looked up at me sheepishly, clearly hesitant to catch my eye.

"Hello," I said and cooed at the tiny girl in her mom's arms. "She's beautiful."

Layla bounced the baby on her hip and gave me a sad smile.

"Thank you. Heard about the new principal from away. Good luck with the school. Rocky's in first grade this year." She gestured to the boy who was lost in his game.

"I look forward to getting to know your family." I gave her another smile and watched as she slunk away, eyes fixed on her son. Great. Literally everyone here hated me.

Was it my outfit? Maybe the yellow sundress and heels were a little too much, but I'd added a denim jacket because it was freezing here. I'd thought it appropriate for my first meeting with the superintendent, but I hadn't expected him to show up smelling like a river and covered in fishing gear.

Bobby and I talked for another hour or so. Bernice even refilled my coffee once, which I counted as a minor victory. I left her a generous tip. We were going to be friends eventually, so I may as well start now.

As I headed to my car, the weight of my decisions slammed into my chest. Lovewell, Maine, was not what I had expected. This job was not what I had expected.

I hadn't even lived here for twenty-four hours, and I was already tempted to hightail it back to Massachusetts. The hope and badass confidence I'd had when I left Havenport dwindled more by the minute.

So I sat in my car and took in the town. I surveyed the pretty park and the buildings and the people milling about. Absorbed the sense of peace the mountains and the great forests that defined this region and this state exuded. I'd arrived in Lovewell determined to win this place over and make a difference. And I refused to quit.

I took a moment to neatly package all those doubts and store them in the back of my mind. Then I turned the key in the ignition and headed back to my new cabin. I was here, and I would make the most of things. I'd work my butt off and stay true to myself in the process.

WOOD You Be Mine?

The old Alice would have apologized profusely and bent over backward to win every person in town over. The old Alice would have baked cookies for everyone she met, including the fucking moose, to make amends. But Old Alice was dead and gone. And New Alice wouldn't take any more bullshit.

Chapter 4
Henri

Beautiful. She was beautiful.

My neighbor. My tenant. The new principal.

She was beautiful, but that was beside the point.

She had mouthwatering curves. But they were irrelevant.

And her confidence? Irresistible.

None of it mattered. She was off limits.

An outsider.

I had been burned before. I wouldn't make that mistake again.

It was for the best. Why was she always smiling? Every time I ran into her, catastrophe struck, but she kept smiling and joking. What was she so happy about? She was stuck in Lovewell, Maine, for God's sake, not Disneyland.

She was probably the kind of woman who came to town thinking she could help, that she could change things. And she'd inevitably leave after several disappointments. Lovewell had seen a lot of people like her over the years.

Developers from Boston promising to revitalize the town.

Fresh faced social workers and teachers, trying to help without understanding our ways.

And the worst. City people.

People who thought our town was "cute" or "quaint" and tried to reduce us to some bullshit rural stereotype. People who came, took photos for social media, and then left.

So although the vision of her would probably live rent free in my head for the rest of my natural life, I turned my attention back to the task at hand.

I sipped my coffee and studied the floor below me. My office was at the top of a small staircase. The second level had a catwalk that overlooked the inside of our facility.

The place was bustling with employees doing maintenance on equipment, cataloguing and storing tools, and grabbing food from the kitchen, which we kept fully stocked at all times.

Woodsmen tended to be a hungry bunch, and my mother came by daily to restock, usually bringing me a sandwich on her way.

Offices lined the back walls, some of which were now empty, another reminder of what we had once been.

Dad had died a year ago, and my siblings and I had been working nonstop to preserve his legacy and that of the family business my great-grandfather had started with one hundred dollars and a dream in the 1920s.

Like every Monday, I had shit coming at me from all directions. Remy was at camp, supervising the repairs to the road. Paz was dealing with the DEA subpoena we had received recently. And the feller was down, which meant Adele had probably spent the weekend taking it apart, and I would find it in thousands of pieces in her shop.

I called down to Paz, who was pacing the floor with his phone to his ear, probably talking to one of the lawyers. He spent a lot of time on the phone these days. Better him than me. I wasn't exactly known for my diplomacy.

And although we kept our family business clean, drugs were a reality up here. For decades, traffickers had used the private logging roads to run their products in from Canada. Hell, back in the day, my grandfather had turned a blind eye to bootleggers who did the same thing with moonshine.

I hated drugs and hated what they did to our rural communities, but I hated the law up in my business almost as much. We did what we could, and we certainly didn't tolerate any of that shit, but with twelve hundred square miles of wilderness, it was impossible to guarantee nothing ever slipped by.

I'd been a grumpy bastard my entire life. I was happiest out in the woods with my dogs or curled up with a book in front of the fire. As a kid, I'd wanted to be a forester, out in the woods, studying the trees and preserving our forests for future generations. But here I was, running the show, despite my dreams. It was ironic—the guy who hated people managing one hundred people. The guy who wanted nothing more than to be left alone responsible for the town's largest employer.

After Dad died, there was no choice. My siblings were all smart and motivated, but I was the one who'd worked by Dad's side for so many years. I knew every part of the business and the people who had been part of Gagnon Lumber for generations.

But that meant I had to shoulder the weight of responsibility for this company and its employees. And take a hard look at our business and make some truly heart-wrenching decisions.

Dad wanted to grow. And he had a growth-at-any-cost mentality.

Which could explain why he got behind the wheel that day.

He'd always dreamed of Gagnon Lumber becoming the biggest and most successful company in Maine—certainly bigger and better than the Heberts.

And to do that, he overextended himself. He often pulled sixteen-hour days, and he accepted every contract that came our way, even the ones with unfavorable terms and low pay rates.

We pushed. And pushed and pushed. Pushed our bodies and minds, our equipment and the earth for more timber and more profits.

Instead, I inherited a company saddled with debt and shitty contracts in a marketplace that was becoming more competitive by the day.

So I'd worked relentlessly to right the ship, undo the damage, and create something sustainable. Both environmentally and financially.

I had begged my brother Paz to come home and help me run things. He'd been in Portland, doing his thing after getting his MBA. And he, the good man that he was, had sold his condo and was in our office within a week of Dad's passing.

Together, we made a plan that required a lot of difficult choices. Downsizing had been the right decision. We sold off extra equipment, lowered our quotas, turned down new contracts, and renegotiated as many existing contracts as we could.

We capped the hours our guys could work and the size of the load each truck could carry. That cut down on worker burnout as well as accidents and lost timber.

And we eked by. Paz and I forfeited our salaries for the foreseeable future so we could reorganize the company and work to be more efficient and sustainable.

Thank God for my rental properties. I wasn't rich, but damn, those summer rentals helped out a lot.

I closed my eyes and thanked my dad for encouraging me to buy land, to build my own home, and to take an interest in the local real estate market.

And it made sense. Why not build cabins? I had access to the finest timber Maine had to offer and certainly had land to spare. So I built the cabin on my property. Then a house in town came up for sale, and I grabbed it for a steal when the Oswalds retired to South Carolina and wanted to sell quickly.

The river lodge was a bit of a splurge, but the massive timber structure booked out a year in advance, and the interior designer I hired from Portland had outfitted it lavishly enough to justify the insanely high price tag.

I'd be just fine until Gagnon Lumber got back in the black. For now, we had to grind out every dollar.

I ran down to the shop.

"Adele."

My sister emerged from inside a massive rig, wiping her hands on her pants and heading toward the laptop perched on the hood.

She flipped me the bird while typing furiously.

"Good morning, sunshine."

"I'm busy," she replied without taking her attention from the screen. Adele had the kind of God-given talent that most people dreamed of. Since she was a little girl, she had excelled at taking things apart and putting them back together.

My parents couldn't keep her from rewiring toasters and building go-karts from scrap in our backyard. Taking her to work and letting her loose on the machinery was a no-brainer, even when she was young.

She graduated from the University of Maine *summa cum laude* with a degree in mechanical engineering—no surprise there. And there was a time I assumed she'd be designing rockets for NASA, but she was happiest taking apart engines or fixing hydraulics. She ran the shop here, supervising a team of three mechanics and maintaining our massive fleet of vehicles and equipment. The crew was fiercely loyal to her and would work twenty-four hours a day if she asked. She was queen of her kingdom and hated when I got involved.

She finally looked up at me, her dirty blond ponytail sagging to one side. "You look different." Still eyeing me suspiciously, she backed away from her laptop and strode toward me. "Something is off. What happened?"

My sister's ability to take things apart and study them also extended to people. She could read all of us easily. And she loved to mess with us.

"I came down to talk about the feller." I winced. Adele had made it clear from the second she took over down here that she ran her shop and her team, and we did not interfere. She hated when we pulled the big brother rank and questioned her. As CEO, I agreed that leaving her alone and letting her run her side of the business was the best solution for everyone. Because happy Adele meant happy machines that ran smoothly and made us money.

She raised one calculated eyebrow, and I had to resist the urge to protect my genitals. "Working on it. Trying to order parts and log the upgrades to this fucker," she patted the hood of the truck she was working on, "but please interrupt my precisely scheduled workday for another update."

"It's critical."

"I'm aware. So what's up with you? You seem grumpier than usual."

"No reason."

She nodded, slinging a rag over her shoulder and wandering back to her makeshift workstation.

"I'm getting some new diagnostic software," she said,

sipping coffee and still not facing me. "I think it may be time to get Dad's truck."

I sucked in a breath. We had been fighting about this nonstop since Dad passed away a year ago. "No," I said curtly.

She whipped around, the ends of her ponytail smacking against her stony face. "We need answers, and you know it." Adele blamed herself for Dad's accident. But investigators ruled that the truck had rolled because of bad weather and muddy road conditions. There was nothing my sister could have done to prevent what happened that night. And I refused to watch her fall back into depression over something that truly was not her fault.

"We have the answers. The safety investigators' report told us everything."

"Weather and road conditions?" She rolled her eyes and huffed. "Bullshit." After the shock of Dad's death had worn off, we had a lot of questions. Why was he driving a truck that day? It wasn't totally abnormal; he was the kind of guy to roll up his sleeves and help where he was needed. But why did he turn off the main road, which was maintained and generally safer, onto a small side road that was no longer in use?

These questions plagued me every day, but we had the official report. It would do us all good to put all the wild theories out of our heads and accept his absence, even if the acceptance didn't lessen the pain. Continuing his legacy and maintaining the business was hard enough. Watching Adele fall apart again was something none of us could handle.

"He could have been tired—" I snapped my mouth shut when she narrowed her eyes at me.

The look on her face was so cold it could stop a man's heart.

"You can't go down this road again," I said softly, changing tactics. "The truck stays in the junkyard. It's been a year. There are no other answers."

"Why was he on that road, Henri? Why change course and not radio it in? What happened out there?"

I squeezed the bridge of my nose, feeling a headache coming on. Adele and I had this fight at least once a week.

I stood there as she sipped her coffee and continued to type furiously.

"You're dismissed," she said, not bothering to look up.

I hadn't even made it back to my office before Ellen was flagging me down. "Remy's on the radio for you," she said, waving a hand at my office door.

I ran up the stairs and hit the receiver button on my desk.

"Tell me you have good news," I said, praying there were no more issues.

"Good news," he replied. "Road is repaired, the drainage fixed, and trucks are moving."

"Thank Christ."

"No. Thank Gus Hebert. He had all the crews coordinating and called in some friends from Quebec with another grader."

"Motherfucker." The Heberts were assholes. A rival timber family from Lovewell full of liars, cheats, and dicks all around.

Unlike my dad, who took pride in being an honest businessman and helping his community, Gus Hebert's dad, Mitch, was a slimy prick. He consistently ran his employees into the ground, underbid contracts, and cheated subcontractors. His reputation was shit, but the big corporate-owned mills didn't care whether his crews were unsafe or his ethics were bad.

So while the town continued to decline, the Heberts got richer, ignoring our responsibilities to sustainability, constantly violating environmental regulations, and probably doing a bunch of other shady shit I hadn't even thought of.

The Hebert boys all got cars for their sixteenth birthdays,

grew up on a huge estate outside of town, and generally thought their shit didn't stink.

"He's a piece of shit. Things went well today, but that doesn't mean we can trust him."

Remy let out a defeated sigh. "Dude. We all gotta survive out here. Get the massive white pine out of your ass." He was the fun Gagnon. The kind of guy everyone liked the instant they met him. He was funny and extroverted and could get along with anyone. But he was also too trusting and easygoing.

"Just be careful," I warned. "Cooperate for the sake of the road, but nothing else." The Golden Road, the main logging thoroughfare that stretched from Northern Maine to Canada, was privately owned by a collective of four lumber companies. If we didn't work together to maintain it, we would have no business. The four organizations had controlled this section of Maine's forests for decades, and a begrudging partnership had to be preserved.

Thousands of miles of unpaved wilderness roads were no joke. Without the roads, there would be no wood, so we all chipped in to keep things going. But it was an almost impossible task. The Heberts, being the most successful of the lumber companies, had bush planes and a helicopter to check road conditions. Without the same kinds of resources, the rest of us had to depend on the scraps of information they shared.

"He's not all bad," Remy replied.

I tried to suppress a gag. "Whatever. As long as the trucks can run. Just stick with Richard and keep me posted."

"We've got to build up slowly this season. After such a rainy summer, the mud is still a problem, and we can't afford more damage."

"Got it. I'm getting the schedule ready for November. Stop by when you're back, and we can talk through the plan."

Remy's job was one of the most important but also one of

the most difficult and disliked. He managed the camp up north. During the season, he'd stay up there for weeks at a time to oversee everything. His workday sometimes started at two a.m. if he was needed on the crane.

He was the youngest Gagnon, the charming, silly one, but he got the job done. The guys up at camp loved and respected him, even the old-timers. And the wilderness was his playground, as it had been when he was a kid. Remy was a champion athlete, and could probably go pro if he wanted to. I was sure he'd be climbing trees and throwing axes as soon as he got off work today.

His fiancée, Crystal, often stayed with him in the small cabin we'd built. She would cook and help out and sometimes even drive a truck if she had to.

Would Alice be the type of woman who would go up to the woods in the dead of winter for weeks? Give up the creature comforts to live off the land and make a living?

I shook the thoughts from my head. Definitely not. She didn't know how to start a fire in a wood stove or what to do when confronted by a moose. I could only imagine how high-maintenance she was. She wasn't likely the kind of woman who would get what this business meant to our family and the community. Or put up with the long days, the busy season, and the constantly fluctuating prices.

She seemed like she'd go for the corporate type. Some guy who wore a tie and flew to Europe for meetings. A guy who drove an imported luxury car.

Not a fourth-generation logger. Best to just keep working and forget about my too-sexy-for-her-own-good neighbor.

Chapter 5
Alice

I gave myself a full minute to fantasize about walking out the door. Straight into the bright Maine sunshine and not stopping until I hit the ocean. Leaving all of this behind. Until it was nothing more than a strange blur in the recesses of my mind.

But then I lifted my chin and got to work.

Because every day, I was taking teeny tiny baby steps toward becoming the most real version of Alice Watson.

Every day, I tiptoed closer to the woman I wanted to be. Every day, I fought the demons that had held me in place for so long. I fought the disapproving voices of my parents and the pressures of society that threatened to keep me *where I belonged.*

The Lovewell Community School was a work in progress, but the administrative offices were a certified disaster zone. I made a note to ask Superintendent Redmond if a pack of feral raccoons had thrown a rager in here.

Papers, folders, old computers, and broken desk chairs littered the office.

Ancient file cabinets sagged with files that should have been digitized a decade ago, and the ceiling tiles were water stained and cracked.

Instead of a bright and cheery place that welcomed students and families, this resembled the intake department at a poorly run prison.

My own personal office, if you could call a windowless room with cinderblock walls an office, was even worse. Stained carpet, and a 1960s tanker desk with a broken leg that was propped up on a brick. What a loose brick was doing in an elementary school was an even bigger question.

And that was just the tip of the shitberg. There were several open positions, delayed maintenance on the building, and a smaller budget than I could have ever thought possible.

When I had first seen my hiring budget, I almost fainted. How could I run a functional school in a crumbling building with limited staff and rapidly declining state test scores? I wanted to pack up the truck and head straight back to Havenport. To my safe home and my safe job and the small life I had created for myself. My mother's voice echoed in my head, dripping with judgment and derision. My parents had been horrified when I told them I was moving. Not happy for me, not encouraging. Nope, that had never been their style.

Instead, they judged and tutted at every choice I made, condescendingly telling me I would fail and reminding me that they wouldn't be available to "bail me out." They had never once bailed me out, so I was under no delusions that they would start now.

But I had come here in search of growth. A challenge. And by the looks of things, I'd have to stretch myself so far that I might snap.

So I took a series of before photos and got to work, cueing up the girl-power playlist on my phone, plugging in my earbuds, and cranking up the box fan I had bought at the hardware store in town.

Within two hours, my trunk was filled with trash and debris, and I was feeling optimistic. I was sitting on the one decent chair I'd found, scrolling through my phone, in search of a place where I could rent an industrial carpet cleaner, when I heard a light knock on the door.

A man in his late twenties with wavy dark hair and round glasses gave me a wave. "Are you Principal Watson?"

I stood up and straightened my old T-shirt, trying to look as presentable as I could after I'd spent hours cleaning and sweating. "Please call me Alice," I replied, holding out my hand.

"Dylan Markey. Middle school science and temporary vice principal." He looked like a science teacher, from his wild hair to his T-shirt, which featured the periodic table. His voice was deep, and his demeanor was calm. I liked him immediately.

"Ah, yes. I'm thrilled to meet you."

"A bunch of the other staff have been in this week, setting up their classrooms, but you'll meet everyone at the meeting tomorrow."

My first staff meeting was scheduled for the following day. I had been so lost in my demolition derby of the offices that I'd conveniently forgotten that I had to face my staff and find some way to motivate them. Me. The outsider, the idealistic Masshole. I was going to rally this group of exhausted educators? Awesome.

I had read Dylan's bio, and those of the other teachers, on the school website last night while prepping for my first staff meeting. They were a mix of young and veteran teachers who were beloved by students and faculty alike.

"We're really glad you're here," he added awkwardly.

I waved him into the office and pointed to a plastic storage tote filled with files that was the closest thing I had to a chair for guests.

"Things have been so rocky these past few years."

"I'm glad to be here. Just trying to get caught up and ready for next week. My plan is to schedule one-on-ones with everyone, but I'm a big fan of casual drop-ins. Please come by anytime. I want to get to know you and your students."

Dylan laughed. "Be careful what you wish for. There will be a line of teachers at your door tomorrow begging for supplies and new equipment."

I winced. There was so little to go around. Based on the state of the administration offices, I could only imagine what the classrooms lacked. "Since you're the first person to stop by," I said, "tell me what you need this year. How can I best support you in your classroom?"

He scratched his chin, which was covered in a few days' worth of stubble. "Hmm, iPads. And 3D printers. Licenses for a few software programs. To start."

I mentally saw the tally going up in my head. If only math teachers still worked with rulers and protractors and notebook paper like when I was in school.

"But I would settle for dry erase markers and a printer that actually works. The dinosaur in the faculty lounge only works about every other day and occasionally prints in only yellow ink."

I took an orange Post-it off the pad and wrote *printer* on it and stuck it to the wall next to my desk. Maybe I could find a reasonable repair person? Or buy a quality used one? Commercial printers cost as much as small cars, but there had to be some way. I could only imagine how demoralizing it must be for the teachers not to be able to print things for their students.

I looked at the ancient desktop sitting on top of my metal tanker desk. "Do we have IT support?" I smiled hopefully.

Dylan burst out in a fit of laughter, slapping his thigh. "Sorry," he said. "That's just funny. The district has someone who pops in once or twice a year. Other than that, we figure it out ourselves or ask the students. They're better at this stuff than we are."

He wasn't wrong. Most tweens these days were extremely tech savvy. Hmm...maybe we could find a talented kid who could fix the damn printer.

"And office staff?" I asked tentatively. The lack of information about administrative staff in the binder I'd received didn't leave me feeling hopeful about the possibility that the district had front office personnel.

"Lucille Dupont retired at the end of last year. She ran this place. I really don't know how we're going to get by without her."

My heart sank. Of course the seasoned admin had retired. Fuck my life. I took a look at the mountain of files filling my office and wanted to cry. "Any chance she still lives in town?"

"Nope. Headed to Florida a few weeks ago."

Crap. I wrote *find an admin* on a Post-it and stuck it up next to the printer note. I'd have to track her down and see if she'd be willing to at least answer some of my questions. Maybe she'd help me recruit some new office staff if I bribed her with what was left of my savings. Or a kidney.

Dylan blew out a long breath, probably sensing my despair. "We're really happy to have you here, Alice. This community is hurting. We've seen better days, but we have wonderful students who need the support and structure school offers. They need our attention and our time."

I smiled at him, grateful to know his whole heart was in this. The kids. They were why I was here. Why I'd gone into education in the first place. The children of Lovewell deserved so much more than they were getting.

"On the surface, things seem terrible. I get it. But it's not so bad. We've got each other. And trust me, the most important thing is winning over the faculty. We can move mountains if motivated enough."

I thought of the poor first impressions I had made on most of the town. How could I get through to this team? How could I get them on my side and convince them to trust me?

And then it came to me. Food.

"Is there a decent pizza place nearby?" I chewed on my pen.

"I love what you're thinking. Yes, there is. I can call in the order and pick it up before tomorrow's meeting."

"Great. I'll give you my credit card. I'll hit up the diner for coffee and pie, and you pick up pizzas." I mentally scrapped my carefully planned agenda. "I want tomorrow to be informal. I think I want to start my time here by listening, not talking."

Dylan's eyes lit up, and I knew I had said the right thing.

Chapter 6
Henri

Despite every impulse telling me to stay far away from Alice, I couldn't shake the feeling that she might need my help. And given how challenging our first two meetings had been, establishing a more friendly rapport seemed necessary.

I'd meant to come by earlier, but we had run into some mechanical issues, and Adele and I had spent the afternoon fighting about one of the yarders. After several hours, emergency peanut butter M&M's, and almost losing an ear after she threw a wrench at me, we finally got it up and running.

I ran my hand through my hair. I should have stopped home for a shower, but my mother would never forgive me for being inhospitable. I had even managed to remember the loaf of banana bread she had specifically *requested* I deliver to my new neighbor.

When she pressed it into my hands this morning, she'd looked at me pleadingly and told me to be nice. Why my mother insisted I act like Lovewell's welcoming committee was beyond me. Everyone knew my brothers were much more likely to be good company. Me? I enjoyed fresh air and silence. And the only companions I needed were my dogs.

The lights were on, and there was that red hatchback parked out front. Just another reason why this woman was a disaster waiting to happen. That clown car would not make it through a Maine winter.

When I knocked on the door, I could make out the low hum of music, but there were no shuffling feet or responses. After a few minutes, I knocked again, louder this time. And Heathcliff barked.

And then I heard it. A crashing sound. Shit. My heart rate doubled. Was she in trouble? Was she hurt?

I twisted the doorknob. It was unlocked, of course. Jesus. An animal could have gotten in. Bears had been known to enter homes in areas like ours—or worse.

There had been several break-ins this summer. Mostly addicts from up north targeting tourists. Unfortunately, Lovewell was not as safe as it used to be. I pushed the door open, my heart in my throat. I prayed I wouldn't come face to face with a bear or a junkie desperate enough to hurt someone who stood between him and his next fix. The cabin was spacious and bright, with large windows in the back facing the mountains. On a really clear day, one could see all the way to Katahdin.

But right now, the only view was a very naked, very wet woman. Screaming.

The loudest, shrillest, most ear-piercing noise I had ever heard shook the walls of the cabin and made my stomach churn.

I was no stranger to noise, but I could have used my ear protection in this moment.

I dropped the loaf of banana bread as my eyes, without my consent, roamed over the goddess standing in front of me. Long hair, large round breasts, wide hips, and thick thighs. Acres of creamy skin and the kind of curves that rendered me temporarily paralyzed. I should have looked away or turned around. Hell, I should have run out of the cabin and never come back. I'd sell the entire property if I had to. But my paralysis persisted.

"Get out of my house!" she yelled, her voice shaking. "Or I'll call the police." She picked up a frilly pink throw pillow to cover herself, but her eyes were fiery. "You're breaking and entering, motherfucker. And I will prosecute you to the fullest extent of the law."

She was so angry and sexy, and tiny drops of water were pooling on the oak floors beneath her feet. I tried to avert my gaze and ended up studying her toenails, which were turquoise. Cute.

I turned my back to her and crossed my arms. "Go for it, but since it's my house, the police probably won't do much. Just tell Chief Souza I say hi."

She muttered something unintelligible, then the bedroom door slammed.

It was then that I recognized the song playing. "Build Me Up Buttercup." I smiled. It was so Alice.

I looked down and caught sight of my dogs, who were gleefully ripping apart the aluminum foil and feasting on my mom's famous banana bread. Assholes.

Alice reemerged a few minutes later, wrapped in a silky blue robe, her damp hair soaking the fabric on her shoulders.

"I'm sorry I scared you. But the door was unlocked, and I heard a crashing sound."

"That doesn't give you the right to barge in. I knocked over a box and stubbed my toe while I was dancing. The incident hardly warrants breaking and entering."

"You should lock the doors."

She shrugged and let out a haughty huff. "I forgot. I never do it at home...I mean...in Havenport. It's that kind of place, you know? Postcard-perfect small town. Everyone knows everyone, and the crime rate is almost nonexistent."

I couldn't suppress my growl. This woman was totally unprepared. "Lock the damn doors. A bear could walk right in. They've been known to do that."

She rolled her eyes and crossed her arms over her chest, inadvertently pushing up those gorgeous tits. "So far, you're the only grizzly that's broken in."

I ignored her. "And second, we have break-ins and crime just like any other place. This is rural Maine, not wherever the fuck you're from."

"Havenport, Massachusetts."

I snorted. "A Masshole. Figures."

She put her hands on her hips and narrowed her eyes. "I've had a shit day, so you have two choices. Turn your ass around and get out of my house or help me unpack while I make some tea."

After I cleaned up the mess my dogs made enjoying Mom's banana bread, Alice put me to work unpacking the kitchen. It was filled with neatly packed plastic storage bins, each clearly labeled.

She put a pink kettle on the stove and rifled through one of the boxes.

"Here it is," she announced with a proud grin when she produced a wooden box stained a dark coffee color.

I eyed her suspiciously. "What's that?"

"Tea," she said, pulling out a strange spoon thing with holes in it.

"It's loose leaf. I order it from London. I fell in love with Fornam & Mason when I visited earlier this year. It's this wildly overpriced store that sources exotic tea from around the world."

She just kept talking. And I found myself fascinated. By the dimple in her chin, the way her hair was beginning to curl as it dried around her face, and the slight rasp in her voice. She was covered up now, but my mind kept replaying the sight of her naked—the vision was burned into my retinas.

I grumbled the first thing that came to mind. "Oh God, I hope you don't plan to host tea parties in my house."

She set the box down and frowned at me. "I'm paying rent, so I'll do whatever I want. I may not be a lawyer, but I read the lease carefully, and there were no clauses prohibiting the consumption of tea. Or any other hot beverage, for that matter."

From a distance, her eyes were brown, but upon closer inspection, her irises were flecked with gold and green. Hazel. And stormy at the moment.

"Oh Jesus. You're a mouthy one, aren't you?" I said, further inserting my foot into my own mouth. I wasn't a great conversationalist on a good day, but Alice Watson had completely unnerved me. Maybe it was the memory of those glorious breasts. Or the way she clearly took no shit.

"So what if I am?" she challenged. She tapped her chin and studied me. "Let me guess. You're one of those grumpy, closed off mountain men. You probably shower monthly and can count your teeth on one hand."

I laughed. And laughed. She talked too much, but she was funny and had a backbone. I liked it. Her sarcasm and wit were in direct opposition to the silky robe and the throw pillows and the fancy fucking tea.

"Laugh it up, Brawny Man. Because I am having. A. Day." She threw her hands up and paced around the kitchen, abandoning the fancy tea box on the counter. "I swear to God, every single thing in this town, including the goddamn pine trees, hates me. I have never felt so unwelcome in my entire life."

Well, shit. Lovewell was a great place, filled with really good people. But we were wary of outsiders. It was just our way. The number of times we'd been burned over the years made it impossible not to be suspicious.

"So you can growl and grimace and glare at me all you want, buddy. You can bring your pack of feral animals here to intimidate me. You can break in and stare at my naked body. But I'm here to stay."

I fought the urge to smile at her ranting. She really had a head of steam going, and I felt no need to interrupt. Especially because I'd said the wrong thing each and every time I'd encountered her so far. This woman had my brain spinning. I could barely trust myself to stand here quietly, never mind engage.

"And one more thing." She poked me in the chest with her finger, and I stared down at her. She was short, but it wasn't holding her back. "You're welcome."

I raised an eyebrow, willing my quickening heart rate to slow.

She took a step back and crossed her arms. "For the free show. Because let's face it, my boobs are spectacular. Yeah, they're a lot bigger than most, but they're round and bouncy."

My blood pressure skyrocketed, and my face went hot. She wasn't wrong. They were spectacular, just like every other inch of her. And just having this conversation was making me hard. I dropped my gaze and inspected the floor, wishing I'd had the good sense to turn around and go home before I'd opened the damn door.

"I'll consider that my good deed for the day, even though you've been nothing but unwelcoming to me. Why don't you

Daphne Elliot

head home now so you can laugh and roll your eyes at the new person? What is that obnoxious phrase? I'm 'from away'? I'm here now, and you've seen all of me. You're dismissed."

"I'm sorry."

She looked up at me, her eyes wide and her lips pursed.

"I shouldn't have come in like that. I was worried. It really isn't safe to be in the house alone with unlocked doors. We're out in the woods here, and as your landlord, I'd feel a lot better if you would keep the house locked up."

She nodded—a small victory.

"And I'm sorry you've had a hard day. I would offer you my mom's famous banana bread, but my asshole dogs ate it all. The town will come around. Our school needs you, and we all know it."

Her eyes softened, and she dropped her arms to her sides. "Thanks. I appreciate it. I grew up in a small town, but as it turns out, it's nothing like Lovewell. I got myself all psyched up to move here, thinking I'd fit right in, but people are instantly distrustful because I'm 'from away.' What the fuck does that mean? Is that even English?"

"It's just something we say. And maybe insulting grammar isn't the best way to make friends in a new town." I gave her a wink.

Her shoulders slumped. "Sorry. I don't know what has gotten into me. I'm not usually like this. It's been a weird day, and this entire town feels like a Stephen King novel."

"He lives just down the road in Bangor. You can walk right by his house."

"Jesus." She shuddered.

"You can tour the sites he included in his books. There are several companies in the area that host them. The cemetery that inspired *Pet Sematary* is a big hit with the tourists."

Her eyes widened.

44

"Not a big fan of the woods, eh?"

"I love nature, and I thought I would love it here. But the Maine I pictured isn't really matching up with the reality."

The kettle whistled, and I grabbed two mugs from the box and filled them with boiling water.

She sat at the table and methodically measured the tea, then put it in the spoon thingies and mixed them with the water.

She slid one mug my way, and I took a sip. *Shit, that was good.* "Lemme guess. You envisioned lighthouses, friendly townsfolk, lobsters walking down the street doing choreographed songs and dances with a moose or two?"

"Don't even say the word moose to me right now," she snapped. "But yes. I guess I was sort of stereotyping the place."

I scratched my beard. "You grew up in Mass, but you spent summers in Maine. Am I right? Mostly Kennebunk or Wells. And once in a while, you ventured up as far as Boothbay. You've seen the lighthouses, enjoyed fresh lobster, posted shit on social media?"

She sipped her tea and nodded. "Yup. That's pretty much it."

"Well, buckle up, buttercup, because shit is about to get real. But I can help."

She smiled. "Okay, Brawny Man. Educate me on the Mainer ways."

"You should take notes. First, footwear. Always waterproof and always insulated. Second, Deet is your friend. It's mosquito season, and we don't mess around. They're considered the state bird for a reason. Third, you need a truck, or at the very least, a large SUV."

"My car is great in the snow. It has all-wheel drive."

I rolled my eyes. "Think back on this conversation when you're driving up an unpaved mountain road that hasn't been plowed. That car will be spun out and in a snowdrift by Halloween."

Before I knew it, an hour had passed, and Rochester was nudging my leg, ready to go home. *Strange.* I wasn't much of a conversationalist by any stretch of the imagination, especially with people I didn't know. It wasn't like me to sit around chatting. So I took the dog's hint. I rinsed out the mugs and let myself out.

Alice was funny and sharp and had a healthy chip on her shoulder. She was a Masshole who talked too much, but I couldn't help but like her.

Chapter 7
Alice

I nstead of drinking away my sorrows, I settled for a walk. Over the past year, walking had become a necessary part of my day. My sister Sylvie had introduced me to the mental health walk or MHW. She found it on TikTok and spent months talking incessantly about it.

It started with a half mile around my neighborhood. Then I invested in a few pairs of cute leggings and a supportive pair of sneakers and worked my way up to three miles every day. I would walk around town, listen to a podcast or music, say hello to the townsfolk, and just think.

The mental clarity that came with being outside and moving my body led me to being more mindful about my choices. I started to consider what I was really capable of and what I really wanted out of my life instead of remaining in the mental and emotional rut I'd been living in for years.

Walking in Havenport was easy. It was full of gorgeous cobblestone streets and well-kept walking trails, including a path that led to the beach and one that outlined the harbor dotted with coffee shops and parks and public art.

In Lovewell, though, there were few sidewalks, and half the roads weren't even paved. Everywhere I went, I was confronted by views of forest, mountain, lake, or river. But the views were beautiful, and I was embracing the change. There were trails around the cabin, and the road to town had enough of a shoulder that I could walk during daylight.

So although it was getting late, I laced up my sneakers, layered on a fleece jacket, and set off, pushing my pace and trying to suck up as much clean mountain air as I could after two days in that dingy building. I hoped the familiar activity would help me work through all I had learned about the school and inspire me to come up with solutions.

Halfway through Taylor Swift's new album, something wet touched my hand. I jumped back in shock, ready to run, and found myself staring at the snout of a very happy looking, wiggly dog.

I took out my headphones, only to hear the voice I was dreading right behind me.

"What are you doing?" Henri snarled.

I turned around, hands on my hips. My sister Maeve said this was a power pose, and it seemed I unconsciously adopted it whenever Henri was around. I scrutinized him, the lumber-snack who had haunted my dreams since I'd given him a free show the night before.

The kind eyes and empathetic ear were gone. He looked angry and powerful, and God help me, I kind of liked it.

He narrowed his eyes and glowered. He looked especially scruffy today, and his normal baseball cap had been replaced by a navy knit hat. "What are you doing?" he asked again, his tone no less menacing.

"Taking a walk," I replied primly. "Are you familiar with the concept, Brawny? Or do you just stomp around, swinging your axe and scaring the wildlife?"

"It's not safe."

With a small huff, I rolled my eyes. "I'm fine. Thank you for asking. I'm not going deep into the woods or anything. Just getting some fresh air and exercise."

"It's dusk. Forget about the danger of tripping over a tree root. What about animals? Do you even have bear spray?"

"What's bear spray?" I asked before I could stop the question from leaving my mouth.

He squeezed the bridge of his nose. "It's a type of pepper spray you use if a bear is coming at you. It's one of the most effective ways to defend yourself if you insist on hiking in the woods."

His condescending tone made me want to punch him. "Thanks for the tip. I'll be sure to pick some up next time I go to town."

He walked toward me, pointing to the fanny pack I wore slung over one shoulder and across my body. I was thrilled when Maeve had told me that fanny packs were trendy again.

"Do you even have a flashlight?" he asked as I took a few deep, calming breaths, trying to quiet my heart rate. He was dangerously close, and I could see gold flecks in his dark brown eyes. His gaze never wavered, and I could feel his large, masculine presence in every cell in my body. His proximity sent chills down my spine. Another step closer, and he was unzipping my fanny pack and using one finger to move the items inside around while he studied the contents.

"I have lip gloss," I offered weakly, both welcoming and dreading the lecture he would inevitably launch into.

But he didn't respond. Just zipped me back up and whistled for the dogs, who came running out of the brush toward us.

"Well," he said impatiently, "let's get going."

I shook my head. "What?"

"If you insist on clomping around in the woods this late, the dogs and I are coming with you."

"Oh no," I protested, shaking my head. "I need to be alone. This is a mental health walk. I'm supposed to relax, tune into my body, and plan world domination. I can't do that with you hoofing it with me."

"Tough. The boys and I are coming along. We'll be quiet."

I growled under my breath and took off walking toward the tree line, ignoring him. He followed behind me silently, and the dogs panted and ran alongside me, trotting ahead, then circling back to check on us before doing it again.

I turned around. "Why are you being so quiet?"

"You told me to."

"It's weird now. You're just walking behind me like a flannel-clad bodyguard. What are you even doing?"

"Honestly? I'm staring at your ass."

I turned around and threw my hands up. He was impossible. Kind and sweet one minute, and grumpy the next. And sometimes unexpectedly flirty and sexy. All way too much for me to handle in my current state. "Go away, Brawny. I can see my cabin from here. Please, just leave me in peace."

"You asked what I was doing." He shrugged. "Don't ask if you don't want to know. And no, the dogs and I will accompany you back."

My face flushed, and I itched to yell at him—a sensation I was unfamiliar with. I rarely got exasperated by men.

Annoyed? Yes.

Disappointed? Frequently.

But my heart was racing, and I was sweating despite the chill in the air. And I refused to give him the satisfaction of getting to me.

So I started walking again. Backward.

"You're going to hurt yourself," he warned.

Huffing at him *again,* I scowled. I didn't want him staring at my ass. I wasn't ashamed of it. In fact, I liked my round hips and big butt. For the last few years, I'd been slowly making peace with my body. The MHWs helped with that too, but right now, I was itching to fight, even my own tush.

"The view is even better from the front, buttercup. You're not exactly upsetting me."

I turned over my shoulder to check where I was going, then continued on the way I was, arms crossed and glaring.

Was it too much to ask for some time alone with my thoughts? All I wanted was to process my day and get ready for tomorrow.

And here I was, in a staring competition with this grumpy bastard who had the really obnoxious habit of looking at me like he wanted to devour me. It was my own fault, dancing around naked and giving him a show. But he didn't like me, and I didn't like him.

There was no need for him to be so primal about it.

Because that was Henri. Primal. He had caveman energy, and between the sheer size of him and his beard and clothes and old, scuffed up boots, he was the poster child for knock her over the head and drag her back to my cave type.

And I hated that type of man. The arrogance and bristly nature. Hated the "leave me the hell alone" persona and rugged look.

Or at least I thought I did.

Brawny was making me reconsider my penchant for quiet, skinny, nerdy types. The beta men I had dated for years. And who, frankly, had never really satisfied me, sexually or emotionally.

But I didn't have time to think about Henri like that. My goal was to be the best damn principal this town had ever seen.

And to live my life the way I wanted to, judgment and consequences be damned.

I did not want to be distracted and confused by this oaf. That was for sure.

But before I could come up with something quippy to say, it happened.

My heel hit a tree root, and before I knew it, I was falling ass over teakettle down the grassy hill. Followed by a yelling lumberjack and his two barking dogs.

Chapter 8
Henri

I went from admiring those gorgeous curves to carrying them over my shoulder in the span of seconds.

Alice, wearer of rainbow leggings, drinker of fancy tea, and tormentor of my soul, tripped and tumbled right down the hill, screaming all the way.

The dogs reached her first, but in typical fashion, they only licked her face and took turns barking at me to hurry up.

She lay in a heap, covered in dirt, hair a mess, and panting. And as absurd as it sounds, I almost had to adjust my pants. This woman was under my skin in the worst way.

"You okay, buttercup?" I crouched low and inspected her. There was no blood that I could see. Her arm was scraped up, but she was massaging her ankle.

"Did you twist it?"

She nodded, so I gently untied her sneaker and pulled lightly on the heel, trying to ease it off her foot. Before I could remove it, though, she groaned and reached for it again. It was already swelling, so I decided it was best to leave the shoe on.

"Let's get you back to the cabin." I set her foot down as

gingerly as I could. "I can clean those scrapes and look at this ankle."

"I'm fine," she snapped, but her eyes welled with tears. "I can walk." She pulled her knee in and tried to put weight on her foot, but pain radiated across her face with the movement.

The tears fell freely, then. I wanted to wipe them away and hold her. Tell her that shit happened and there was no need to be embarrassed. But I'd probably get a punch in the dick for my trouble, so I abstained.

"I'll carry you back."

"Absolutely not. You can't carry me."

I smiled. "Oh buttercup, you know I haul logs around all day, right?"

She studied her hands. "I weigh a lot." Her voice was small, ashamed. "I don't want to hurt you."

I snorted. "Good one. I assume you're trying to insult me, but I'll be a gentleman and let it slide."

I grabbed her hands and hauled her up so she was balancing on her good foot. Then I slung her over my shoulder and headed back toward the cabin, ignoring her protests.

"This is absurd. Put me down."

"Keep wiggling, buttercup. I enjoy it," I said, resisting the urge to give her ass a quick smack. From what I'd seen from her so far, she was the type who would require a good spanking now and again, and I itched to give it to her.

That shut her up quick as we made it down the hill toward the cabin.

"Keys," I barked.

"It's open," she mumbled over my shoulder.

My eye twitched. "What the fuck, buttercup? I told you to lock the doors." The thought of her vulnerable and in danger made me see red.

"Save it, Brawny. I don't want a lecture right now. Deposit me in my house and leave, please."

I opened the door, and before I could get more than a foot past the threshold, the dogs pushed their way in and sniffed every surface they could reach, making themselves at home. I deposited Alice on the couch and set off to look for ice and a first aid kit.

The bathroom closet was perfectly organized with colored plastic bins, all bearing typed-out labels. I reached to the top shelf to the one labeled *first aid*, but as I did, my attention caught on something in the back.

I pushed the bin full of Band-Aids and Neosporin aside and pulled out a pink box that was labeled *toys*. I unlatched the plastic lid and peered inside, almost passing out in the process. Inside, carefully laid out, were several vibrators, a box of condoms, and a large bottle of lube. I resisted the urge to study them further—my glance revealed one shaped like a V with ridges all over it, and that was enough snooping—and instead put the lid back on and shoved it back where I'd found it.

I cursed myself for leaving my phone in the kitchen. I should have snapped a pic to study later. Research what she likes. For purely scientific purposes, of course.

"Stop it. I can take care of myself," she growled when I stepped out of the bathroom with first aid supplies.

"I think you'd secretly love it if I took care of you." I gave her a wink as I put ice cubes in a plastic bag.

"No, thank you. I prefer men with manners. Not whatever this caveman shit is." She pulled the disinfectant wipe out of my hand and swiped at the scratches on her forearm. "Women don't like to be ordered around and growled at. We prefer evolved men who listen and have nice manners."

Her prim and proper attitude while covered in dirt and scrapes was both absurd and sexy. I kneeled beside her, leaning in until our faces were inches apart and her heaving chest practically brushed mine.

I ran my knuckles down her cheek, slowly continuing to her neck and grazing her collarbone. Her body arched toward me, just slightly, but I'd count it as a victory. I yearned to kiss her, to shut her up and to satisfy my curiosity about what she tasted like.

"Oh buttercup, I think we both know you like my manners just fine," I growled as her breathing sped up. "And if you gave me the chance, I'd show you just how rude I can be."

She pulled back, giving her eyes a dramatic roll. "How about you leave the first aid kit with me and go back to your own house?" She snatched the bag of ice from my hand. "I've got to ice this ankle because school starts in three days, and I've got a to-do list a mile long."

"Anything I can help with?"

"No. Somehow I don't think your grumpy mountain man skill set lines up with my needs."

I raised an eyebrow, and she flipped me the bird, settling back onto the couch with her ice pack.

"What kind of needs are we talking about?"

"Go away, Brawny." My mind flashed to the pink box in the closet. I envisioned grabbing it and using all of those toys on her, discovering which was her favorite, and teasing her for hours.

"I'm clearly distracting you with my damsel in distress energy. Go home and let me wallow in peace. I don't feel like watching you drool over me tonight."

Her drooling comment wasn't far off. I was as bad as my dogs, salivating over the gorgeous treat laid out in front of me. I wanted to stay all night and touch her and taste her and figure out what the fuck those NASA looking sex toys were for. I wanted to lose myself in Alice, in her curves and her sassy attitude, until I could forget about all my troubles. About work and Adele and my dad's accident and the Heberts.

But I didn't have time for a distraction. What I needed was distance. And probably to do a better job of hiding my attraction to her.

I cleared my throat. "I'm not drooling. I'm helping. So you might as well tell me why you feel like a failure."

"You're a therapist now too, Brawny?"

"I told you. I have many talents." I waggled my brows. "I run a company with almost one hundred employees and many temperamental machines. I'm used to listening and helping when I can."

She fussed with the bandages for a few moments and pressed her lips together in contemplation. Probably trying to wait me out with her silent routine. The joke was on her, though, because silence didn't make me uncomfortable. I'd wait here all night if it meant I could help her.

And before I could encourage her to open up again, she burst into tears. The big, messy kind. Not teary eyes, but full-on blubbering and hiccupping sobs.

Stoic was my default setting. I had seen my fair share of shit in my life and could usually deal. But there was one thing I could not abide, and that was a woman crying. My sister Adele knew this, and she used it to her full advantage. Especially when she wanted an insanely expensive tool, and it hadn't changed since I was a kid.

The sight of Alice crying gutted me. I froze, still crouched in front of her, not sure what to do and racking my brain for solutions.

Without any other options, I sat on the couch next to her and pulled her into my chest.

I acted without thought, and it felt right. She fit perfectly. I rested my chin on the top of her head while she sobbed into my shirt. She didn't hug me back, but she stayed tucked in my embrace for a few minutes.

I closed my eyes and soaked in the feel of her for a moment. It had been a long time since I'd held a woman and comforted her. And I liked it more than I should.

After several minutes, she pulled back, sniffling.

"I'm such a failure," she cried. "I swear, I came here with the best of intentions. I work hard. I'm a kind person. And everything is such shit."

I handed her a tissue from the end table, and she blew her nose.

"Everyone hates me. Even the fucking moose."

"Don't worry about Clive. He's wary of newcomers."

"This job is too much," she said after clearing her throat and straightening her shoulders. As hard as she tried to feign composure, her eyes were cast downward and her voice was small. "I feel like I'm drowning every day. Morale is in the toilet. The teachers, the students, even the printer, have given up on me.

"I want to help them all. But the superintendent is more concerned with fly-fishing, and the last principal embezzled a bunch of funds we can never recover."

I considered her confession for a few moments. "There are a few things you need to know about Lovewell," I said, pressing my hands against my thighs and regarding her. "This is a town of survivors. A town built on resilience and struggle."

"Okay. A lot of small towns are."

"True. But things are a bit different here. The town grew in the late nineteenth century, especially after the railroad came in to bring the timber south to Boston. The town rode out the highs and lows, but then the sawmill closed in the late nineties. That devastated the entire region. So much timber manufacturing has moved to China, and things never fully rebounded."

She nodded.

"But seven years ago, the paper company closed too. And that changed everything. Overnight we went from a prosperous, vibrant community to one struggling with unemployment, drug addiction, and neglect."

"That's terrible," she said, her eyes soft with genuine concern.

"And Lovewell lost its identity. The blueberry festival was canceled, people stopped booking weddings locally, and the hotel started to crumble. And year after year, we lost jobs and citizens. And now here we are."

"That explains a lot," she responded, her head tilted thoughtfully.

"The people here are proud, but we're tired. Over the years, so many outsiders have come in with their savior complexes, trying to fix Lovewell. They've either failed outright, like some of the real estate developers, or they've cheated and stolen from the town, like the last school principal."

She twisted her hair up into a ponytail while she listened, and I was momentarily distracted by the curve of her neck, but I continued.

"It's why my siblings and I work so hard. We've had so many offers to sell the company, but keeping things running, keeping our family's legacy and the legacy of this community going, is important to us. It's fucking hard. Trust me. Sometimes it's tempting—the idea of selling and spending my days lying on a beach somewhere, but it's not who I am. And it's not who the citizens of Lovewell are."

"That's very noble of you."

"It's mostly stupid, but thank you for the compliment."

Her tears had dried, and her face was lit up with excitement. "You are amazing," she said, leaning over and giving me a kiss on the cheek. "I have a million ideas right now."

She jumped up off the couch, groaning when she realized how sore her ankle was, and hobbled over to the kitchen table to get a notebook. She asked a few more questions and took some notes, tapping the pen on her chin as she thought. It was absurdly cute. I tried to stay focused on the information she was requesting and not on how incredible it felt to have her lips on my skin.

"I'm not telling you this so you'll pity us," I continued, "but just think about your approach. Because all the smiles and kind words in the world aren't enough to win people over. Listen, observe, and be willing to put in the work."

"I am willing." Her face was earnest—I could see it. The determination in her eyes, the grit in the set of her jaw. I hoped that she could do it. "Slowly, if you follow through, you'll win the town over."

She bit her lip and stared at me. "So tell me, have I won you over, Brawny?"

Chapter 9
Alice

I took Henri's advice, tabling my inner cheerleader and approaching my next staff meeting from a position of listening and learning.

I was on a mission to make a positive impact in Lovewell. Because every single man, woman, and animal I had met in this town—with the exception of Dylan, the friendly science teacher—had greeted me with nothing but hostility since my arrival. And it was not getting easier.

Even Jerome, who owned the service station in town, had eyed me suspiciously when I stopped by to gas up my car. Yes, the town was wary of outsiders, and the last principal had been a complete disaster, but this was out of control.

So I buckled down and put a plan in place. I dragged tables and chairs into the newly decluttered office and propped a massive white board against the wall. I brought in pizza and snacks and purchased a bulk supply of Post-its for suggestions. I dressed casually in hopes of coming off as approachable, welcoming, respectful.

The meeting started off rocky, but I shook it off and stayed focused. Because there were things bigger than my ego and feelings at stake. These kids needed my best. So I sucked it up, plastered a smile on my face, and kept listening.

And it worked. Sort of.

By the end of the day, my board was covered in requests. The kindergarten classroom needed art supplies, the science labs were using twenty-year-old equipment, and the fourth graders were sitting on tiny chairs because there had been no budget to order bigger ones. There were critical needs for textbooks and computers, and the gymnasium roof had a terrible leak that had destroyed the basketball court floor and all the mats.

Turned out, all the teachers at the Lovewell Community School had long wish lists. And big appetites. They destroyed the pizzas and then put away the four blueberry pies I had bought from Bernice. She still eyed me suspiciously, but at least she'd sold me the pies without argument. It was progress.

But as the meeting unfolded, the staff became more and more comfortable. I learned who the leaders were among the faculty. The queen bee was clearly Lydia Huron, a Lovewell grad who had come back to teach second grade after attending college in Boston. She was around my age, with waist-length red hair and a fiery attitude to match. Dylan couldn't seem to keep his eyes off her.

I made a mental note to ask her to go for coffee. Winning her over would be a huge step in the process of creating reciprocal respect and trust with the staff.

But as I listened, I got more than just a shopping list. I learned about the students, their struggles, and the educators who showed up every day to help them.

A run to the liquor store on my way home this afternoon moved up to the top of my personal priority list. Even my finest Darjeeling tea wouldn't cut it after all these revelations.

My clothes were dirty, my feet ached, and my head throbbed.

It was this negative death spiral. The better the school performed, the more money it got. But the schools with the greatest needs were the weak performers. So as test scores dropped, so did state funding for Lovewell schools. And with no resources to improve performance, we didn't have a prayer of changing that any time soon. We were trapped in a catch-22.

My brain spun with ideas interspersed with panic. At the very least, the educational team was solid. Yes, several people pulled double duty, and we needed admin staff, but they were a team, and they were loyal to one another, as well as their students. And hopefully, if I inundated them with loads of compassionate listening and pizza, they would let me lead them.

This school needed a miracle. And I, Alice Watson, was no miracle worker. But a small part of me was excited. This was why I'd come. Because it was hard.

Because I could do hard things.

I stood straighter as I knocked on the door, my ankle throbbing, and the cold air deepening the blush on my cheeks.

Why was I even here?

I steadied the dish in my hand. After the incident while on my walk yesterday, a recalibration was in order. My thoughts and feelings were all decidedly off balance.

I had been on a Henri-themed emotional rollercoaster since arriving in this town. And it was time to get control over my errant thoughts and feelings. Today had been huge. I had made serious progress at school, and it was an important reminder of why I was here. I had a job to do. And I was going to do it my way while taking care of myself and living my life on my terms.

The problem was, Henri made me feel so many different things at once. He was much more than a grumpy landlord. He was funny and gruff and sexy and maybe even sweet? But mostly confusing. Because sweet was my personal downfall.

Too much sweet, and all the resolve I'd built up would crumble around me.

Because I had the terrible habit of falling in love with every man who treated me kindly.

I had a list of daddy issues long enough to fill several psychology textbooks, and trust me, I was working on it. But the chubby middle child inside me still desperately wanted attention and validation.

Sandwiched between my sisters, I'd longed to feel special. Maeve was the perfect overachiever, and Sylvie was the free spirit musician. Both beautiful, both talented, and both sucking up all the attention. Which left me sitting patiently, waiting for someone to notice me.

So Henri was dangerous and distracting. And I needed to stop my brain from running away with romantic fantasies about my hunky landlord. So I was standing on his doorstep, wearing an adorable dress, my hair and makeup freshened up, and holding a lasagna. Because I had to tip the scales back. Show him I was not a damsel in distress and put him firmly back in the neighbor category. Make it clear that I was grateful for his help, but that was all.

After the way he looked at me after he helped me into the cabin and set out to take care of me, the boundaries needed to be firmly established.

Because my brain was spinning out so many possibilities. Many of which involved him removing his shirt. So I had to stop myself. My stupid brain got me in trouble all the time.

Romantic fantasies, grand gestures, heartfelt soliloquies. All the stuff of Hallmark movies but not real life.

And Henri? He was dangerous. He was big and imposing, with just a hint of gentility.

Nope. Not my type. I went for the shy nerds, the academic types. Guys who could discuss poetry but didn't know how to change a tire. Who needed clear instructions and several attempts to find my clit.

Henri's burly mountain man energy was knocking me off my game. I was so jittery after he left last night that I spent the hours staring at the ceiling, studying the grain in the wood logs. I would shut whatever this was down. The flirting, the lingering gazes, the wild fantasies in my brain of those strong hands all over my body.

Shut it down, Alice. Shut. It. Down.

So there I was, dressed up and bearing food. Not because I wanted to see him again. Nope. Not a chance. Because I wanted to say thank you and be the prim and proper principal I knew I could be. To make my brain stop thinking about him and his sexy shoulders and the feel of being tucked up against his broad chest.

I couldn't afford the distraction. Or more heartbreak. Because despite being unexpectedly kind under the gruff exterior, Henri wasn't interested in any more than the way I looked. He couldn't be.

The old Alice would have hidden in the cabin and avoided him forever, while creating vivid fantasies about weddings and hot mountain sex. But the new Alice lived in reality and had a school to save and a town to win over and didn't have time for such nonsense. The new Alice knew that real life never lived up to the fantasies. And that men like Henri, despite his protective streak and fascination with my rack, didn't go for girls like me.

And that was fine.

It was great, actually.

Thank God my life wasn't filled with hunky mountain man distractions.

Because I had a lot to get done.

I knocked again. It really was getting colder every day. I thought longingly about Havenport, where people were still using their boats and wearing shorts in mid-September. At this rate, I'd be breaking out my winter parka next week.

The door finally opened, but instead of Henri or the dogs, I was greeted by a tall woman with dirty blond hair piled on her head in a messy bun.

"Hi." I said, my heart in the pit of my stomach. I had massively misjudged this situation. Did he have a girlfriend? Or a wife? I'd checked for a ring on his finger the day we met—old habits die hard—and hadn't seen one.

Maybe they were one of those modern couples who didn't believe in rings. I could never do that. I would want every woman my man crossed paths with to know to keep her grubby hands off him, thank you very much. But then again, I was possessive and jealous. Probably the opposite of this cool girl standing before me.

She was tall, like supermodel tall, and built like one of those Amazon girls in the *Wonder Woman* movie. Her skin was clear, and her cheeks rosy. I tried to dislike her, but the disarming smile on her face made that almost impossible.

"I just came over to drop this off for Henri. I'm Alice. I'm renting the cabin." I waved vaguely in the direction of my place.

Blondie opened the door wider and smiled. "Alice? You're Alice? Fucking awesome. Come on in."

Before I could make it all the way through the door, the

dogs rushed up to me, tails wagging and clearly excited about the food I brought along.

"Henri," she yelled loudly. "The hot neighbor is here."

He emerged from the kitchen slowly, a dish towel slung over his shoulder, which made him look even sexier. "Alice," he murmured.

"Here," I said, shoving the dish into his hands. "It's lasagna. To say thank you."

Before I could run away in shame, another man walked out of the kitchen. He was tall and broad and looked like a more clean-cut version of Henri.

"This is Alice?" he repeated, his eyes wide with astonishment.

The woman rushed forward and grabbed my hand, shaking it vigorously. "It is such a pleasure to meet you. The entire town is thrilled to have you. The last principal was a disaster."

I nodded, stunned, as she gripped my hand. Then I cleared my throat. "It hasn't exactly felt like people are thrilled," I replied, finally getting my hand back.

She shrugged. "It's the Lovewell way. Most of us make people work for our affection. Not me, though. I'm always desperate for new faces around here, but the rest of them?" She tipped her head at the two men and rolled her eyes.

"Adele, stop being rude. Jeez."

I was overcome by the sheer awkwardness of my introduction to...these people...whomever they were. Never mind the way Heathcliff had his nose stuck up my skirt. Bastard.

And that was my cue. Not only was I shutting down due to my discomfort, but my stupid heart and my stupid brain were feeling extremely upset about Henri's Amazonian girlfriend.

All the more reason to shut it down, Alice. He's taken.

I should have been relieved. I would never, *ever*, think twice about a man who was taken. So this discovery removed him as a possibility for me. Even so, I was regretting all the time I wasted curling my hair into these soft waves.

"Adele, stop gawking at her." Henri sighed. "Alice, please come in."

Adele. Figures she'd have a gorgeous name.

"I don't want to impose," I rushed out. "I just wanted to bring you a lasagna to say thanks for your help." I gave them a forced smile. I hoped it looked friendly, but with my luck, it probably looked maniacal. "You were so helpful," I continued, uncomfortable with the silence.

"How's the ankle?" he asked softly, like he and I were the only two people in the room.

I shrugged. "Better."

Adele looked between the two of us with a huge smile on her face.

"I am so heating this up." Adele snatched the lasagna from Henri's hands. "What temp?" she called over her shoulder, already heading toward the kitchen.

"Um, 375," I replied, turning to leave.

I hadn't made it two steps before a strong hand landed on my shoulder.

"Don't leave." It was a commend. And I'd be damned if my thighs didn't clench.

I paused, reveling in the feel of his touch. *Shut it down. He's taken.*

Turning, I gave Henri a tight smile. "I have a lot of work to do at home. I hope you have a nice evening."

"Stay."

I jolted. I didn't want to like being commanded by him, but my body disagreed.

He dipped his chin and ran a hand through his hair. Then he blew out a long, almost nervous breath. "Let me introduce you. Alice, this is my brother Pascal and my sister Adele."

I shook Pascal's hand and waved at Adele, who was turning on the oven.

"Sister," I ruminated.

Adele's head snapped up. "I hope you didn't think...*ew.*" She gagged. "Gross. Henri is single. Very single. So single we couldn't pay a woman to date him. And trust me, Remy and I have tried."

My face flamed as I searched for a way to remove my foot from my mouth.

"Why don't you stay for a bit?" Henri asked sheepishly. "I had planned on a quiet evening with a book, but my siblings have this habit of showing up when they feel like it. Adele brought a bottle of fancy wine."

The sensible part of my brain was screaming at me to go home and work through my budget spreadsheets. Budget spreadsheets were safe. There was no risk of romanticizing budget spreadsheets and getting my heart broken.

But Henri's house was gorgeous and cozy and warm, and Adele was already pouring the wine.

"Okay. I'll stay."

Chapter 10
Alice

"**W**ait," I said, holding up my glass so Adele could refill it. "Let me get this straight. You cut down trees for a living?"

They all nodded.

"And in your free time, you compete in a sport where you... cut down trees?" I scrunched my nose.

"They're already cut," Adele explained. "We just chop them or climb them or roll them or slice them."

"There are a bunch of events," Pascal patiently explained, "and we all have our specialties." He looked like a thinner, clean-shaven version of Henri, but they could have not been more different. He was outgoing and flirty, and from the looks of things, preferred the current trends versus his brother's rugged, necessary apparel.

"It's pure," Henri said, leaning back in his leather chair and absentmindedly patting Rochester's head. "The skills reflect what this business is all about. What our ancestors did."

"Plus the business is totally different. We use complex machines, computer programs, and science."

"I keep 'em running!" Adele said, lifting her glass.

Pascal shook his head and smirked at her. "It's about quotas, weight, truckloads, and negotiating orders. But timbersports. The real shit. It's a man—"

"Or a woman," Adele interjected.

"Sorry. A *person* with a blade and a log, and that's it. It's about precision, strength, and strategy. We've been doing this since we were kids. Adele was the college champion in the block chop."

Adele flexed her impressive bicep, and I gave her a thumbs-up. I had no earthly idea what a block chop was, but I supported female excellence. She was friendly and, despite her intimidating physique, hilarious. She certainly loved to tease her brothers. It was fun to watch her rile Henri up. I'd bet she was the only person on earth who could get away with speaking to him like that.

They chatted more and more about an upcoming competition and their business, then speculated about a rival lumber company I had never heard of. The rapport between the siblings made me ache for my sisters. We hadn't been very close as kids, but now they were my entire support system. Leaving them behind in Havenport had been difficult, but they had jobs and partners and exciting lives to lead. And I had to strike out on my own.

"I should get home," I said after loading the wineglasses into the dishwasher.

"I'll walk you." Henri jumped out of his chair, the dogs following right behind him.

"No need." I waved him off. The last thing I needed was chivalry. Then I would be tumbling ass first into a crush, and that would cause a lot more pain than a twisted ankle.

Since I'd arrived, Henri was constantly rushing to my rescue. But I was not helpless. In fact, I was far from it. And even more, I was terrified of what his constant rescues were doing to my insides.

I was a romantic at heart. Where Maeve was practical and Sylvie had her head in the clouds, my mind swirled with romantic fantasies. Mostly driven by Disney movies and the Harlequin romance paperbacks I discovered in high school and devoured.

The desire to be chosen, to be worthy, was an unhealthy fixation I was working to break out of.

I was naturally optimistic and hopelessly romantic. After years of romantic disappointments, I could no longer assess whether I genuinely liked a person. Instead, my misguided brain and my bruised heart told me lies, and I discovered I liked men who were willing to date me. Not because of how they treated me or our commonalities.

I became hyper-fixated on how they perceived me and what they wanted from me.

After years of desperately wanting to be worthy and concocting romantic fantasies in my head, I lost objectivity about men. I no longer knew what I liked or didn't like. And that kind of conditioning would take years to undo. So I'd chosen to take a long break from dating to recalibrate and rediscover who I was. New Alice had a lot to accomplish before tackling her lackluster love life.

All the flirting with Henri and the chivalry and the Brawny mountain-man masculinity was lighting the fire of crazy in my brain, but I couldn't let the flames burn out of control.

"I'm walking you home," Henri said, his tone firm. "It's dark, and we both know you have a penchant for tripping and falling." For the second time tonight, it was as though we were the only two people in the room. When Henri focused his attention on me, everything else faded away.

I looked up at his dark, stormy eyes and glared. "I don't

need an escort."

"Tough luck. I can either walk with you, or I can sling you over my shoulder and carry you again."

My face heated as Adele and Pascal exchanged a look. Adele looked positively giddy, and I could only imagine what she thought of me.

"You're being unreasonable," I said, tipping my chin up in challenge but knowing I wouldn't win this fight.

"Humor him," Adele said, grabbing her keys. "He's a grumpy bear. Sometimes you just need to let him go all alpha male. He means well, even if he's unpleasant about it."

She grabbed me by the shoulders and pulled me into a tight hug. She and Pascal had been so kind tonight. It was a welcome departure from the rest of this town. Like maybe we could be friends. The thought made my heart soar.

But then I looked over at Henri, whose jaw was clenched as tight as his fists as he paced near the door, like he couldn't wait to usher me out of his home.

"Let's go," Henri said, opening the door as I was saying goodbye.

We walked in silence down the hill to my cabin. The wind had picked up, and the cool air chilled me to my bones. Henri walked next to me, close but not touching, his masculine presence unnerving me.

About halfway down the hill, he stopped and unbuttoned his flannel shirt, exposing a tight white T-shirt and what looked like intricate tattoos in the moonlight.

He handed it to me without a word.

"Thank you," I said, wrapping it around my shoulders.

He just grunted and kept walking as I tried to keep up.

What was his deal? He was constantly annoyed by my existence, yet he insisted on being an overprotective ass. Not to mention the random and unpredictable flirtation.

Once he'd walked me up the porch steps, I unlocked the door and turned to him. "Good night," I said tersely.

"Thanks for the lasagna," he said from the second porch step. In this position, he was eye level with me.

"Thanks for carrying me home yesterday."

"All in a day's work." He swallowed thickly. "And thanks for hanging out with my family."

I shrugged. "I like them. They're so charming and welcoming. Where did you come from?"

He tipped my chin, and I found myself staring right into those dark eyes. "Very funny. Now get inside safely so I don't have to worry about any more injuries."

"I can take care of myself, Brawny," I said, looking over my shoulder as I walked inside.

"Oh, *I know*," he called over his shoulder, already walking toward his house. "I saw your toy box."

My heart stopped beating. *How did he know about my toys?* Bastard was just trying to mess with me now.

"You're stuck with me, you know," I called out as he and the dogs walked back up the hill to his house. "You, the school, the town. I don't scare easy. No matter how much you growl at me."

I stood in the doorway, watching as he walked back up to his cabin. He was about halfway between his place and mine when I realized I was still wearing his shirt. I could have yelled out and offered it back to him, but I liked it too much. It was big and warm and smelled like pine trees and man. I wrapped it tightly around my body and took a big whiff of his scent.

Then I went back into my little cabin, a sense of satisfaction sinking in. I was here to stay. I would be the best damn principal this town had ever seen. And nothing and no one would stop me, especially the grumpy lumberjack next door.

Chapter 11
Alice

Since Kindergarten, I'd loved the first day of school and all it entailed. The butterflies that took flight in my belly, the clean classrooms ready to welcome young minds, and the unlimited possibilities that awaited. Granted, things had changed since I was a child. Heck, since the previous school year, and I was so nervous I had barely slept the past few nights. But there was something truly inspiring about a new year.

The day had started out strong. The previous day, I had taken a road trip to Bangor and hit up a Staples and a Walmart, and I'd filled my car with supplies. I'd even purchased a smart new tote bag for myself. It was red leather with sturdy handles and lots of pockets.

It was similar to the dozen or so I already owned, but something about this one said, "I'll make you look like a real principal. Someone worthy of respect and admiration." The soft leather and contrast stitching convinced me that it would balance my checkbook, teach all my students, and manage to touch up my roots in the process. This bag would dissolve my anxiety and give me the confidence I needed to walk into a struggling school and fix every problem with ease.

So I bought it, in addition to every crayon, dry erase marker, hole punch, Post-it, and glue stick in the state of Maine.

I visited each classroom first thing, depositing gifts like Santa. Despite our limited budget and suboptimal facility, the teachers had gone all out, decorating and arranging their class-rooms. The effort they put in to welcoming their students and creating engaging learning spaces inspired me to work even harder to find solutions for our budget and crumbling building.

The printer was still a problem, but my gifts seemed to brighten each face as I dropped them off. And I'd purchased extra to stock the supply closet in the main office. My savings would recover eventually.

I would win over my staff, and I wasn't above bribery. I only hoped it would help me get through to this ragtag group of jaded educators.

Making my rounds, I greeted students, parents, and staff, popping into classrooms, and leading the kindergarteners in the Pledge of Allegiance. I soaked in the hustle and bustle and giggles and laughs. And I couldn't help but smile as the kids filed out onto the playground or sat together reading in their classrooms. My to-do list was long, but my heart was full. This had been my dream. It was hard, but I was finally living it.

I was headed back to my office, hoping to get some time with the curriculum plan, when I came face to face with a mountain of a man. He was taller than tall and looked kind of like a sexy Viking from one of those TV shows.

"Hello?" I said sheepishly, wondering what the hell could have happened before 8:40 a.m. to warrant a parent meeting already.

He gave me a broad smile. Shit. I was a sucker for dimples like his.

"Just wanted to introduce myself." He held out a large hand. "Finn Hebert."

The interaction was far friendlier than any I'd had with the citizens of Lovewell—not including Adele. And he undeniably attractive. His polo shirt stretched across his broad chest. A chest that was probably more suited to a fireman of the month calendar than my dingy office. "Principal Alice Watson. You can call me Alice."

"The whole town is so grateful," he said. "This school has had a bad run. And as a parent, I'm glad you're here."

"A parent?"

"Oh yes. My daughter Merry is in second grade." He whipped out a phone and enthusiastically showed me photos of a smiling girl with braids and missing front teeth.

"She's adorable. I can't wait to meet her."

"She's a handful. Don't be afraid to call if she acts up."

"I'm sure that won't be necessary."

"Trust me. Since my divorce, things have been rocky. We're involved parents, and I hope we can be partners. This school has great kids and great teachers, but it needs strong leadership."

Maybe I was reading him wrong, but his tone shifted at the end, like maybe his words were a warning.

"I understand. I've only been here a week, but I'm working hard to support the students in every way I can."

And I meant it. I was here, and I was doing this.

But then the problems started. Seventh graders smoking in the parking lot, a clogged toilet, multiple teachers complaining about their rooms—from the temperature to problems with their computers—and by midafternoon, my office wall was covered in multi-colored Post-its organized by urgency.

I focused on putting out the fires first and organizing the other to-dos into short- and long-term priorities. I needed more bodies—aides, substitutes, and special subject teachers—but had no budget to pay them. I drew a question mark next to the Post-it that said *art*.

Before I could contemplate how to accommodate an art class, there was a knock at my door, and George Harris led two children into my office.

"I'm sorry, Alice. I left my class to deal with this. I gotta get back."

A boy, probably eleven or twelve, with shaggy, unwashed hair and clothing too big for his scrawny body, stood just inside my office door clutching a pink backpack and holding the hand of a small girl.

She had blond curls and a tear-stained face.

I approached them slowly and crouched low, giving them a big smile.

"Hello. My name is Principal Watson. What are your names?"

The girl burst into tears, and the boy put his arm around her. "I'm Tucker. And this is Goldie."

"There's no reason to be scared," I soothed. "I'm here to help. Do you want to sit on my beanbag?" I gestured to the large fuzzy beanbag chair I'd bought in Bangor.

Goldie's eyes lit up, then she darted across the room and plopped into it, the boy perching on one edge.

"Now, can you tell me what happened?"

Goldie buried her head in Tucker's shoulder.

"Rocky Allen stole my sister's backpack and took her lunch," Tucker explained. "And when she started crying, I came over and tried to get it back. She's hungry, and he took her chips and threw them in the trash."

"What about the rest of her lunch?"

"That's all she had," Tucker explained, staring at his feet, his cheeks pink with embarrassment. He flicked his bangs out of his face and grimaced. "We didn't have anything at home, so I bought her a bag of chips at the gas station on our way to school with a few quarters I found."

Nausea rolled in my belly. That was all these kids had to eat? I took a deep breath and surveyed the kids while I worked out a plan. Goldie was tiny for her age and was wearing flip-flops so small her toes curled over the edges.

"I didn't mean to hurt him," Tucker explained. "I was just so mad. I'm not a bully, I swear."

I nodded, my heart in my throat. Fuck. This never got easier.

"Okay," I said, clapping my hands together. "I have more questions, and I'll need to speak to your parents. But right now, I'm hungry. How about we go down to the lunchroom and eat together first? Then we can do the boring stuff."

"The lunchroom is closed."

"Not for me." I grinned and pointed to myself. "Principal, remember?"

"We don't have any money." His eyes were firmly trained on the floor in front of him, that long hair hanging over them.

"Not a problem when you roll with the big boss."

Over Sunbutter and jelly sandwiches, I gleaned more information, and none of it was good. They'd done a few stints in foster care, both together and separated, and they currently lived with a foster family in a place called Mountain Meadows. The shame in his expression when he said it made me want to hug him hard. Tucker was a protective brother and clearly doing his best.

I told him about the programs that would allow them to get lunch and even breakfast if they'd like. All they needed to do was bring home some forms. Tucker did not look convinced, so I assure him that I'd call their foster parent this afternoon to get it all worked out.

Tucker was guarded, but once I got him to open up, it was obvious that he was bright. He spoke lovingly about *Dogman*, his favorite book series, and boasted, his narrow chest puffed slightly, about helping Goldie learn to read. He was a good kid who had reacted poorly, and I'd be following up with the kids' teachers and their parents to get to the bottom of things. But at the moment, I was impressed by him.

Maine had adequate school meals programs, and although the paperwork was a pain in the ass, it was worth it. I mentally added a call to their foster parents to my afternoon to-do list, noting that, depending on how that went, I may have to follow it up with a call to the Offices of Child and Family Services.

I walked them both back to class, my unease still bubbling. I needed an admin and an infusion of cash, and now I needed to make sure Tucker and Goldie ate every day.

Chapter 12
Alice

Sweet mother of Jesus H. Christ.

Had I died and gone to heaven?

Did I get eaten by Clive the moose and ascend already?

Because there was simply no other explanation for what I had stumbled upon.

That man. Wielding an axe.

His body moving like a ballerina on pointe.

The rhythmic flex of muscle.

The powerful swing, each movement precise, not a single breath wasted in the action.

I froze midstep, not making a single sound.

A massive pile of logs littered the ground around him. He would grab one, place it on a tree stump, and then swing the axe, splitting each one perfectly. Then he would neatly stack them in a pile and line up the next log.

He was so precise. Strong.

It felt wrong to watch. Indecent even.

I'd needed fresh air and exercise after day two at school had turned out to be even more exhausting than day one. So I'd thrown on my yoga pants and laced up my sneakers. But I never imagined coming upon a scene like this.

But I was rooted to the spot on the edge of the path, unable to take my eyes off Henri.

But then he stopped. And sweet mother of lumberjack muscles. He took off his flannel shirt, revealing a plain white T-shirt that clung to every rippling muscle. With suspenders.

Yup. Suspenders.

Lord have mercy, I was going to hyperventilate. Never in my life had I considered suspenders on a man. But they were decidedly my new kink.

Between the white T-shirt, the tattoos that covered his arms, and the fucking suspenders, I was sunk.

I was being tortured. How was I expected to resist this?

After spending far too much time gawking, I worked to create a strategy that would hopefully allow me to exit while avoiding detection. My best bet would be to double back toward the woods so he couldn't see me. Then hustle home and straight to my toy box.

But then came a familiar bark.

Shit motherfucker fuck shit.

And Henri turned.

The suspenders looked even hotter from the front. Damn it all; of course they did.

His baseball cap was dirty, and his chest was heaving from exertion. I almost swooned on the spot.

He held his hand up to shield his eyes from the sun. "Alice?"

I gave a small wave, pretending to detangle my earbuds like I'd just pulled them out and noticed him. It was no use. I had been blatantly devouring him with my eyes. And by the heat crawling up my neck, I was sure my face was beet red, making any lie I could come up with useless.

The dogs came charging at me, so I crouched to give them some love, taking advantage of the opportunity to avoid making eye contact with Henri. The more I petted them, the more his gaze bored into me. *God, what was wrong with me?* A hot dude with an axe, and I lose all my dignity on the spot?

In my defense, what I had just witnessed was obscene. Unholy. There had to be some loophole in the empowered woman handbook about chopping wood. Because I only had so much inner strength.

But it begged the question: How could this man be single?

I contemplated this as I petted the dogs and let them nuzzle me. Maybe he was a serial killer? Shockingly, that didn't bother me. Shit, I needed to stop reading so much dark romance.

By the time I stood and brushed the dog hair off my leggings, he was walking toward me, looking as grumpy and hot as ever.

"Come here," he said, gesturing with his meaty paw. Up close he was sweaty and his white T-shirt clung to his sculpted chest, which, if I wasn't mistaken, had a nice dusting of dark hair. My thighs clenched involuntarily, and I stooped low again to pet the dogs, hoping to cover my horny desperation.

"I've got to go. Taking my walk!" I trilled, embarrassed and desperate to extricate myself from this situation.

He gently grabbed my elbow, steering me away from the path.

"Since you were enjoying the show, you might as well learn something useful."

Shit. I had been ogling him like a piece of meat. He may not be my best friend or anything, but he didn't deserve that. He was a person, and I shouldn't be getting all tingly over his shoulders.

"Come on." He grunted. "Those shoes are not ideal, but they'll do."

"For what?"

"Chopping wood, buttercup."

What on earth was he talking about? I held up my hands in surrender. "No, I'm good. Thanks. I should get back to my walk. Good to see you."

"Nope. If you can watch, then you can chop." He steered me over to the stump where he had a log set up.

"I can't."

He turned and regarded me, his arms crossed. Fuck. The crossed arms with the white T-shirt and black suspenders were extremely distracting. There were any number of things I would happily agree to at that moment. Just not manual labor.

"You live in a home heated by a wood stove."

I nodded, studying the vein in one of his biceps.

"How do you think you get the wood to put into the stove to heat the house?"

What was with all the questions? I was in no headspace to engage in logical conversation. I couldn't move past the feeling that *this* had been missing in my life for so long. White-hot lust.

I hadn't experienced this degree of want before. At least that I could remember.

And it was terrifying. How could a woman function day in and day out when her nipples were rock hard and her clit throbbed incessantly?

How did women with hot boyfriends or husbands get out of bed every morning and go about their lives? Did one build up a tolerance to the hotness? Like spicy food or alcohol?

"Sorry," I said, shaking my head to pull myself out of my stupor.

"You chop the wood. That's how you get it." He ambled to the large shed and rummaged around for a few minutes. Then he came back with a small axe gripped in one of his massive hands.

"This should work for you." He held the handle out to me.

"I don't need an axe."

"It's a maul, not an axe. We're not chopping the tree down. We're splitting logs. Different job, different tool."

I nodded, not comprehending a single word. All I could focus on were his full lips and the hint of a grin dancing across his usually stoic face. Did he know how distracted I was? Could he sense that I was barely keeping my clothes on at the moment?

"And since I got a good look in your bathroom closet, I *know* you have no problem using the right tools to get the job done."

Wait, *what?* My lungs seized. Oxygen was no longer needed to sustain me because I was dead. D.E.A.D. Mr. Grumpy Lumberjack just called me out for my sex toys?

Was I embarrassed? Ten thousand percent yes.

Was I a bit turned on? *Yesyesohfuckingyes.*

He held the maul out a little farther, and I took it, avoiding his eyes.

"Don't judge me," I said primly, examining the tool. It was heavy, with a long wooden handle and a thick metal head. I could probably do some damage with this thing.

"I wouldn't dare," he retorted. "Just making an observation."

Ugh. Hot guys were the worst. What gave him the right to comment on something as intimate as those toys? I was a sexually evolved thirty-four-year-old woman living in the goddamn woods where moose outnumbered the eligible single men thirty to one.

Suddenly annoyed, I growled, "Men like you"—I pointed a finger in his direction—"are always threatened by toys." I finally tipped my chin and glowered at him. "You know they get the job done better than you ever could, and your fragile male ego can't handle it."

He seized the handle of the maul, pulling me closer and looking me straight in the eyes. My heart was pounding so hard, Clive the moose could probably hear it on the mountain.

"Let's get one thing straight, buttercup. I am not threatened; I'm intrigued. Big difference."

He took a step back, running his thumbs under the straps of his suspenders, as if to straighten them. It did nothing but ramp up my sexual frustration by at least ten degrees.

"Okay, buttercup." He turned to the stump, as if we'd been having a pleasant conversation about the process of chopping wood. "Time to earn your keep."

He lined up a small log for me.

"The key is how you use your hands. When you start, your left hand should be on the bottom of the handle and your right at the top. While swinging, slide your right down to meet your left."

I shook out my shoulders and lined my hands up.

"When the head hits the wood, both hands will be at the end, giving you maximum momentum for your swing and more power," he explained. "Watch."

He split the log effortlessly, the smaller tool looking tiny in his massive hands.

"Your turn. Let me show you the movement."

He stepped behind me, his chest touching my back and the heat of him soaking through my top. My body went hot at his proximity. He was so big and so powerful. Yet I wasn't scared; I was intrigued.

"Open up your stance." He kicked the instep of my right foot with his boot, maneuvering my legs where he wanted them to go.

"Now slide your right hand down like this." His breath tickled the back of my neck. "It's all about finesse and precision."

He took a step back, giving me some space. "Now try. Give it a swing. But go slow."

I lined it up and swung, coming down over my shoulder and trying to remember to let my hand slide down.

It landed with a thud. I hit the log, but the maul got stuck about halfway down.

"Not bad."

He stepped forward, wiggling it out from where it was wedged and handing it back to me.

"Use your legs more. This takes your full body."

"There's no way I'm splitting this thing, Brawny."

"Just get the technique down, and you can do this whole pile." He gestured to the massive log pile nearby. There were hundreds of them.

"This is only a fraction of what I need for the winter. To make it up here, you need to be willing to get your hands dirty." He took the maul and effortlessly swung it, hitting the spot I had split and cutting it right through.

He tossed the pieces onto the pile and lined up another log.

"Try again. You're going to be really cold in January if you don't learn."

I cocked my head. His holier than thou attitude was really pissing me off. "Can't I just buy firewood?"

"Sure. If you want to be the laughingstock of Lovewell."

I sighed and closed my eyes. It was probably too late for that, but these days, I was far more concerned with the mountains of work at school than making friends with a town full of people who disliked me.

"Trust me," Henri said, as if reading my thoughts, "if I go into the diner tomorrow and brag about how you split wood like a true Mainer, Bernice may finally give you almond milk for your coffee."

I whipped my head around. "She has almond milk?"

"Of course she has almond milk. This is Maine, not Mars. We've got dairy allergies just like the rest of planet earth. She's got almond milk, but you have to earn it."

"You're not making this easy."

"Never said it would be easy, buttercup. Now get to swinging. We gotta get through this pile before sunset."

I had always taken great pride in being an independent woman. I had been on my own since I left home at eighteen, and I happily took out my own trash, shoveled my own snow, and built my own maddeningly complicated Swedish furniture.

But every time I saw Henri, I felt womanly and in need of assistance. Which was not a feeling I enjoyed.

There was something intriguing about the idea of chopping wood so I could stay warm on a cold winter's night. And since he wouldn't be using his stupidly sexy body to keep me warm, I guessed I'd have to take matters into my own hands.

So I grabbed the maul and lined it up like he'd shown me. I took a deep breath and swung, bringing the maul down with all my might.

The log split in two, both pieces tumbling off the stump and landing with thuds on the grass.

I turned to him, enjoying the look of astonishment on his face.

"And that's how we do it in Massachusetts."

Chapter 13
Alice

Stepping inside the Chop Shop was nerve-racking. But it had to be done. The trendy salon occupied a corner spot on Main Street and looked a bit out of place in rural Maine.

But I walked in with my head held high and waved at Becca, the owner. Tall and curvy, with a sleeve of tattoos and an eyebrow ring, she was intimidatingly cool. Earlier in the week, she had stopped by my school office and introduced herself to me. She and her daughter Kali had moved to town after her husband passed away last year.

She had given me her card and invited me to her salon, which had recently opened downtown. Given that she was by far the most welcoming person I had met in Lovewell to date, I took her up on it. Not only did I need a friendly face, but I also needed a trim. The faculty and staff were meeting for happy hour tonight to celebrate surviving the first two weeks of school. It was my first opportunity to socialize since moving here, and I was excited about the chance to bond with my staff.

She threw her arms around me, pulling me into a hug. "Principal Watson. I'm so glad you came!"

"Please call me Alice. And I hope it's okay that I just walked in." Under normal circumstances, I would have made an appointment, but I was already downtown running errands and figured it wouldn't hurt to see if she could fit me in.

She gestured to the empty salon. "Clearly, I'm not busy. Come sit down. First, we have coffee. Tell me all about yourself and whether my kid is being a little shit." She was so disarming and funny. It was impossible not to like her. "And then I'll give you the haircut of your dreams on the house."

"I couldn't possibly." Especially since she was new in town too, and the place was dead on a Saturday afternoon.

She shook her head. "Nope. You spend your days taking care of kids like mine, and you're a new friend, so the first one's free. Corporate policy." She put her hands on her hips and narrowed her eyes good-naturedly.

"Okay," I acquiesced. I got the sense that she was used to getting her way. "Let's start with coffee."

Becca was easy to talk to and a lot of fun. Unlike the rest of Lovewell, she smiled genuinely at me and asked questions about my life like she was interested in knowing me. I told her about Havenport and my sisters. About my old school and why I needed a change.

"My story? It sucks," she said when I shifted topics to her. She ran her hands through her long black hair, ruffling the deep blue streaks, and sighed. "Dan and I were meant to be. Met in our early twenties bartending in Philly. I was going to cosmetology school, and he was a drummer in a moderately popular local grunge band. We fell hard and stayed together.

"We grew up, became responsible adults, and eventually did the very thing we had sworn never to do." She cringed teasingly. "We got married."

7

I feigned a gasp.

"I know, right? So not rock 'n' roll. But we grew and evolved together. And then we had Kali, and things were perfect."

She wiped a tear away, managing to avoid smudging her perfectly applied cat eye. "And then he was gone. Taken away from us suddenly."

I leaned forward and squeezed her hand.

She swallowed thickly and cleared her throat. "And I had to pick up the pieces."

"I'm so sorry."

"Thanks. And now we're starting over. It's only been a year, and it feels like ten. But I'm trying."

"You opened a brand-new business and got your daughter settled—happily, I might add—at a new school. I'd say you're crushing it."

She wiped her tears and let out a laugh. "Hardly. I can't wrap my mind around this place sometimes. Girl, I'm from Philly. And while I have street smarts to spare, I can't for the life of me figure out this mountain living." She shook her head and smiled sardonically. "Too many things that could kill me here. Moose? Bears? The potholes alone could take out a tank, never mind my little Subaru."

I laughed. "Oh I got you beat. My second day here, I stepped out of my car and came face to face with an enormous bull moose in my front yard." Sometimes, when I closed my eyes, I could still see his giant eyes staring right at me.

"No shit?"

"Yup. I was ready to turn around and go home right then. Most days, I still question why I'm here."

"I probably would have gotten in my car and never looked back. I'm terrified of wildlife. But I gotta get over it, right? I'm a Mainer now. Dan grew up here. His mom and dad are wonderful and wanted to downsize, so they sold me the house he grew up in for pennies, and Kali and I moved so we could keep part of him with us while starting over.

"And I needed support. His parents are here, and his brother lives in Orono with his wife and kids. They both teach at the university. I just want Kali to have family."

She set her mug on the counter, and I followed suit.

"That's beautiful."

"It's something." She waved a hand, motioning me over to the shampoo station. "I've got her in every type of therapy and watch her mental health like a hawk. But I'm sure I'm screwing something up terribly anyway."

"I think you're doing great," I said, sitting and lifting my chin so she could drape a smock over me. "And for the record, Kali is not a little shit at school. She is engaged and helpful. You're doing an amazing job."

"Thank you for saying that. Sometimes I need a pep talk." She guided me back and pulled my hair out from behind my neck.

"It's the truth. Trust me. I appreciate how difficult it is to start over." I closed my eyes as she brought the sprayer to my hair. "I'm up to my eyeballs with challenging kids this year, and this town doesn't make it easy for outsiders. I'm always available if you need to talk."

"Thank you. I'm sorry you're having a hard time. This place has seen some hard times, and people here have been burned by outsiders."

"I appreciate that. I just want to make a difference, but it feels impossible between the unwelcoming townsfolk, the underfunded, under-resourced school, and my own lack of experience as a principal. I just worry I'm failing already."

"Don't you see? You're already making a difference just by being here. By showing up every day for this town and these kids. You just can't see it yet, but you will."

"Now who's giving the pep talk?"

"Maybe we give each other pep talks?" She leaned over, eyeing me with a smile.

"I think we're officially friends." I grinned.

A lightbulb went on in my head. Lovewell was a small town. A really small town, where everybody knew everybody. "Do you know anything about the Fournier kids?" I asked. "Goldie is in Kali's class."

"Not much." Becca shook her head. "Goldie doesn't go to the birthday parties, and her mom certainly isn't on the class text chain."

I frowned. "I figured."

"Their mom has been gone for a while. I've heard rumors of addiction issues. I wouldn't be surprised if there was neglect too."

I nodded. I couldn't divulge confidential information about students, but I'd do what I could to gather all the intel available.

"And my mother-in-law knew some of the family. They're all long gone, but they weren't kind people. But those foster parents up in Mountain Meadows?" She shook her head. "I haven't heard good things."

I flinched. Every sense in my body was telling me those kids were not safe. And I had to do something about it. My call to the Office of Child and Family Services was the first step. It would take months to get any oversight, and even then, there was no guarantee that changes would happen. I shuddered at the thought. If my suspicions were correct, there was a lot more going on.

"I'll keep my ear to the ground. See what I can find out."

"Thanks." I gave her a small smile. "Just trying to get to know all my students."

She arched an eyebrow and smirked. "Sure you are. They're lucky to have you looking out for them."

"Now let's talk about this hair." Becca's hands moved through my long, mouse brown strands. "What are you thinking?"

After she washed my hair, she guided me to her workstation and combed through my wet hair.

I shrugged. "Not sure."

"Judging by your lemon print skirt and purple nails, I'd say you have awesome style and need hair to match."

I blushed at the compliment. I was secretly thrilled, but I wasn't the type of girl who usually stood out.

But a few months ago, I started to branch out little by little. It started with going to the nail salon, and instead of my usual light pink, I chose a deep turquoise. For a girl who was raised to believe that I had to wake up every single day and blend in, it felt like rebellion. And I liked it.

And it might have started with turquoise nails, but it didn't end there.

Next, I booked a vacation. Alone. I had always dreamed of traveling to London. I had been fascinated by the castles and palaces and the history and the literature. So I booked a ticket, and during April school vacation, I flew across the Atlantic all by my damn self.

April in London can be quite dreary and rainy, but I packed a raincoat and didn't care. While I was there, I bought a pair of turquoise Wellington boots that I wore every single day as I splashed along the sidewalks, taking in all the sights, riding the tube, eating fish and chips, and spending hours upon hours upon hours in the world's finest museums.

And I realized something. There's nothing wrong with taking a solo vacation. I spent my time getting lost in beautiful exhibits and museums and wandering around a foreign city, soaking up the feeling every single day.

Before that trip, I had been sitting in life's waiting room, making excuse after excuse for why I wasn't really living. And once I realized that. There was no going back.

Soon I'd pushed all the black and navy to the back of my closet and was wearing cute vintage-style dresses and colorful accessories that made me feel like *me*. And if a skirt made my ass look big? So be it. My ass was big, and I liked it anyway.

Before I moved to Lovewell, I donated all my boring black clothes—the sensible pants and the sweater sets and the long jackets.

I went to Jeanius Bar in town and spent a small fortune on skinny jeans and cute tops and colorful skirts. Then I went online and found Modcloth, a site that sells size-inclusive vintage-style clothing. I ordered more sundresses and circle skirts and cropped cardigans and beautiful, wild clothes than I knew what to do with.

Things I would have never dared to wear before. Never dared to even consider.

Things I felt my body didn't deserve.

And I looked damn good. I looked like a sexy pinup instead of a sad girl who sat around waiting for her life to actually start.

With the resurfacing of those memories also came that same rebellious urge. "I've always wanted to be blond," I blurted out.

Becca paused, her focus on where my hair was still in her hands. I cringed. I shouldn't have said that to a hair stylist. It was the kind of thought I kept to myself most of the time. But dammit, I was curious. And although I didn't know Becca well, I'd already come to trust her. And if anyone could give me awesome hair, it was her.

"That's brilliant," she said, continuing to run her fingers through my strands, studying my hair carefully. "You would look so good. I'm thinking honey blond with lowlights and a few more layers around the face." She walked around the chair, examining me from multiple angles. "Yes. Yes. The more I think about it, the more I love it."

"Really?"

"Fuck yeah. You're going to be one hot blonde. And fair warning: I tend to get obsessed with hair, so I will literally harass you to death if you don't just let me do this now."

"Um. Okay?"

Becca did a fist pump and danced over to the color station. "You're going to look smoking hot, Alice," she said over her shoulder, mixing the color. "Too bad it will be wasted on this podunk town."

My mind wandered to my grumpy neighbor. Maybe this makeover wouldn't be totally wasted after all.

Chapter 14
Henri

Friday night. Just me, my dogs, a cold beer, and pages and pages of financial documents to sort through. This was usually Paz's department, but since I was the only one who could read Dad's handwriting, deciphering the random notes, scribbles and handwritten agreements usually fell to me.

And something was off. There were payments that didn't line up and missing inventory. Chrissie, our bookkeeper, usually kept meticulous records, but from the looks of things, Dad had made some agreements off the books. Of course, Dad had always gone a thousand miles an hour without stopping to dot any i's or cross any t's, so I suppose the discovery wasn't a total shock.

But the financial confusion piled on top of the constant doubt I had about Dad's death. Adele wasn't wrong. Things didn't add up. But the constant disagreements surrounding it were exhausting. Mom, Paz, Remy, and Adele argued over their differing theories regularly. And I was stuck in the middle, mediating and trying to keep everyone calm.

Fighting and screaming would not bring him back. The best way to honor his life and memory was to save the family business. So I put everything I had into that mission and did my best to keep everyone busy and distracted.

As a result, things were progressing with the road repairs, bills were being paid, and the winter season was on the horizon. Next week, I'd head up to camp to attend a series of meetings with our forestry consultant. At times like these, I wished we could still afford to keep a pilot on staff. Walt, one of my dad's old buddies, had retired a few years ago, and we'd sold the bush plane to cover expenses.

I must have been seven or eight the first time I went up with my dad and Walt. We took off in the floatplane from Lake Millinocket and soared above thousands of acres of untouched forests. Places with no roads, just endless trees and wildlife stretching as far as the eye could see.

My dad would talk about the beauty and power of the trees. Our responsibility to care for this land. How these trees had built our family business and fed multiple generations of Gagnons. In those moments, even as a little boy, I swore I would do everything in my power to protect this land, to raise my own children to value and respect it.

But pilots and planes were expenses we'd save for another year, when things were steadier again. Right now, we were surviving season to season, keeping our people paid and logs moving to the mills.

I was just settling in my chair near the woodstove when my phone beeped on the side table next to me. I glanced at the screen, expecting a meme from Remy, but instead saw a text from Adele. I grabbed the phone. Adele could handle herself—hell, I'd seen her in action more times than I could count—but it didn't stop my big brother instincts from kicking in.

WOOD You Be Mine?

> You should come down to the Moose. Fun night.

I rolled my eyes. My siblings were far more social than I was. Most weekends, they'd happily partake in Lovewell's nightlife. Which consisted of one bar. A dive called Duck, Duck, Moose.

Remy and Crystal would be there dancing, and Adele would be set up at the dartboards, hustling most of the locals out of their paychecks. But I had cold beer and a comfy chair here. Why would I drag my ass all the way into town?

> Your girl is here. Come get her.

> I don't have a girl.

> My mistake. Your tenant, Alice, is here, and she's a bit tipsy. Finn Hebert is making her laugh.

I was out of my chair and looking for my boots in the span of a heartbeat. The thought of a Hebert flirting with Alice made my vision go red. Those assholes thought they were entitled to everything and everyone in this town. But not tonight.

Shit. I guess I was going to the Moose.

I jumped out of my skin when I saw her. She was all blond hair and pale skin and womanly curves, wearing one of her frilly dresses. It was sky blue with white and yellow flowers. It dipped low in front in a way that was probably intended to be demure, but at the moment afforded me an excellent view of her ample cleavage. All she had over it was a flimsy little sweater. And it did nothing to keep Finn away from her.

I stomped over to her, furious and confused. I should have turned around. I had no business being here. I had no business with Alice.

But I kept going. Because I had more rage than sense.

"What are you doing here?" The words were harsher than I meant them to be.

Alice turned toward me slowly, eyeing me up and down before frowning.

"It's great to see you too, neighbor." She tipped her head to the side and gave me a lovey smile. Tipsy was right.

We'd had fun chopping wood together. It had been damn near impossible to keep my hands off her, especially in those stretchy yoga pants, but I'd survived the afternoon. And she had glowed with the exertion and pride. Maybe it was the stress relief, or maybe the desire to do something on her own, but either way, she'd gotten all flushed and adorable. And it had taken every ounce of willpower I had not to kiss her right there in my yard. Since then, I had devoted hours to reliving that moment: The joy in her eyes when she split the log. Her pink cheeks and bright eyes. Those damn kissable pink lips.

But I had more important things to focus on at the moment, like getting this asshole far away from her. "Hebert," I said, not taking my eyes off Alice's face.

"Always good to see you, Henri," Finn said, clapping me on the back. "Let me get you a beer."

"Fuck off," I replied.

He ignored me and turned to get the bartender's attention, leaving me locked in a staring contest with Alice.

"What are you doing?" I asked again, clenching my fists.

"I came out with my team to celebrate a successful start to the school year. Not that it's any of your business." She twirled a lock of hair around her finger. "I have every right to be here. Last time I checked, I'm a citizen of Lovewell and a member of this community. So even I, the terrible, idealistic Masshole, get to drink at the local dive."

Shit. As usual, my grumpy scowl had given her the wrong idea. But before I could correct her assumptions, a group of people crowded the bar, led by a woman with striking red hair.

"Henri!" the redhead exclaimed, throwing her arms around me. "Do you want a moxie bomb?" She signaled to the bartender, who shook his head at her. Jim was older than dirt and meaner than a trash can full of raccoons, but he had served the population of Lovewell for years. Since his wife passed, he spent all his time tending bar and scowling at people who were having a good time. But he mixed a hell of a drink.

I shook my head. I would rather chug battery acid than a shot of Jägermeister dropped into a glass of Moxie. But I watched as Alice and the other teachers gleefully partook.

"Do you know Lydia?" Alice said, tipping her chin at the redhead.

Ah. Lydia. How could I forget Paz's high school crush? She had certainly grown up since I saw her last. I looked through the crowd for my brother, but he was chatting with a brunette on the other side of the bar. Typical Paz.

He was the friendly, charming one, after all. The good brother.

I was the asshole.

"Thanks for giving our principal a place to live," Lydia said, holding her empty glass and grinning. "We're so happy she's here. She showed up on the first day of school with bags of classroom supplies like Santa and personally plunged a clogged toilet." We both watched as Alice was pulled into a conversation with her colleagues.

She narrowed her eyes and leaned closer, whispering into my ear. "Don't scare her away. We need her."

I pulled back and scowled. My siblings had said the same

thing. Since when did I scare people away? I kept to myself and minded my own business, unlike the busybodies in this town. But I couldn't help that I was confused and unnerved by her presence.

"Don't play dumb, Henri." She leaned in again and quirked a brow. "I see what's going on. You're here, which means you're interested. But you're acting grumpy and aloof, which means you can't identify and process the feelings you're having."

"You don't know what you're talking about, Lydia."

"Oh, but I do. I'm in therapy to avoid falling in love with your type again. But enough about me. Either show her a good time or go the fuck home." She turned on her heel then and joined the group of teachers—including Alice—who had moved to the cluster of high-top tables.

I picked my jaw up off the floor. Was I that transparent?

I had been restless and on edge since Alice showed up; that was true. Things hadn't been right in my head since I saved her from smoke inhalation, and my thoughts had only gotten more jumbled after I saw her naked and carried her down the hill with a twisted ankle.

I was attracted to her, obviously. But attraction had never stopped me from getting shit done before. The world was filled with pretty women. So why did this one have me tied up in knots?

I sipped my beer as I watched her chat with the teachers and take selfies with several of them. She claimed the townspeople hated her, but she'd quickly been pulled into the fold.

Paz and I grabbed a booth when one opened up, and I ordered a burger, keeping an eye on Alice. I hadn't pegged her for a party girl, but she sure was letting loose.

"Wanna tell me what's going on?" Paz asked, stealing the pickle off my plate.

"Nothing." I shrugged. "Work is crazy. We've got our hands

full gearing up for the winter season and getting the roads repaired."

He nodded. "Still in denial, I see, big brother."

Before I could respond, a large, dumb shadow crossed over our table. Ugh. I hated those fuckers here, in our bar. They thought they were better than everyone else and had more money than sense. Why didn't they just build their own town and leave us be?

"Do you need something?" Paz bit out.

"You're protective of our new school principal, Gagnon," Finn said, crossing his arms.

Just the sound of her name from his mouth filled me with the overwhelming desire to punch him in the face. He was a big dude, but so was I. It would be a fair fight. "Fuck off. Shouldn't you go home to your daughter?"

"She's at my mom's tonight. Thought I'd blow off some steam. Maybe get laid. But then you came barreling in here like a bull moose and cock blocked me."

I stood up, knocking over my beer glass and clenching my fists. "Stay away from her," I growled.

Finn eyed me up and down, taking a step back. "I meant no offense. I didn't realize she was taken."

I narrowed my eyes. "We're not together."

"Then you're dumber than you look, Gagnon. Fair warning. I'm interested." He gave Paz a nod and headed toward the door.

Paz laughed, crossing his arms and leaning back in the booth while I mopped up the spilled beer and sat back down.

"I knew it. I fucking knew it."

"Shut up," I grumbled.

"It's a good thing—you getting territorial over a woman. It's about time you showed interest in something besides trees."

I grabbed a fry and dipped it in the puddle of ketchup on my plate. "I hate you."

"Nope. You don't." He tipped his beer glass in my direction. "Go talk to her."

"I'm not having this conversation with you."

Paz leaned back and waved to our sister, who was celebrating another win at darts. She sauntered over with an annoyed expression on her face.

"What?" she barked. "I'm on a winning streak."

"I was just noting that our brother here has taken a keen interest in our new school principal. And should maybe act like a grown man and ask her on a date instead of growling at her every time he sees her."

Adele steepled her fingers like a super villain and grinned. "Yes, please. I actually just overheard her saying she needed to get home—"

I stood, dropped a few bills on the table, and headed straight for the high-top tables where she was still mingling.

"Need a ride?" I pushed my way between her and a guy wearing a cowboy hat. What the fuck is that shit? It's Maine, not Montana.

"We were just talking," the cowboy dumbass protested from behind me.

I ignored him, instead snatching Alice's purse off the table and handing it to her. I held out an elbow. "What do you say, buttercup? Can I drive you home?"

Chapter 15
Alice

"You need to stop rescuing me." I slumped in the front seat of Henri's monster truck after I'd heaved myself into it without the aid of a ladder—barely. I briefly let my mind wander. Was the big truck compensating for the size of something else?

I shook my head and buckled my seat belt. Those were the exact types of thoughts I had to stop. The more I thought about Henri, the more my dumb brain got attached. This is what always happened: I took every small gesture, every kindness, and turned it into a great love affair in my mind. But he had made his disinterest clear already. Henri Gagnon was just a good guy, the realization of which only made him more intriguing.

Sadly, the alcohol had rendered me incapable of proper mental discipline, so instead of being a mature adult, my mind was running wild with theories about his penis.

"You don't exactly make it difficult."

"I hate you for saying that. And I hate that it's true. I just want this all to work so badly, you know? I came here, a new

Alice, ready to slay. But it's been so much harder than I thought it would be. And you've had a front-row seat to all my failures."

"You're not failing. It looks like you made plenty of friends tonight."

There he went with his kindness again, making my drunk brain feel warm and fuzzy.

I shrugged. "I'm trying to support my staff. And tonight, they needed alcohol. I just wished I hadn't drunk so much. And Moxie? What is that shit?"

"It's the official state drink of Maine. It's horrible."

"My mouth. It tastes like burnt coffee and cough syrup."

He chuckled. "Just wait till tomorrow."

I groaned.

"You'll need half a gallon of water, aspirin, and a pound of bacon in the morning."

While I'd never say no to bacon, I dreaded the hangover. Since I turned thirty, more than one drink rendered me useless for days. But it had been so long since I'd been swept up in the camaraderie and fun of a night like tonight.

"How about you just solve all my problems, Brawny?"

"Try me. I bet I can." His cocky attitude was even more annoying in my exhausted, inebriated state. But damn if my drunk lady parts weren't buzzing with attraction. His kind eyes, honesty (even if it was brutal sometimes), and generosity didn't hurt, either.

And despite the mountain man aesthetic, he smelled deliciously like pine trees and was always impeccably groomed, his hair neatly combed, and his thick beard trimmed.

The beard was new for me. I had always been attracted to the clean-cut type. But damn if I wasn't curious about how that scruff would feel against my neck. And maybe other places too...

"Go on," he said, bringing me out of my woodsy sexual fantasy, "tell me your problems. I bet I can help fix them."

I regarded him. He took up a lot of room, but he fit the space in his truck perfectly. He was at ease navigating the dark roads. I yearned to reach up and gently stroke the nape of his neck where his hair was starting to curl.

"I need a school admin. Not that I can afford one. There's so much work to be done, not to mention answering phones and dealing with the students."

"Easy," he deadpanned. "You can have my mom."

"Excuse me?"

"My mom. She's been really down since Dad passed last year, and she did administrative work in our office for years. She's bored and lonely. This would be perfect for her."

"No way."

"Yes way. I'll drive to her house right now. It's two miles down the road. You can interview her."

My face went hot. I did not want to meet Henri's mother while I was tipsy and had mascara smeared under my eyes. "That's not necessary."

"Tomorrow then. She will be thrilled to help out."

I turned my attention back to the road and clasped my hands in my lap. At this point, I'd take a moose if he could answer the phone and digitize the student records. "Okay. But please don't force her."

"Trust me, buttercup, no one forces Mama Gagnon to do anything. You'll see."

Back at the cabin, Henri insisted on walking me inside and forced me to chug two glasses of water.

When I'd finished, he stalked to the wood stove and fussed with the logs, making things perfect. He wore a sexy look of concentration, and his muscles rippled as he restacked firewood into neat piles.

"Hey, Brawny?" I asked, feeling a bit saucy.

He turned and gave me an annoyed look that only made me want to torture him more.

"You saw me naked."

He ignored me and went back to stacking firewood. "Go to bed, Alice."

Before he turned away, I watched his cheeks turn pink, and I relished the feeling of knowing I was making him blush.

"You seem embarrassed."

He continued to ignore me.

"If anyone should be embarrassed, it's me. But you're over here ignoring me like a teenage boy who has never seen a pair of boobs before."

He stood abruptly and stalked toward me with fire in his eyes. "Drop it, Alice. It's not my fault you dance around naked."

"I can do whatever I want in my own house." I poked him in the chest, feeling my anger rise up. "You could have knocked like a civilized human being."

"Who dances around naked?"

"I do. And it's fucking great. You should try it sometime."

"I'm going home." He turned toward the door, but I grabbed his arm, bringing him to a sudden halt.

"Actually, I think we need to even the score. I showed you mine, so you should show me yours."

"Fuck no."

I trailed my fingers down the front of his shirt. "Come on, Brawny. Show me the goods."

"You're drunk." His face was a deep shade of crimson, and I was loving every second. This man had seen me literally fall on my ass, but I finally had the upper hand.

"What is it you're hiding under the flannel and Carhartt gear?"

He grasped my hand and dipped his chin, looking directly into my eyes. "Go to bed and dream about it." And with that, he turned and strode out the door.

I woke up bleary-eyed with a pounding headache. I had never been a big drinker, so what on earth had possessed me last night?

But when I checked the time on my phone, I was confronted by a slew of texts from my staff. They shared photos from our night out, and each one thanked me for organizing the group happy hour. It wasn't my most professional moment, but it felt like I'd broken through to a few of them. If they could see me as an ally rather than an enemy, we had a chance at turning things around at school.

I sat up and reached for the glass of water on the nightstand and chugged, relishing how it soothed my cotton mouth. My head throbbed and my stomach churned. *Fucking Moxie.* Once I'd finally heaved myself out of bed, I padded across the hardwood floor, desperate for more water. I ignored the one boob trying to escape my tank top, and judging by the crusties in my eyes, I definitely had not removed my makeup before falling into bed.

As I swung open my bedroom door, I was hit by the most intoxicating scents. Sizzling bacon and strong coffee.

But my euphoria was short-lived, because then I spotted Henri Gagnon wearing one of my yellow aprons—this one with butterflies on it. He looked awake and freshly showered and was wearing jeans that did some magical things to his thick lumberjack thighs. And he was standing at my stove, frying bacon. A sexy man cooking was the last thing I wanted to see in my current physical state.

"Morning, buttercup," he said in a chipper tone I'd never heard from him.

"What are you doing here?" I asked, trying to put my boob away while petting the dogs, who were circling my legs in search of affection.

"Solving your problem. Or *problems*, I should say." He turned from the stove and set the spatula down. "First, taking care of your hangover. Have some coffee. It's the good stuff. Paz orders it from an organic farm in Costa Rica. We make fun of his fussy tastes constantly, but I stole a bag for emergencies."

He handed me a mug that said Lovewell RiverFest 2002 on it, filled with a dark, steaming life force. I closed my eyes and inhaled deeply over the mug. It smelled strong enough to take the paint off my car. Perfect.

"And then I called my mom. She would love to work at school and is ready to start today."

"It's Saturday."

"Gagnons don't believe in weekends," he said cheerily —*weird*—taking a sip from his own coffee mug. "Not when there's a job to do."

I groaned. The plans I'd made for today consisted of sleeping and watching Bravo.

"And she's waiting for you to show her around school."

"Fuck," I said, slumping against the counter and chugging the piping hot coffee, burning my mouth in the process.

"Go clean up. And maybe put on a bra? I enjoy the show. But you are the principal and all."

I threw a dishtowel at him and stalked off to the bathroom, hoping to shower off my shame and poor decision making.

Chapter 16
Alice

Loraine Gagnon was a force to be reckoned with. It had taken her less than half a day to establish herself as completely indispensable and totally in charge. I was a little bit in love with her.

She found an old desktop in a closet and bribed a couple of eighth graders to set it up for her. Then she figured out how to work the PA system in a matter of minutes.

Kids stopped by to say hi to Mrs. G every morning and at the end of each day. When she told Brian Oulette to take his hat off in class, he did so immediately and without complaint. The faculty loved her and popped in during their planning periods to say hello and to help her with whatever she was working on.

Over the past two weeks, the front office had been transformed. The mildewy boxes had disappeared, and a dozen metal filing cabinets had replaced them, all lined up and shiny and alphabetized.

She created a massive, colorful bulletin board for school

announcements and the lunch menu and another to display the kindergarten class's artwork.

The transformation was nothing short of magic. Especially since it mysteriously happened after school hours. She was clearly an organizational witch in pastel separates.

"We need to discuss your pay," I said for the tenth time since she had started. The woman refused to fill out a single form and changed the subject or came up with excuses before taking off to handle yet another situation. Despite her unwillingness to give me the information I needed to add her to the payroll, she showed up every morning, sometimes with multiple loaves of banana bread in tow.

"Oh, I don't want to be paid, dear," she said, as if it were a silly suggestion.

"This is a job," I said firmly.

"It's pro bono. The least I can do. My four children attended this school, as did my late husband. It's my public service." She tucked her immaculate auburn bob behind her ears and gave me a sweet smile tinged with steel.

I leaned forward, putting my elbows on the desk. "I know it seems like we're in dire straits, but I can offer you a paycheck and benef—"

"I don't want it," she interrupted, crossing her arms over her chest, then turning back to the stack of folders she was labeling.

I bit the inside of my cheeks and took in a deep breath. "Legally—"

She held up one hand to stop me. "Fuck legal. Sweetheart, look around." She gestured to my sad prison office. "We're in Lovewell. Things aren't exactly done by the letter of the law here."

She wasn't wrong. But I wanted to make this a professionally run, organized school environment.

"My stubborn husband, God bless him, had life insurance.

I'm comfortable and provided for. Use that money to buy books or art supplies or a new printer, for Christ's sake. I need something to get me out of the house. I'll fill out your HR forms, but I work for free."

I smiled tensely. This woman was not backing down.

"There is one thing you can do for me, dear." Her tone softened suspiciously.

My anxious brain ran through multiple scenarios. What kind of favor would Loraine Gagnon want? A kidney? Help with a money laundering scheme? A dark magic ritual? I could probably manage any of those, as long as she kept running the front office smoothly.

"My son. Henri." She studied me, her eyebrows raised. "Look after him."

That was so far from money laundering or black-market organs. "Sorry, I don't understand."

"You live on his property."

"Yes."

"And the busy season is upon us. I know my Henri. He will work himself to the bone."

I nodded, unsure of how I fit into this.

"He gets angry when I interfere." She rolled her eyes dramatically. "So just keep an eye out. Bring him a meal once in a while. Make sure he's eating and sleeping."

"Um..."

"Don't be shy, dear. Just keep an eye on him. You're right next door. And my daughter tells me you're an excellent cook."

"Thank you?" I tilted my head and pressed my lips together. "But I'm just not sure..."

"Sweetheart." Her tone was syrupy sweet, but her eyes were pure ice. "I'll make your life so much easier here at school. Just help me out and do the same for my sweet boy, okay?"

I nodded, but no words came to mind. This had officially

been the most awkward HR conversation of my professional life.

She stood, brushing the legs of her immaculately pressed slacks. "Now give me a hug. That's how we finalize agreements up here."

I let Loraine pull me into a tight hug, enjoying her floral scent and her strange manipulation tactics.

"Now," she said, stepping back. "If you wanted to ask him on a date too, that would be fine."

"Mrs. Gagnon!" I almost dropped the mug of lukewarm coffee I'd picked up off my desk.

"Oh please, call me Loraine."

"Loraine," I enunciated, trying to calm my racing heart. "That's not going to happen."

She shrugged. "Why not? He talks about you nonstop."

"Really? He's never struck me as the chatty type," I snapped back.

She chuckled. "In his own way, he talks about you all the time. And Pascal and Adele were positively giddy about the prospect of you two dating."

I had to nip this insanity in the bud. It was bad enough I was letting this woman work for free and with no employment contract. I couldn't have her thinking she could play match-maker in my school.

"This school needs 100 percent of my focus and energy at the moment. And while I'm sure Henri is a lovely person, I'm simply not interested in dating."

She laughed. Laughed and laughed. She laughed so much that I began to get offended.

She put a hand to her chest, a smile on her face. "Oh, you can take the girl out of Massachusetts, but you can't take the granite stick out of her ass. Loosen up, sweetie. Winter is coming. It'll be cold and long and lonely. Having someone to snuggle up with is not a bad thing." She gave me a wink and then sauntered out of my office.

I rested my cheek on the cool surface of my desk and stared at my door. Thankfully, I had hung it back on the hinges last weekend after watching half a dozen YouTube tutorials. A coat of paint had transformed the cinderblock walls into... cinderblock walls painted a soothing blue. And bit by bit, this was becoming a place where I could speak to teachers, students, and parents comfortably.

It wasn't much, but it was mine.

And things were taking shape. I had finally gotten through to the University of Maine. An art professor I had found on Facebook was helping me recruit undergrads to teach art classes and workshops for class credit. There were a lot of hoops to jump through with the university, but Jenni thought it was possible. I surveyed the wall next to my desk. It was still covered with neatly lined Post-it notes, color-coded by priority and cost. Inhaling a deep breath, I moved the one that read *bring back art classes* from the goal section to the work in progress section. It was a start.

But before I could pick up the phone, there was a knock on my door, and a small head of shaggy hair popped into the door-frame. Tucker.

"Hello, Ms. Watson," he said, shuffling his feet and studying his hands. He was wearing athletic shorts that were too short and a threadbare T-shirt despite the forecast of highs in the fifties this week.

"To what do I owe the pleasure, Tucker?"

He settled into the fuzzy beanbag chair and sat perfectly still for a moment, like he was reveling in the comfort before facing the true reason for his visit.

"Mrs. Stroud sent me here."

"For fun?"

He pushed the hair out of his eyes, but his gaze stayed locked on his feet. "Nah. I got in trouble."

I rested my elbows on my desk, giving him a moment to come clean.

"She's mad because I've been fixing stuff instead of doing schoolwork." He finally looked up. "And then she saw Jackson McAvoy give me money, and she got super mad."

"Back up. Why did he give you money?"

"His Switch wasn't working. So I fixed it. I fix stuff sometimes, and kids pay me."

I shook my head. "You fix stuff?"

"Yup." He sat straighter in the beanbag chair, the Styrofoam beads inside rustling with the movement. "I'm good at it. Last year, I lived with a foster family in Bangor and did this STEM summer camp. It was so cool." He grinned, which was a rare sight. "I learned all about circuits and taking stuff apart."

"Ah." I fought the urge to walk around my desk and pull him in to a tight hug. The pride in his voice was unmistakable and rare. This was not a kid who got a lot of opportunities like STEM summer camp. It broke my heart that kids like Tucker and Goldie didn't have equal opportunities for growth and development or loving, stable homes.

"But that family couldn't take Goldie, and she didn't like being away from me. So I came back here. But I still remember everything. And I use YouTube if I don't know something."

"And you're doing this during school time?"

He shrugged his skinny shoulders. "Sometimes. I need the money. And Jackson gave me ten dollars for fixing his switch. I'm going to take Goldie to the diner after school, and we'll both get our own slices of blueberry pie."

Nausea rolled in my belly. Fuck, this job was so hard sometimes. I took a deep breath, pulled a granola bar out of the top drawer of my desk, and tossed it to him.

He caught it in midair and had half of it shoved into his mouth before I closed the drawer.

"Tucker, I know earning money feels important, but as a kid, your job is to come to school and learn. There's plenty of time for fixing stuff after school or on weekends or even when you're eighteen and have a diploma."

He rolled his eyes at me. He was only eleven and already jaded.

His foster mother had been thoroughly uninterested in speaking to me, and even less interested in assistance with free lunch program forms. There had been a baby screaming in the background, so she'd made an excuse and quickly ended our conversation. The second time I called, she flat out hung up on me.

My calls to OCFS were equally frustrating. Their case worker, a sweet man name James, was concerned but over-whelmed by his caseload and promised a follow-up in two weeks.

"We were doing math. I'm good at math. I don't need to do another worksheet about division. I got division up here." He tapped his forehead. "I just wish I could get a job, you know? It would be easier."

I steepled my fingers and tried to find the right words. As a principal, I knew what I was supposed to do. But the reality of life for this tiny human in front of me was far more nuanced and complicated than I had witnessed before.

"What if I gave you a job? After school?" I asked.

He nodded, chewing the rest of the granola bar.

"We have this giant printer and copier." I waved in the general vicinity of the outer office.

"I've seen it."

"It hasn't worked in years. We can't afford to replace it, and

I spent a lot of money on a repair man who said we should throw it in the trash."

"I don't know if I can fix it."

"You said yourself that you can fix anything. Maybe you could watch some YouTube videos. I downloaded the manuals online. We can study them together, see if we can do it."

He scooted forward on the beanbag, his eyes lighting up, but he bit his lower lip nervously. "What if I can't do it? What if I make it worse?"

"It doesn't work. How much harm could you do?"

"And you'll pay me?"

I nodded. "I'll pay you, and Goldie can read or color in my office while you do it. Deal?"

He jumped up, offering his tiny hand. "Deal."

"But," I said, keeping hold of his hand, "you only get the job if you focus in the classroom and stop taking on repair jobs during school hours. I want to hear good reports from Mrs. Stroud."

He nodded happily before grabbing his battered backpack and walking out of my office.

"Starts today at three p.m. sharp," I called.

Once he was out of sight, I put my head on my desk. It was only eleven a.m., and I was exhausted. But I sat up straight, and I mentally went through my to do list, sipping my now ice-cold coffee.

A walk around the building would help me clear my head, and it would give me an opportunity to check in on the classrooms.

I grabbed my travel mug and headed in the direction of the teachers' lounge, where I had recently added a brand-new Keurig machine, courtesy of the Walmart in Bangor, to help build morale. As I waited for my cup to brew, I scanned the space. The room looked cleaner and lighter than it had previously. Someone had washed the windows and removed some of the old furniture.

The chairs were neatly arranged around the tables, and the office supplies were organized and stacked on shelves in the back of the room. I rested a hip against the counter and sipped my coffee, reminding myself to notice the small changes and take pride in the tiny victories.

I strolled down the halls, noting the clean classrooms and the attentive, smiling faces. Lovewell was nothing like I had expected. I was working harder and smarter than I ever thought possible. But things were improving slowly.

Every day, I fell more in love with this school, its staff, and its students. And no matter what it took, or how hard I had to work, I would do my best for them.

Chapter 17
Henri

"You ready?" Pascal stood in my office, wearing a suit and shiny shoes. My brother had always been the corporate type. In grade school, he would save his Halloween candy and sell it at a premium price to the other kids after theirs had run out. At the sight of him now, I was hit with a pang of guilt. He didn't belong here. He should have been behind a desk in a skyscraper in Boston or New York City. But he'd come home. For me, for us, for the company.

Just another reminder of how badly I was screwing things up.

"Yeah, yeah," I grumbled, closing my laptop and running my hands through my hair. I bit back a yawn when I stood and stretched. Lately I'd lain in bed, tossing and turning every night. Not even a glass of whiskey before bed helped. I suspected part of my insomnia was due to my curvy neighbor, but I shut down those thoughts the moment they popped into my head—which was a regular occurrence. I needed to be on my game today.

"I don't understand why this is necessary." Today we were

dragging our asses all the way over to the Heberts' corporate headquarters for this bullshit.

When we arrived at the multi-generational lumber company offices—although the place looked like a midtown Manhattan law firm—a smiling receptionist doled out tiny bottles of water and led us to a conference room that sat twenty and had a massive projector screen on the back wall.

The hallways were covered in professionally framed black-and-white photos of the Hebert ancestors logging in the woods, dragging logs with chains and horses, and driving them down the river. Like these people invented cutting down trees, for fuck's sake.

We were joined in the ostentatious conference room by members of the Clark and the LeBlanc families. Our four families jointly owned the Golden Road and controlled most of the commercial forests in the state. We generally tolerated each other since our families had been in business together for decades. But everyone hated the Heberts.

After we'd been kept waiting for a stupid amount of time, Mitch and Paul Hebert entered. My fists clenched, an automatic reaction every time I laid eyes on one of these people. Paz elbowed me hard. Unlike me, my brother had the corporate nice guy smile plastered to his face.

It pained me to see these assholes still walking the earth while my own dad, who'd spent his entire life working hard and raising his family, wasn't. Every time I had to deal with them, it reminded me of how unfair life was. These jackasses hadn't driven trucks in decades. They didn't jump on a crane when someone called out sick. They didn't visit their employees in the hospital or pay for their kids' braces or show up to coach little league after working for twenty-four hours straight.

My dad died because he worked too hard, and because he loved his business and his family too much. He shouldn't have been driving that day. But weather and illness put us in a bad position, and Dad jumped in with two feet like he always did.

What would have happened if I'd gone instead? It was hard not to wonder how things would have played out if I had been behind the wheel when the truck rolled. If Dad was still here to run the company.

Instead, I was stuck here with these fools, trying to keep my ears open and my mouth closed.

The lawyers from Boston we'd hired to help us deal with issues related to the roads were in attendance today as well.

"How can they do this?" Lucy Clark asked.

The attorney who was running the show was Peter Wright, a Mainer from Downeast who, despite that fact, was deeply trusted by all the families. He sighed, clearly annoyed at having to drive all the way up here to speak to paying clients. He was a fiftysomething man, pale and doughy from a life spent at a desk and sporting a watch that cost more than my house. He was accompanied by two other attorneys. A young woman in a dark suit with bright red hair and a serious-looking young black man who kept pushing up his glasses. Each typed away furiously on laptops, clearly terrified of their boss.

"The roads are privately owned. Both by this collective and by your individual companies. Technically there is limited jurisdiction. But we're talking about the federal government. They have threatened to come back with warrants," he explained.

"It's not safe to have random agents out there."

"They understand that. Which is why giving them a few days to set up surveillance, map the area, and conduct their investigation is the best course of action."

"The Golden Road isn't some kind of drug superhighway," Martin LeBlanc insisted. "This feels overblown. We'll lose so much business."

Murmurs of agreement went up around the table.

Mitch Hebert slammed his fist on the giant mahogany table, startling the group into silence. "It's all bullshit," he growled. "They can't do this. I won't allow it."

"Mr. Hebert," Peter pleaded, "what we've suggested is the best path forward. I assure you."

"We've got businesses to run. My trucks are on that road twenty hours a day. We got quotas to make, orders to fill," Mitch bellowed.

I tensed at the rage that emanated from him. The yelling seemed inappropriate, given the circumstances and audience.

"Bullshit's right!" Paul shouted, always in agreement with his brother. His son Cain, the heir apparent to their empire, pumped his fist in agreement. He was a certified grade-A dumbass, and the last person who should be at management level.

Mitch Hebert was a proud, stupid, cruel man. He was tall—taller than me—and bald, his face red from years of drinking and yelling at his five sons. Most of them were not involved with the business, save for the eldest, Gus, who ran a camp up north. Mitch didn't seem to think much about his kids. I couldn't stand a single one of them, but I would have been devastated if my dad had pushed me out of the family business. It had been my dream to run this company with my dad since I was a little boy.

The Heberts might have had money, but they were assholes who didn't value family. My parents had taught us right, so no matter how many trees they moved, we would always be richer. That's why I did this. For the family. For the future. To keep things going for the next generation. To take my kids out into the woods like my dad did, teach them about the trees and the forests and the incredible gifts nature gave us.

"Calm down," Lucy Clark urged, narrowing her eyes at

Mitch. She was the matriarch of the family, widowed for years, and not one to mess with. Her company was small, but her employees were loyal, and no one messed with them.

Mitch ignored her and continued to rant about freedom and the unfairness of it all.

And suddenly I couldn't take it anymore. "If you're going to act like a dumbass, we're leaving." I stood, gesturing for Paz to follow me.

"Sit the fuck down, Gagnon," Cain snarled.

"Drug running is not our problem," Mitch insisted. His face was beet red, and a bead of sweat ran down his temple. The man loved money more than his own family—that was a fact—but his reaction today was extreme.

I *should* have bitten my tongue. And I should have listened quietly and let the lawyers handle it. But I was not my dad. Anger and resentment bubbled to the surface and spewed before I could think twice. "You're such a fucking prick. Of course it is." I stood straight again, my blood boiling and my fists clenched. "How many employees have we lost to addiction? How badly has this region been hurt? Look around. This is a crisis. Opioids are destroying lives and communities. We own these roads; we profit off these roads. If they're being used in this way, we have a responsibility to help stop it."

"You're a goddamn idealistic fucker, just like your father."

"Stop right there," I growled, leaning over the table.

Paz put a hand on my arm. He always had my back, of course, but it was a warning. I was dangerously close to crossing a line.

Peter finally found his balls and spoke up. "It's inconvenient, of course. But as Mr. Gagnon said, this is a public health crisis. And there is tremendous pressure to address this proactively. Do you think the governor cares if you stop hauling logs for a few days? The US Attorney? The families of people lost to addiction? There is a bigger picture here."

I sat back and considered his words. Paz sat, scribbling notes, likely running the numbers, calculating how much we stood to lose.

"Gentlemen," Lucy interrupted, "enough. We gotta defer to the lawyers here. And then I've got to get back to work. I can't fuck around all day in your boardroom." She raised an eyebrow at Mitch.

He looked slightly chastened. No one messed with Lucy Clark, but that didn't stop him from continuing to rant. "They're full of shit. There are no drugs on those roads. We're out there all the time. Do you see sketchy drug dealers lurking around?"

Peter gave another huff of annoyance; we were probably taking time away from his golf game. "Modern drug trafficking is a professional and strategic operation, Mr. Hebert. You'd be surprised how unlikely you are to pick up on these types of activities."

"We've got thousands of miles of roads, plus all the outposts. It's impossible to monitor every mile of road and square foot of land constantly," Paz added, earning a small smile from the female lawyer. He'd probably get her number before we left today. Paz loved redheads, and they loved him back. After so many years in the city, he had returned with a bit of a reputation. I had assumed his game would suffer after he returned to Lovewell, but clearly, I underestimated my brother.

I, on the other hand, had no game. I could barely string a sentence together most days, hated crowds, and preferred the company of animals, so a pickup artist I was not. I had my fair share of casual relationships, mostly with women in Bangor or Orono who eventually got sick of me. But it had been a good long while since I'd felt even a flicker of interest in a woman.

Until Alice. And her presence was messing with my head, because what I felt was so much more than interest or curiosity. It was frustration and annoyance and this powerful pull toward her. I wanted to yell at her and then kiss her and then spank her and then drift off with her in my arms. Was it any wonder I couldn't fucking sleep?

Now add all these concerns about drugs, business shut-downs, and the law crawling all over us. Maybe Paz would take pity on me and knock me unconscious tonight. Though my brother was not a fighter. Maybe I could find Clive the moose? He'd probably kick my ass for a two-pound bag of carrots from the market.

In the truck on the way back to the office, my adrenaline waned, and bone-deep exhaustion was taking over. "How are we going to afford this?" Paz asked.

"Dunno," I replied, unbuttoning the top button of my shirt to eliminate the strangling sensation. "For now, we've got to keep things going and figure the rest out as we go."

"It's what Dad would have wanted."

Regardless of how bad business was, Dad would have never tolerated drugs on his roads.

So I'd keep hustling, keep juggling, and pray we could keep things afloat.

For Dad. And for Lovewell.

Chapter 18
Henri

I hated crowds and I hated socializing. But I never missed the fall bonfire. It was a combination of my favorite things. Cold weather, lots of fire, and beer.

The last weekend in September used to be reserved for the annual Lovewell RiverFest. It was a huge festival that drew tourists from all over New England. That was back when the inn was open and could accommodate a slew of out-of-town guests. The festival consisted of an art fair, sporting events, food trucks, and all sorts of shit that tourists ate with a spoon.

But the town hadn't hosted a RiverFest for a few years now. After the paper mill shut down, things sort of fell like dominoes. First the inn closed, then a good percentage of local restaurants. Shortly after, the town didn't have the funds or sponsorships to run the festival anymore.

The only remaining tradition was the bonfire. And it was for those of us who'd stayed in Lovewell. It wasn't the big event it used to be, but we showed up religiously each year with chairs, food, and drink.

The Timber Trio, our local cover band, was playing

familiar bluegrass music just outside the heated tent area set up with games and crafts for the kids.

I'd devoted my life to this community, and that would never change. Because that's what my dad had done. He got up every day to provide for not only his family, but the other local families too. The responsibility of being one of the largest employers in town was a big one, but he bore it well.

These days, I appreciated more and more how heavy this burden could be.

I wandered over to the food tent filled to the brim with incredible-looking sweets. Every table was covered in pies and cookies and to-go hot chocolate.

The sign attached to the tent and strung with lights read: *Bake sale to benefit the Lovewell Community School after-school programs. Help fund the homework lab, STEM club, and sports programs!*

Alice was there, smiling and hugging an older woman.

"This is amazing," she said, arranging the pies.

When I realized who Alice had just released from her hold, I tipped my chin. "Bernice," I said cordially, never wanting to make an enemy of the owner of the diner and best pie baker in the state. "How'd you get Bernice to donate pies?" I asked once she had walked away.

"She already hated me, so I had nothing to lose. She turned me down initially, but then I reminded her that her grandkids go to our school and could really benefit from after-school enrichment."

"And she started to appreciate you?"

"Fuck no. She still hates me. But she did donate a dozen pies, and that's all I really care about."

"Fair enough."

"To think I used to be afraid to ask people for help! Never

wanted to burden anyone. But then I realized I'd have to if I wanted to make a difference at the school. So I stopped in every shop downtown and asked. I can't believe how many people were willing to help." She was fighting a grin and bouncing on the balls of her feet.

I studied her face—the excitement in her eyes and the blush creeping up her cheeks. Every once in a while, she would reveal a small detail about her past that simply didn't compute for me. The Alice I had known these past few weeks was bold and confident. I could absolutely see her demanding Bernice donate pies for the school with a smile.

"Those look good." I pointed to dozens of small cookies packaged in clear plastic and decorated with bows.

"Oh! I made those." There went the smile again. "Secret family recipe from my grandmother."

She handed me a cookie from a tray on the table behind her. It was crunchy and sweet and melted on my tongue. I groaned. "What are they called?"

"Baci di Dama," she replied, biting her lip. "Translates to 'lady's kisses.'"

I nodded absently, distracted by her lips and the mention of kissing.

"What'll it be, Henri?" She wiggled her eyebrows, and although my first choice would have been to lick frosting off her spectacular tits, I settled for half a dozen cookies and a blueberry pie.

"Donating to a good cause, I see." Dylan Markey sidled up next to Alice, looking like his usual cheerful self. "You should share those cookies with Remy. He's moping around here somewhere."

He had been Remy's best friend since kindergarten and spent more time at our house growing up than his own. The two of them got into endless trouble together. He taught science now and only raised hell with my little brother on weekends.

I nodded. "How's the school year going?"

"Great. Thanks to this lady over here." He put his arm around Alice's shoulders and squeezed, forcing me to fight back the urge to rip his arm off. The familiarity between them made my hair stand on end.

Alice rolled her eyes. "Ha. The last principal was a train wreck and stole from the school, so the bar was set pretty low."

He nudged her with his hip. "Don't listen to her. She works her tail off for us every day. She organized this bake sale in two days and talked everyone into donating and volunteering."

"She is persistent," I said, never taking my eyes off hers.

Her lips were glossy, and her cheeks were pink from the cold, making her look more irresistible than usual.

"Yeah. We've never been able to offer after-school support for our kids, but Alice is making it happen."

The corner of her lip twitched. "When I want something, I make it happen."

The heat crackled between us. She was baiting me. She was a gold medalist in getting under my skin.

"I don't doubt that."

"You just gonna sit here and stare at the fire?" Remy asked, slapping me on the back and handing me a fresh beer.

"You could join me."

He sat on the camp chair next to me, elbows on his knees, silently sipping his beer. Which was strange in and of itself. Remy was constantly in motion, always talking, laughing, running, climbing. He had been like that since birth. He climbed out of his crib at six months old and never looked back, always trying to keep up with the rest of us. This quiet, contemplative version of my little brother was disconcerting.

"Everything okay?" I wasn't great with heart-to-hearts, but I was observant enough to know that something was off.

He nodded, not taking his eyes off the dancing flames in front of us. "Just thinking."

"Still training?"

"Always. Couldn't stop if I wanted to." Remy was the athlete of the family. Didn't matter what it was, he was great at it. He was shorter and leaner than Paz and me, with lighter hair and more energy. He ran ultramarathons and was one of the best speed climbers in the country. Hell, he was undefeated in the sixty-foot climb.

But his true love, aside from his fiancée, Crystal, was the block chop. Participants had to chop pockets into a log and wedge planks into those pockets so they could climb a minimum of ten feet, then chop off a two-foot-long block of wood from the top. It took agility, strength and speed, and Remy had it all. If he kept training the way he had been, he had the potential to go to the world championships in Finland someday.

Remy rarely took anything too seriously, though, so the long-term devotion he'd need wasn't a certainty. But I envied his happy-go-lucky attitude. And that he had found a partner, a true partner.

Speaking of... "How's Crystal?"

"Busy," he replied flatly and tipped his beer bottle to his lips.

"Everything okay?"

"Fucking great," he snapped. "You talk to Adele?"

"Not since yesterday." Which was surprising. She loved the bonfire even more than I did. "Spent most of the day at a bullshit meeting with the logging families."

"She's got a new boyfriend." He finally looked my way and arched one eyebrow.

Adele had terrible taste in men. Horrific. And I wasn't just saying that as her older brother. She truly had a bad picker.

"How bad?"

"Another professor."

"Ugh. The worst." Adele had a type: know-it-all, superior, snobby professors from the University of Maine. Not only had she earned a degree in engineering summa cum laude, but she'd also developed an affinity for the glasses and elbow patches type.

She was lonely sometimes, sure, but these guys tended to be brainy blowhards who treated her terribly, looked down at our family business, and, more often than not, cheated on her with undergrads.

It was officially a pattern, and we were tired of picking up the pieces once things inevitably went south. "She's in Orono with him tonight. Probably won't see her for a while."

That was another part of the pattern. My sister's boyfriends rarely made the effort to come to Lovewell, so she exhausted herself driving back and forth to see them. She always felt like she needed to chase these guys, like she wasn't good enough on her own.

But she was thirty-two years old. I couldn't force her to see sense. I couldn't force her to do much of anything. Just like I couldn't force Remy to tell me why he was sitting here silently instead of singing with the band, carrying his fiancée around on his back, or doing cartwheels to entertain the kids.

I couldn't control their lives. I was just the big brother— here when they needed me and when they didn't. We sat in companionable silence, watching as the crowd thinned and the fire dwindled. Letting the cold air fill my lungs, I pushed thoughts of Remy and Adele aside and tried to decompress from the day. With my head tilted back, I studied the stars and silently begged my dad for guidance. How could I keep the business on track? My siblings? This town?

And when I tipped my chin down again and looked past the fire, there she was. Her hair was down and wavy and tucked under a purple knit cap. Her long coat did nothing to hide the dangerous curves hiding beneath.

"Thanks, Dad," I muttered. Of course Alice, looking like a sexy angel, would be the thing I saw first. My body wanted to get up and walk over to her. But my mind convinced me to stay put.

It was so hard to stay away from her. And even harder to resist asking my mother about her. It seemed they had become friendly in the few weeks they'd known each other. Which made sense. My mother was a no-nonsense roll-up-your-sleeves type, and I was learning that Alice was very much the same.

I'd already respected her hustle and her positive, can-do attitude, and since seeing her naked, I hadn't been able to think about anything else. She was under my skin; that was certain. And it was killing me that I couldn't let myself do anything about it.

Chapter 19
Alice

The bake sale tent not only sold out, but Dylan and some of the other teachers mercifully folded up the tables and tent and volunteered to bring them back to school for me.

I was dead on my feet, but my heart was soaring.

Tonight had been a huge success. I had met so many people and received so many compliments. Not just on my cookies, but about school as well. Maybe my strategy of busting my ass twenty-four seven was finally starting to pay off. I hadn't won Bernice over yet, but she'd brought pies, so I was calling that a win.

Day by day, week by week, Lovewell was opening up to me. People smiled and chatted and shared more a little at a time. And the details mattered. Which kids struggled with reading, which parents worked night shifts and couldn't help with homework, which townsfolk I could coerce into helping me with a last-minute bake sale.

I filed away every single detail. Every piece of information learned was a gift I would treasure. Because Lovewell was a complicated puzzle, but I was slowly solving it. And the answers were even more important and heartbreaking than I ever could have imagined.

The bonfire had been a great opportunity, both for community-building and fundraising. And the bake sale had been a stroke of genius on my part. I hadn't slept for two days, but by the end of the night, we'd sold every last creation. And more importantly, I'd gotten my face out there and had shown what I was doing to improve the school. And I was learning that went a long way in a town like Lovewell.

After decades of decline and disappointment, this town needed people who would show up and do the work. Plans and proposals wouldn't impress them. Little did they know I was just getting started.

As the night wore on, most of the young families left, and the circle grew smaller as people huddled around the bonfire for warmth. Henri had been nearby all evening, doing his usual grump-in-public routine. He'd be exactly as nice as the situation required, and then he'd go back to his resting grouch face.

"Having fun?" I asked, nudging him.

He nodded. "You sell all your pies?"

"Every last one."

"I'm not surprised. They're a town favorite."

"I wouldn't know. Bernice has never allowed me to have a piece."

He looked over one shoulder, then the other, and then he leaned in and whispered, "I'll share some of mine with you."

I fanned myself dramatically. "Aren't you a knight in shining armor?"

"But don't tell anyone. If Bernice finds out, she may cut off my supply."

I held up my glove-covered pinkie. "I swear."

As the night wore on, my eyelids started to droop and my

limbs got heavy. "I should get home. I've been baking too much and not sleeping enough." I suppressed a yawn.

"Do you need a ride?" He nodded at the paper cup in my hands.

"Just hot chocolate. But thanks."

"Then let me walk you to your car."

"No need."

And here came the grump face. "It's a long trek to the parking lot, and you tend to trip and fall in daylight. I'd hate to see what you're capable of in the dark."

"I do not need an escort, Brawny." I crossed my arms over my chest and huffed. Here he went with his grumpy demands.

"You're getting one, buttercup." He stood and offered me his arm.

After a very brief internal debate, I took it. I only had so much strength, after all.

As we walked across the large field toward the parking area, an unexpected warmth and contentedness seeped into me. It had been quite a night, and walking with Henri under the bright stars made my head spin with a number of unwelcome thoughts.

"You did good," Henri said quietly when we reached my car.

My heart swelled, and I bit back a grin. Henri was not the type of man who gave out undeserved praise. A compliment from him had to be earned.

And suddenly, instead of saying thank you or getting my ass into my car, I did something truly dumb.

I stepped closer, stood on my tiptoes, and kissed him. It was sloppy and haphazard, and I missed half his mouth, getting more beard than lips.

Because Henri made me feel things beyond attraction or flirtation. He made me feel seen and beautiful. He may have been a pain in my ass, but the way he looked at me, the way he regarded everything I said, the way he treated me with respect, was overwhelming.

I pulled away, confused and more than a little embarrassed.

"What was that for?" he growled.

I stared at my feet and wrung my hands. I was such an idiot. "I don't know."

He put two fingers under my chin and tipped my face up until I was looking into his dark eyes. "Tell me."

"I felt something and decided to act on it, okay? I'm sorry."

The corner of his lip twitched, and his eyes narrowed. "What did you feel?"

I turned my head away, feeling almost burned by his gaze. "None of your business. It's gone now."

Henri took a step forward into my space so that his strong chest brushed mine, sending a small shiver up my spine. "Nope," he said authoritatively. "It's not happening like that."

"I don't know what you mean." I had to tip my head back to look him in the eye.

"You want a kiss, buttercup," he growled. "We both know you do. So give me a chance to make it a real one. None of this random peck bullshit."

My heart raced as I studied his face. Was he serious? Or was he messing with me? Given how much we had been flirting recently, anything was possible.

Why had I done that? Why couldn't I just keep my damn lips to myself?

"Forget it," I said, my voice wavering.

He stepped forward again, forcing me to move back and caging me against the door of my car. With his strong arms on either side of me, he angled in, ghosting his lips over my neck and up to my ear.

He paused, his breath tickling my earlobe. "Just say you want it, buttercup. I'll give you anything you want."

My lungs seized. My heart stalled. And I swear the earth stopped rotating on its axis. Because in that moment, I was nothing but need and want.

"I want it."

Then his mouth was on mine, and my hands were in his hair, and he was pinning me to the truck. Lips and tongues and teeth everywhere, frantic and needy all at once. Desperate for connection. Desperate for friction.

I pawed at his chest, feeling the flannel of his shirt between my fingers as he kissed along my jawline, eliciting a needy sound I could swear I'd never made before.

This wasn't sweet or gentle or tentative. This wasn't a dip-a-toe-in-the-pool kiss. This was free diving into the endless ocean abyss.

He slid his hands down my torso until they landed on my hips, which he gripped tightly as he found my mouth with his again, our rhythm in sync and our bodies flush.

And before I could process what I was experiencing, the size of him, the way he manhandled me and made me feel possessed and treasured at the same time, it was over.

He pulled away and fixed his gaze on me, gently running his knuckle along my jawline.

The firelight danced across his face, highlighting his gruff expression but also the tenderness in his eyes. He was handsome, checked all the boxes; tall and broad and strong. Dark hair and beard and the kind of shoulders that could pick up small cars for fun.

But there was more. The curiosity mixed with that tender look in his eyes, the way he chose his words so carefully. The thoughtfulness and care with which he approached simple tasks.

And the clear love and admiration he had for his family, this town. Not to mention the dogs. My heart melted every time I saw one of them snuggling with him. It wasn't fucking fair. Because I wasn't that girl anymore.

The girl who begged for the guy to pick her. The girl who was so desperate for affection she'd give up all the important parts of herself.

That girl was long gone. And the new me? She knew this flirtation was just that. A distraction. And one scorching hot kiss. And that's all it could ever be.

Chapter 20
Alice

We sat on the metal bleachers, eager for the competition to begin. The area was filled with people milling around and small flatbed trucks filled with perfectly proportioned logs.

A massive stage area was rigged with generators and lights while trucks and booths dotted the open area next to it.

When Becca had called me this morning and instructed me to grab comfortable shoes and layers and meet her at the salon, I hadn't anticipated piling into her Jeep with Lydia and Kali and heading an hour south to a town called Belfast for a lumberjack competition. The girls were all decked out in plaid, and Becca had a cooler of snacks and warm blankets.

Although it wasn't how I'd planned to spend the Saturday of my long weekend, a lumberjack competition was just too good to pass up. If anything, it would give me more to talk about with my sisters, who were coming to visit tomorrow.

"Explain again how this works," I requested.

"It's really easy," Kali explained with the kind of worldly

annoyance rare in a first grader. "There are a bunch of different events. The people have to cut logs or climb trees."

"And the fastest person wins?"

"In some," Lydia added. "You'll get the hang of it. Each event is different, but we'll teach you. The whole region comes out for this. A lot of people from Lovewell, so we have to represent."

My mind immediately caught on one possible competitor. A certain neighbor who seemed quite adept at chopping wood.

As if reading my mind, Lydia said, "Yes, Alice, the entire Gagnon family competes."

I blushed. Clearly I wasn't any good at hiding my teeny tiny crush on Henri.

"And the Heberts too," Becca added.

"They hate each other. Have hated each other for generations," Lydia said. "My grandma dated a Hebert in high school and said all he ever did was pick fights with the Gagnons. And that was back in the sixties."

"And they all do...this stuff?"

"Yup." Lydia popped the *P*. This is just a regional competition, but there are professionals who train and tour year-round. Lots of prize money and sponsorships. Timbersports are a big deal."

"Wow."

"It's really competitive. Lots of Maine athletes have gone to the national and world championships."

I didn't know Lydia well, but I liked her. She was intimidating, but she genuinely cared about Lovewell and was an excellent teacher. Between her and Becca, I was starting to have a smidgen of a social life.

Soon, our section of the bleachers filled with people from town. Loraine was there with some older ladies, including Bernice, drinking Irish coffee out of pastel travel mugs and cheering the loudest. I recognized some kids from school and waved.

The atmosphere was electric. Everyone surrounding us was smiling and talking animatedly. I hadn't attended a ton of sporting events in Havenport, and when I had, they'd generally involved children. Not grown men and blades. This was sure to be interesting.

Competitors were called up to the stage as the crowd roared. Some looked totally serious, and others waved and laughed.

Most of the participants had the same sort of look going on. Wide, rugged guys wearing the requisite uniform of Carhartt pants and some kind of flannel shirt. Each had a beard of varying length and wore work boots. It was a little disorienting but very satisfying to watch them strut around.

The first event involved sawing giant logs with chainsaws. It seemed the objective was to make a perfect disc in the shortest period of time. It was not the most thrilling sport I'd ever seen, but it was certainly easier to understand than football.

Then, as they were preparing the stage for the next event, I saw him. He was standing on the sidelines with two men who had to be his brothers. I vaguely recognized Pascal, who looked a lot more rugged in a tight white T-shirt than the last time I met him. And next to him was a smaller man I had to assume was Remy.

Henri stood between his brothers, looking intimidating. He was wearing a blue plaid shirt with the sleeves cut off, revealing thick muscled arms covered with ink.

My heart picked up its pace, and I felt slightly faint. No wonder he'd had no trouble carrying me when I twisted my ankle. The guy was built like a goddamn tree. I had never exactly been immune to his physical charms, but my body and brain were in overdrive now. I hadn't felt this amped up since I'd gone to a Backstreet Boys concert with my sisters in eighth grade.

Kali nudged me. "You okay, Principal Watson? You want some of my cotton candy?"

I smiled at her and cleared my throat, trying to pull myself together.

And then the event began.

Henri and a few other men set super long saws up next to massive logs.

"They're called misery whips," Lydia explained, pointing to the equipment. "Takes a ton of strength."

The whistle blew then, and the competitors got started working the long blades across the logs. I tried not to drool as Henri's powerful legs drove his upper body, and his arms worked the saw in graceful yet powerful strokes.

I was hypnotized by the way his body moved. Such strength and such control in one large, grumpy package. I screamed and cheered. Jumping up out of my seat when his disc fell first, and he dropped his saw.

I was cheering like a complete lunatic, but it wasn't until Loraine turned around and gave me a double thumbs-up that I realized I was attracting the attention of the audience members in my vicinity.

Shit. I looked around, my face hot and my hands sweating, then dropped back into my seat, embarrassed by my display of horny enthusiasm. If a man with a saw was getting me this hot and bothered, I should probably head home and break out the toys.

I pretended to be distracted by my phone as the competitors left the stage. My face still burned with mortification. Logically, I knew the last thing I needed was man drama in my life, but my silly, hopeless, romantic brain just could not turn it off. Especially where Henri was concerned.

He was sexy and smart, sure. But over the past two months, I had grown to appreciate his kindness and generosity too. The way he cared for his dogs, his concern for his mother, and the responsibility he felt for his community.

And then our kiss. My lips still tingled every time I thought about it.

And it didn't help that my life had been far from spicy in recent years. That was something I planned to remedy some-day, but not until I'd achieved my professional ambitions and self-actualization.

I hadn't dated until my junior year of college. Unsurprisingly, I had been cripplingly shy and deeply insecure in high school. And despite being only a size ten back then, my mother had bullied me incessantly about my weight. And so I would spend weekends going on power walks or at the gym instead of parties or football games or participating in any of the activities that my sisters did.

Instead, I was expected to get perfect grades and shrink my body because its size and shape were not acceptable. I was conditioned to believe it made me unlovable and unlikable, so I never even considered the possibility of a boyfriend.

By the time I reached college, I was ready to get away from my mother and her fucked-up expectations. And I did, dating a bit and finally losing my virginity to a very nice guy named Chris from New Jersey.

For the next fifteen years, things were hit or miss. A few relationships, a lot of shitty first dates, and far too much time wasted obsessing about men and what they thought of me.

My fresh start in Lovewell was supposed to be about me. Stepping into my light. Being the main character in my own story. Not about pining for another guy or concocting romantic fantasies in my head that would never come true.

But as much as I tried, I could not shake Henri Gagnon. And yes, the lumberjack sex appeal was part of it. But in the month I had known him, he had proven himself to be thoughtful, kind, and dependable. Plus, he had already seen me naked and seemed to be into it. Which was a major bonus.

While volunteers were setting up logs for the next event, I excused myself. Space from the Lovewell gossip network and a moment to compose myself were at the top of my to-do list at the moment.

"Alice?"

I turned, and there he was. All sweaty and covered in sawdust. I fought the urge to squeeze my thighs together.

"Having fun?" His eyes twinkled, probably because he'd caught my enthusiastic display of support. Great.

"Oh, yes." I tried to play it off. "I'm having a blast. You did, um, great. You won, right?"

He bit his lower lip, the simple action making my nipples harden beneath my bulky sweater. "Yes. I did."

"Well, good job!" I was internally cringing. This was torture. "You are a great saw-er. Um. I mean, saw person. Whatever. You did good."

He tilted his head and examined me. I could almost see my words hanging between us in a speech bubble. My entire body twisted and clenched with all the awkwardness. God, I was such a mess.

But then the wildest thing happened.

Henri smiled. It started small but turned into a broad, toothy grin that lit up his entire face. He went from being grumpy hot to being panty-meltingly handsome in the span of one second. Even with the thick beard, I could see his full lips and straight white teeth. I had anticipated a sarcastic remark or for him to roll his eyes at my idiocy and walk away. But this? This was a choir of angels singing. A beam of light shining down on my face in the middle of a muddy field in rural Maine.

"Holy shit. Are you smiling?" I asked in shock.

He nodded and dropped his chin to his chest for a moment. "Can't help it," he said, locking gazes with me. "You're so cute when you're embarrassed."

My face flushed further, and I swore my eye twitched. This entire day was short-circuiting my brain.

"I don't know if you have plans, but we're all going to the Moose tonight. It's tradition. Loser buys the first round. Most of the town will probably come."

He was still smiling, and my body was positively humming.

"Sure," I said, answering the question he hadn't even asked. "I'll swing by."

I probably would have agreed to sell my organs on the black market if he had asked with that smile. I still couldn't quite process it.

In a daze, I walked back to my friends, wondering who the hell Henri Gagnon was and whether I'd ever been more attracted to a man in my entire life.

Chapter 21
Henri

The Moose was rowdy. Jasper Hawkins and his band were playing, and people were already dancing. He had been working on one of my crews for years but was a talented guitarist on the side. The atmosphere was fun and loud, but I was having a terrible time.

What was wrong with me? I invited her here, and suddenly I could barely speak two words to her. Every time I tried, I either clammed up or barked at her.

It didn't help that she looked so pretty. Or that she was smiling and friendly and winning everyone over. In a few short weeks, she had made friends, built relationships, and created a spectacular reputation for herself in Lovewell. I was impressed and, honestly, a little jealous. I'd lived here my entire life and employed half the town, but people had never greeted me that warmly.

I envied the pure joy radiating from Alice. Today I'd taken a step back from work and had a blast with my brothers. Our three-man team came in second, mostly because Remy climbed trees so damn fast. I was the old man of the group, the dead weight. But even I'd had one of my best days. Mainly because I had seen Alice in the crowd cheering for me.

I was a lucky bastard. I had grown up with a loving, supportive family, but something about a pretty girl cheering for me had made me work even harder.

I'd gone out there and left it all. Gotten out of my own head. Swinging the axe was liberating. I was so focused on cadence and technique that I couldn't think of all the other shit that weighed me down every day.

And when I was done, I got to look up at her big smile. She was interested; that was clear. And so was I. I had spent the week obsessing over our kiss. The way she felt in my arms, the little moan she let out. It haunted me. And I was a man obsessed.

But I couldn't get out of my own damn way. I needed to talk to her, make a move, do something other than sit here drinking a beer with a scowl on my face.

But the prospect was daunting. How could I enjoy myself and drink beer with my brothers and accept the congratulations of my friends when she was over there looking like that? How could I chat and laugh when I ached to touch her?

"You could ask her to dance, you know." Adele nudged me in the ribs with one of her razor-sharp elbows. "It's hilarious. Put an axe in your hand, and you're Mr. tough guy mountain man, but in here? You're a moody preteen at the middle school dance."

"Shut up," I grumbled into my beer.

"You like her. She likes you. Now, while that doesn't say much about her emotional health, it's something…"

I turned and leveled her with my best *don't fuck with me* face. Sadly, my sister didn't scare easily, and instead of dropping it, she laughed in my face.

"And maybe, just maybe, you could open your mouth, say

something nice and, I don't know, just be happy for a minute?" She leaned her head on my shoulder. "I want good things for you, Hen."

I dropped my shoulders and let out a long breath. Little sisters were such pains in the ass. "Thanks. But I don't need you interfering in my love life."

"Of course you do." She elbowed me again. "None of us knows how much time we have left. Look at Dad."

I winced. It was still so recent, so raw.

"You can be grumpy and lonely forever, or you can ask a pretty girl to dance. Think about it."

I did think about it. In fact, I overthought, prowling around and accepting congratulations while keeping an eye on her. When Jasper sang the first few lines of "Hold On" by Dierks Bentley, she caught me staring at her. She waved and raised one eyebrow. It was now or never.

I moved across the room toward her but stopped when a hand landed on my arm. It was Chief Souza. He had been chief of police since I was a kid—mostly because no one ever ran against him. Lazy and generally ineffective, he was tolerated by the town because he was one of our own. Personally, I had no use for the man. Our business was in danger because of drug trafficking, petty crime was way up, and people were dying of opioid overdoses on his watch.

Yet he was here, on a Saturday night, drinking and joking instead of doing his damn job. Usually Paz dealt with him when it came to the business, because my fuse was short and I didn't have time for his bullshit. He loved the town, but things had changed so much recently, and it seemed he wasn't interested in keeping up.

Unsurprisingly, he had received calls from the feds. But he seemed more annoyed about the paperwork than the genuine danger to our community. I truly had no patience for his bullshit right now. There was too much to do, and too many things that could go wrong. The headache that had started after Dad's death had become a constant companion. And I hadn't had a decent night's sleep in weeks.

By the time I disengaged from Chief Souza, I had lost sight of Alice, but I ran right into my baby brother. He was standing by the bar, drinking a beer and glowering.

"Where's Crystal?" I asked. I hadn't seen her in weeks.

"I don't know." He lifted the amber bottle to his lips. This was not Remy. He was usually the first to smile and laugh. He was also usually training for an athletic event and almost always stuck to water.

Remy treated his body like a temple, and for years he had been focused on turning his passion for timbersports into a potential career. Earlier this year, he had met an agent who was helping him get into bigger competitions and working to line up potential sponsorships. Crystal had convinced him to get on Instagram a while back, and he had hundreds of thousands of followers, mostly thirsty ladies who liked watching videos of him chopping wood.

But that was Remy—always happy, always in motion, and always with Crystal.

"Is she okay?" I was beginning to get worried.

Remy turned his attention to me. There were dark circles around his eyes, and his shoulders were slumped. "She's fine, Hen. She went to visit friends."

I nodded, taking the hint. He'd talk when he was ready. "You did great today," I said, trying to divert him. "Who was that guy talking to you earlier?"

"He's from Stihl."

I ran my hands through my beard. "Well, shit." Stihl was one of the world's largest manufacturers of chainsaws. They

WOOD You Be Mine?

sponsored the national competition circuit and were a huge deal in our world.

He nodded. "He thinks I could go to nationals. Wants to talk sponsorship. My agent and I are meeting with him next week."

I slapped him on the back. "That's incredible. And he's right. You're talented Rem."

He nodded but didn't even crack a smile at the possibility of the life-changing opportunity.

I stood next to him, soaking in the atmosphere. This sullen man beside me was not my baby brother. It was obvious he needed support but would never ask for it. So I stood there with him for a few minutes, trying to find Alice in the crowd.

When I finally found her, my heart stopped. She was dancing. With Finn Hebert.

I couldn't identify the soulful song Jasper had moved on to because my heartbeat was pounding in my ears.

She was dancing and smiling, and he had his hands on her. And I was crushed by regret. I should be dancing with her. I should be making her smile and laugh. But I couldn't get out of my own way and make a move.

The woman had stuck her tongue in my mouth a week ago, and I was sitting here hemming and hawing about whether she liked me. Adele was right. I was acting like a boy.

Shame churned in my gut.

Part of me wanted to cut in, push Finn away. But in my current state of mind, I would say the wrong things and upset her. She was having fun. I had no right to interfere because I couldn't handle my feelings.

So I put my beer down on the bar and slipped out the front door and into the cold night air. I took a deep breath and looked up at the stars. The realization that I was just a tiny ant living on a tiny planet careening around the universe always grounded me.

My brain was at war with itself. Angry and sad and confused and longing for Alice. I was tied up in knots over this woman, but it had to end. My life had been perfectly fine before she moved here.

It would be best to go home and go to bed before I let my frustration get the best of me and I threw Finn Hebert through a fucking window. I'd made it a half a dozen steps toward my truck when the door opened behind me.

"What are you doing, Brawny?"

I turned around, and there she was, standing outside the door, frowning at me.

I took three big steps closer, watching the anger swirling in her eyes.

"Why did you storm out?" she asked, arms crossed and shoulders hunched.

She shivered in her thin sweater. All I wanted was to wrap my arms around her, warm her up, and take her back inside. But instead I said, "What do you care? Go back to your dance partner." Not my finest moment.

"Excuse me? You have no right to be angry. I thought you were going to ask me to dance."

I shrugged, going for unaffected but missing the mark by a mile. "I don't dance."

"Shame. Because I wanted to dance with you."

"Oh well." I examined my feet, scuffing the dirt with the toe of my boot.

"You're being a big baby because I was dancing with Finn."

I looked up at her, taking in her beauty. She was so goddamn gorgeous, even in her angry state. And I couldn't pretend any longer.

"I don't want you dancing with anyone. Even Father Tom would make me insane."

She took a step closer. "Why's that?" she asked softly.

"Because you do something to me, buttercup. Something I don't understand and don't enjoy. But it's there. The want is there, and I can't make it go away."

"So don't," she whispered. "Stop fighting it."

I shook my head. That wasn't an option. There were too many conflicting feelings and urges in my brain. I would fight this until it was reasonable and easy to understand. Until I broke it all down so I could manage it.

"You are impossible. You know that? You've been nothing but a grumpy pain in my ass since the day I arrived in this town. I've been kind, I've been helpful, and I even let you kiss me."

I scoffed. "Let me? Buttercup, we both know how badly you wanted it."

She flushed crimson, but she was silent.

I itched to touch her, to put a palm to the warm blush creeping along her cheek. To claim every single inch of her body as mine and never let anyone else, especially trash like Finn Hebert, touch her again.

"I like this song. Dance with me."

"In the parking lot?"

She nodded. "I know you can do it. I saw how graceful you were at the competition today." She grabbed my hand and placed it on her hip. Nothing had ever felt more perfect than her warmth under my hand. I wanted to spread my fingers and grab hold of her and pull her flush up against me, show her what she did to me. But I stood still, watching her, letting her lead.

"Now," she stepped even closer, until her hair tickled my chin, "just dance."

I clutched her tight, and we shifted back and forth in the moonlight, my clumsy feet doing their best not to fuck it up. My body a tightly coiled spring, poised and ready to explode. The feel of her body, the scent of her hair, it was driving me over the edge.

And then she did the most amazing thing. She leaned her head on my chest, the warmth of her body soaking into mine through my flannel shirt.

I tightened my arms around her and rested my chin on her head, just holding her there.

And something inside me clicked. The noise in my brain quieted, and my heart rate slowed.

I took a breath so deep it felt like my first.

Was this what it felt like? When something was right?

After a few moments, Alice looked up at me, eyes glassy and wearing a shy smile. "Will you take me home?"

I froze, unsure of what she meant and desperate to keep holding her for as long as I could.

Clearly feeling my hesitancy, she said, "Let me make myself clear." Then she stood up on her tiptoes and pulled me in for a kiss. A messy, desperate kiss that ignited every nerve ending in my body.

I ran my hands down her sides and let them linger on her hips.

A tiny gasp escaped her mouth, and she bit my bottom lip hard.

"Please? Take me home, Henri. And I don't want you to be a gentleman."

And just like that, my resolve crumbled. Every argument, every reason. Just gone. I would give this woman anything she wanted, regardless of what it cost me.

We raced to the truck, not even bothering to say goodbye to anyone.

"I got a ride here with Lydia," she said when I opened the passenger door and guided her in.

"Text her," I grunted, leaning over her and buckling her seat belt.

I had never been a fast driver. Growing up on the logging roads, I'd been trained to go slow, be aware of my surroundings, and always be on the lookout for wildlife.

But tonight I had to suppress the urge to put my foot through the floor. The thought of Alice in my bed had me losing all sense.

I wanted her underneath me, on top of me, any way she wanted.

Because she was mine. She didn't know it yet, but I felt it in my bones, even though I couldn't verbalize it. I wasn't sure whether we had a shot in hell at lasting, but suddenly I had to try.

Because I could not miss this chance.

Chapter 22
Alice

Henri bolted from the driver's seat and rounded the hood of the truck. The second he opened my door, his lips were on mine. I threw my arms around his neck and kissed him back with abandon, throwing all caution to the wind.

But things cooled a bit when we got inside and had two excited dogs jumping all over us. While Henri fed them and let them out, I sat on the couch, wringing my hands and debating what I should say. *Should I go home? Should I lay out the boundaries up front?*

What was the etiquette in this situation? I had never been a one-night stand kind of girl. I wasn't against the concept in theory, but the logistics of it all seemed unwieldy. And casual sex never really squared with my inner romantic.

But I was New Alice. Practical and organized, even when it came to matters of the heart. Or rather, matters of the ladybits.

Henri came back into the room after a few minutes and took my purse and coat wordlessly, then hung them up in the mudroom.

"We should talk," I said, my voice shaking. "I don't want to make things awkward. But this is just a one-time thing."

He nodded but didn't respond.

"And I want this."

His eyes widened, and heat radiated off his body, but still, he was silent.

"But I just want to be clear."

He held my gaze for a beat, and I immediately began to doubt myself. Had I ruined the moment? Was I misjudging him?

But then he gently took my hand and kissed it, his lips lingering on my skin as he looked up at me, his gaze heated. "I'll give you anything you want, buttercup"

My face burned, my nipples hardened, and every part of my body screamed for his touch. And suddenly, boundaries and rules and talking seemed less important.

I pulled him close, kissing him and gripping his hair. I needed this. There was no other place to put all this pent-up lust and attraction.

He sensed it too, breaking the kiss only to pick me up and throw me over his shoulder. I gasped. I was too stunned—and too turned on—to even respond. Instead, I luxuriated in the feeling of being carried around.

He placed me down gently, as if I were made of glass, in a massive room anchored by an even more massive bed. The space was totally sparse, with a wall of windows looking out at the mountains and the starry night sky.

The bed was made of intricately carved logs and covered with a plush white duvet and more fluffy pillows than I would have expected from a bearded, flannel-wearing lumberjack.

He ran his knuckles along my jaw, tilting my head up to look at him.

"You are gorgeous," he said, leaning down to kiss me, his

hand gently cupping my face. I stared up at him, into those dark brown eyes, and felt a deep, primal kind of desire.

I was no virgin, but my past sexual experiences had been awkward, sometimes pulling me out of the moment or making me feel like we were out of sync.

While I wanted sex, I had never wanted a person so much before. It wasn't the act my body was aching for—it was him. I wanted to feel him and explore him and touch him. I wanted to satisfy the curiosity that had been building within me for months.

And most of all, I wanted to see the real Henri. Not the grumpy neighbor, not the exhausted boss, not even the responsible older brother. I wanted to see Henri the man, stripped bare and exposed. In every way.

He gently kissed down my neck, letting his fingers play with the hem of my sweater. "I don't want to pressure you," he breathed, not stopping for one moment. "We don't have to do anything you don't want to."

I arched my back to give him better access, groaning as he pulled me closer. "I want to."

"Is that right?" He smiled against my lips, and I took the opportunity to grind my hips against him. "Because I have plans, buttercup." He pinched my ass so hard I jumped a bit. "So many plans."

I didn't respond. Instead, I reached down and pulled my sweater over my head and tossed it on the floor in one swift movement.

He drank me in, savoring my green lace bra. "Fuck," he whispered before tangling his hand in my hair and kissing me again fiercely.

"Take off your pants. Show me the body I've been dreaming about for so long."

I giggled. "You've already seen me naked."

"And it was the best day of my fucking life," he growled. "But I need more. I want to savor and appreciate every sexy inch of you. I'm taking my time, and you will not complain."

I nodded obediently, so turned on by his orders. My fingers fumbled to unbutton my jeans, and then I slowly slid them over my ample hips.

When they hit the floor, I was left in panties and my bra.

Henri fell back onto the bed, leaning back on his elbows. "Fucking hell. I've died and gone to heaven."

I bit my lip, luxuriating in the intensity of his gaze. I felt no apprehension. He made me feel like the sexiest goddess. Which was so far from my previous experiences. I usually used every possible trick to hide my body. Total darkness, under covers, strategic lingerie, only certain positions. It was something I had gotten pretty good at, only taking things off at the very last moment.

All those impulses suddenly felt so far away and so unnecessary. It wasn't just that Henri wanted to see me, but that I didn't want to hide anymore.

I was done hiding. I was going to be seen, and I was going to enjoy it.

"Now lose the bra," he rasped.

I reached behind my back and unclasped my bra, letting it fall to the floor.

"Good girl."

My stomach muscles clenched at the sound of those words on his lips. I wanted to please him, to show him just how good a girl I could be.

"Pinch your nipples," he commanded.

I obeyed, never breaking eye contact. My breasts felt heavy and ached for his touch. I walked closer to where he sat, situating myself between his legs, and he took the opportunity to pull me onto his lap, kissing me while his hands explored my naked body.

"Why am I the only one naked?" I arched my back as he kissed down my chest, giving each breast his full attention.

He ignored me, instead letting his hands and mouth roam freely. "You drive me fucking insane."

"You don't exactly make it easy yourself," I replied, slowly unbuttoning his shirt. He watched me as I struggled with each button, the thick flannel stiff between my fingers.

"I can't fucking wait," he said, lifting me up and throwing me onto the bed. He stood and tossed his shirt on the floor, then quickly unbuckled his belt and dropped his jeans.

Before I could stop to appreciate the exquisite specimen before me, he was on top of me, caging my body between his muscled arms and resuming his exploration. I wiggled beneath him as he kissed down my neck, taking a moment to lavish attention on each of my breasts.

His cock, long and heavy, brushed against my thigh and sent a shiver down my spine. My mind narrowed, drowning out all my usual anxieties. All I could think about was feeling him inside me.

I moaned as he stroked his fingers over the seam of my panties.

"Fuck, you're soaked."

"Yes." I lifted my hips off the bed as he slowly pulled them down. "Do you have condoms?"

"Slow down." He swiped one finger down my seam and slowly brought it to his lips. "I need to taste you first."

I shook my head. As amazing as that sounded, I was primed and ready to go. "No. I need you," I gasped.

Henri's dark eyes narrowed, and suddenly I felt his strong hands pinning my thighs to the bed. "I make the rules, buttercup. And I'm tasting this pretty pussy."

He bent down and nipped at my inner thighs, driving me even more insane. A distant voice in my head protested at his bossiness, but it was only drowned out when his tongue met my aching clit. Just the faintest of touches, and I was seeing stars already.

But the gentility was short-lived as he held me down and devoured me.

"Yes. That's just right. Fuck—oh my God." I could barely speak, especially when he eased one finger inside me. I detonated on the spot. My hips rocking, I soaked up every sensation as I cried out in pleasure. He didn't stop. Didn't even pause as I spasmed and clenched around his fingers.

Eventually, I came back down to earth and realized that Henri was kissing his way up my body. The sight of him and those broad, strong shoulders lifted me out of my orgasmic haze. I needed more.

"I want to be on top," I said, my voice shaking slightly.

He nodded. "Perfect. Exactly how I've dreamed about this."

I flushed again, his words strengthening my resolve.

He lay back, putting his hands behind his head, and I took a moment to appreciate him spread out before me. Strong and broad, with thick chest hair and a happy trail leading to a very impressive dick. I wanted to lick every inch of him.

But first I had work to do.

After rolling the condom on, I straddled him and held eye contact as I lined myself up. The look of pure desire on his face only ratcheted up my arousal. I sank down slowly, letting myself feel every inch of him stretching and filling me perfectly. I threw my head back and moaned, letting myself adjust before looking down at him again.

He gripped my hips hard, the rough pads of his fingers

digging into my soft flesh. "Jesus, Alice. Warn a guy. I could have come right there watching your face."

I shrugged and rocked gently. "I'm not sorry."

I rode him with abandon, chasing my pleasure and feeling completely free. I had never done this, never taken this kind of initiative, and I'd never willingly chosen to be on top.

This felt like liberation. And his eyes remained on mine the entire time while his strong hands explored my body, heightening every sensation.

"That's it, buttercup. I can feel you tightening." He gently sucked one nipple while I ground down on him.

"I don't know if I can." I was closer than I had ever been before. Something about the way we fit together was perfect. He was hitting spots I didn't know I had and making me feel so full and so stretched. I loved it.

He snaked his hand up my body and stopped at my neck, pressing against my pulse point with his thumb. The gesture was gentle but sent bolts of desire down to my toes.

"You are so sexy, and your body is incredible. Ride my cock until you come, Alice. I can go all night if I have to."

I clenched around him, my inner muscles heeding his command. My hips sped up, and I cried out, feeling the waves of pleasure overtake me as he tightened his grip on my neck.

"Look at me," he growled, and I did, focusing on his dark eyes as I spasmed and collapsed on his chest, my heart racing.

What had just happened? Obviously, I'd orgasmed, but I had gotten there faster and easier than ever. I hadn't hesitated or obsessed about my body or whether he was having a good time or thought I was sexy. My mind never wandered. I was in the moment, and it felt incredible.

Before I could overanalyze this development, Henri flipped me onto my back and was kissing me again. "Good girl," he growled. "But that was the warm-up lap. Are you ready for more?"

I could barely speak as he slid inside me, dragging out the aftershocks. He was already setting a punishing pace as I wrapped my legs around him and lifted my hips to meet each thrust. "Yes," I cried out, already feeling another orgasm building within me. This was an out-of-body experience. He was everywhere—his hands, his lips, the weight of his strong body, and his thick cock lighting me up from the inside.

He pinned my arms above my head and ground his hips against mine, making me see stars. "Good. Because I'm not done yet. And neither are you."

I probably wouldn't be able to walk tomorrow, but I didn't care. I was swept away in Henri. The feel of his body on mine, the rough scratch of his beard against my neck. I was drunk on his masculine scent and the strength of his body and the way he took total control over my pleasure.

My arms were still pinned above my head as he explored my breasts with his mouth, gently biting each nipple and making me arch off the bed with pleasure.

And then he sped up, going harder and deeper and faster as I clung to him. "You are perfect, buttercup, one night won't be enough for me" he gasped in my ear. "This pussy is perfect. And before I explode, I want to feel you come all over my cock again."

His dirty words put me over the edge, the world falling away as my body responded to his. I was still soaring, reveling in all the sensations of Henri, when he spasmed and collapsed on top of me with a delicious growl.

Chapter 23
Henri

I lay on my back, staring at the ceiling beams, trying to make sense of what had just happened.

Alice's head was on my chest, her soft blond hair tickling my skin.

My body was sleepy and sated, but my caveman brain was short-circuiting with competing thoughts. *Mine? No. Not Yet. Sexy? Yes. Pretty girl? Sleep? Boner?*

I wished I could just turn it all off and go to sleep. But this was better than any dream.

I looked down at her, still naked and snuggled up in my arms. I traced my fingers down her spine, loving her tiny shiver.

We'd had sex.

And it wasn't like any sex I'd had before. Intense. Fun. And rough.

Oh shit. I hadn't been gentle. I hadn't been romantic. I had completely let go, and I think she had too. I hope she wasn't having regrets.

I stroked her hair. "I hope I wasn't too rough buttercup. I'm a growly bastard on a good day. But you make me feral."

She sat up and pulled the blanket around us. She looked sleepy and happy and so fucking beautiful in my bed.

She tucked herself under my arm and kissed my neck. "Tell me what you're thinking."

I looked down at her perfect face and wasn't even sure how to explain all the things I was feeling. "Sorry." I pulled her closer. "That was just...intense."

She nodded, biting her lip. "It was."

"Did I go too far?"

She let out a soft laugh. "No. Of course not. I may not be able to walk tomorrow, but I assure you. Brawny, that's a good thing."

I leaned back against the headboard and exhaled. I had let myself go with Alice, in a way I never had before. She made me feel so free that I had given in to all my impulses. I didn't want her to feel used. I wanted her to feel worshipped.

Cradling her against my chest, I took a moment to appreciate just how damn lucky I was. Not only was my dream woman naked in my bed, but I hadn't managed to scare her off by acting like a wild animal.

She nuzzled closer. "You know, I really liked it." She wiggled, really waking me up. "Sorry, my brain isn't really online right now, you know, after the earth-shattering orgasms and all..."

I smiled, full of pride. "Good. I would never want to hurt you, Alice."

She sat up and stared at me quizzically. "Wait. Now I'm worried." Her body tensed and her eyes widened.

"Why?"

"Because you positively manhandled me. And I liked it. A lot."

She stood up and wandered the room, looking for her underwear and depriving me of her warmth. I cursed myself by opening my damn mouth. Now she was getting dressed and I was being deprived of the greatest snuggles of my life.

She shimmied into her panties. "Jesus. I've never had it rough like that before. You put your hand..." She trailed off, her hand creeping up to her throat. "Around my neck!"

"You didn't like it?"

She stomped her foot, which was adorable and made her tits jiggle. "No, I loved it. I loved the feel of your rough hands on my skin. I've only ever had nice sex before. And now all I can think about is you spanking me and pulling my hair. What's wrong with me?"

"There's nothing wrong with you. Come back to bed."

She clasped her bra, and I wanted to rip it off and burn it. Maybe I could declare my house a no-bra zone? I tucked that idea away for future conversations.

I stood up and pulled her close, tucking a strand of hair behind her ear. "You are perfect," I said, and did my best to show her just how much I meant it with a soft kiss to her lips.

"Really? And you're the expert?"

I kissed her neck, letting my fingers travel up to that damn bra clasp.

"Consensual fun," I whispered in her ear while trailing kisses down her neck, "between two adults who care about one another is never going to be wrong."

She arched her back, and I softly bit her nipple over the lace of her bra.

"Because what we're doing says more about us than it does about you."

"How so?" She dragged her hand down my torso and stroked my aching cock with her fingertips, making me slightly dizzy.

"It says we trust each other. That we want each other, and we can play around as much as we're comfortable with."

I unhooked the back of her bra and let it fall to the floor.

"Because testing boundaries can be really fucking fun."

"I wanted you the first moment I laid eyes on you," I admitted. We were curled up on the couch and the wood stove was roaring. The dogs were behaving, and I took a moment to savor this moment.

"That's because I was a damsel in distress."

"But also because you were sassy and sexy and drove me insane."

"You didn't like me."

"Not true. That's just my shitty personality. It's not you."

She punched my shoulder gently. "Bullshit. You were mad at me for existing."

She was wrong. I was just mad at the world. Angry at my father for driving in bad conditions and leaving me with the burden of a struggling business and my three siblings. And angry that the town I had grown up in was unrecognizable some days.

I had a lot of anger. And none of it had anything to do with Alice.

"I'm sorry I made you feel that way. You just get under my skin. I'm not sure how to explain it. You make me feel things. And most of the time, I hate feeling things. I have too many things to get done, and I try to avoid all this shit."

"Wow. Spoken like a truly evolved lumberjack."

She leaned over and bit my shoulder.

"Ow. What was that for?"

"Not sure. I just felt the urge to take a bite out of you. You were such an ass."

"Still am, buttercup. I'm just the ass that can make you see stars."

She sat back, gathering her hair into one of those messy ponytails. I admired the curve of her neck in the firelight. "Why do you call me that?"

"Because," I pulled her onto my lap so she straddled me, "when I walked in on you naked, the song 'Build Me Up Buttercup' was playing. And it just stuck. Along with the memory of your incredible body. I swear every time I hear that song, I'll get a boner."

She threw her head back and laughed. "Serves me right for trying to dance around naked and managing to stub my toe in the process."

"I enjoyed it. I enjoy everything about you. Especially making you come."

I let my fingers wander up the hem of the T-shirt, which was the only thing standing between me and her naked body. She arched into my touch, and I resisted the urge to rip it off her body.

"That is definitely going in the pro column." She mimed writing on a chalkboard. "Pros: chops wood and delivers orgasms. Con: surly attitude."

"I do chop a lot of wood."

"Trust me. The sight of you chopping wood lives rent free in my brain."

"Is that right?" I smiled. Good to know she wasn't immune to my charms.

"Oh yes. That day you caught me staring? I went straight home and grabbed a vibrator. I don't even think I got my yoga pants all the way off."

Fuck, that was so hot. I closed my eyes and visualized her

touching herself. Great, now I was hard again. I needed more information. Which toy? Which position? How long did it take? Could I do it better? I wanted to know every single thing about her.

"So chores get you going?"

"Fuck yeah. Do you mop floors? Clean toilets? 'Cause lemme tell you, Brawny, that is a major turn-on."

"You're serious?" I laughed and gripped her hips. I liked that she didn't take herself too seriously. And I loved how comfortable she felt with me.

"Oh my God, yes. The axe is hot and all, but fuck, if you want to vacuum shirtless, my panties would probably incinerate in seconds."

I picked her up and put her down on the couch, then jumped to my feet. "I'll get right to work, then."

"Get back here. It's the middle of the damn night."

"Fine."

I sat back down and threw my arm around her, hugging her close and staring at the fire.

"Besides," she said, never looking away from the flames, "I don't have panties on."

Chapter 24
Alice

I missed my sisters. After years of having strained relationships, we had finally grown close. It had started a year ago when my baby sister Sylvie stood up to my parents and essentially told them to fuck off, choosing her music dreams and her boyfriend, Wyatt, over their approval.

Her bravery had inspired Maeve and me to stand up to them in our own ways too, and in the process, we rebuilt our relationships with one another. The three of us were very different, but I loved them deeply.

My parents were prickly, difficult people. They loved us, in their own warped way, but they truly saw their three daughters as reflections of them. And we were expected to toe the line and do what we were told. Be perfect and pretty and well behaved. Get good grades and have high-paying jobs.

I had spent years of my life devastated by my inability to please them or be the perfect daughter they wanted. It wasn't until I hit my thirties that I realized just how toxic those expectations and pressures were. How much they had destroyed my self-esteem and my belief in myself.

WOOD You Be Mine?

These days, my relationship with my parents was frosty. But I had my sisters back, and that alone had made my life so much better.

So I was thrilled when, exactly six weeks after moving to Lovewell, they called me to tell me they were coming for a visit.

They pulled up in Maeve's car, a sporty BMW that had no business on a dirt road in Maine. Sylvie jumped out of the car and darted toward me, leaving the passenger door wide open. When she got close, she threw her arms around my neck without hesitation. My baby sister was a hugger. She was the friendliest of the three of us and was a talented musician and overall lovely person. She enjoyed crystals and reiki, and she lived in a converted garage with her boyfriend, three rescue cats, and dozens of musical instruments.

Maeve exited slowly, closing the driver's side door and taking in every detail of the scenery. The cabin, the land, the road, the mountains. Even Clive the moose would have withered under her scrutiny.

What had previously terrified me now comforted me. Maeve was fiercely protective. She wasn't judging me or my choice to move to Lovewell—she was simply checking this place out to make sure it was good enough for me. What I had spent years perceiving as judgment was really just her way of showing her love.

She walked up slowly, wearing high-heeled snow boots—who knew such things even existed—and hugged me. She was tiny but strong. No one crossed Maeve.

"You look amazing," she said into my hair, giving me an extra squeeze. "We've missed the shit out of you."

"I've missed you too. Come in."

Sylvie retrieved several shopping bags from the trunk—which I strongly suspected contained wine and dessert, her two main food groups—and her guitar case.

Before we could take a step, Maeve screamed and clutched my arm. "Oh my God. What the fuck is that?"

She pointed up the hill toward the tree line. "Calm down. It's just Clive," I said, picking up the shopping bag she'd dropped in her panic.

"Clive?"

"He's a moose."

"I can see it's a fucking moose, Alice. What the hell is he doing so close to your house?"

I shrugged. "He goes where he wants. We had a showdown on my first day here, and then we came to an understanding." I gave Clive a wave and walked toward the house.

"You have a moose friend? Sylvie," she said, turning to my baby sister, "it's worse than we thought."

"We're not friends. We tolerate each other. He doesn't sneak up on me, and I let him eat the grass back there. It's all good."

My sisters looked at one another and then at me, eyes wide with bafflement. They looked like they were minutes from dragging me back to Havenport.

I cooked, Maeve mixed drinks, and Sylvie sat on the couch, playing a few new songs she'd written. She was starting to build her career as a songwriter, and we were incredibly proud of her. I missed being near her and experiencing the way she worked through the pieces she was writing.

We stuffed ourselves with tacos while they filled me in on what was happening in Havenport. I had always loved my hometown and had assumed I'd stay there forever, but I didn't miss it as much as I thought I would when I first struck out in search of a change.

Although Lovewell could not be more different, it was starting to feel like home. I liked who I was here. I could be New Alice. In Havenport, the entire town had known me since birth. I had gone to school there and worked there and visited the same bakery on my birthday every single year. I was stuck there. Here, I was growing and thriving.

"Have we talked about how incredible you look?" Maeve said, topping off our wineglasses. "You're a fucking blond bombshell now. And thank God you stopped wearing all those sad, dark clothes."

"Yes." Sylvie shuddered. "The cardigans. They were awful."

"Hey," I protested. "They weren't so bad." My wardrobe had previously consisted of many iterations of the same boxy, hip-length open cardigan.

"Those cardigans were horrifying and should be burned. You look hot! It's amazing what wearing clothes that fit you can do."

"And you're walking taller. No more making yourself smaller by hunching your shoulders and ducking your chin."

"Maeve, she's got swagger."

"Mm-hmm." She nodded, wearing a smirk. "She moves up to Nowheresville Maine and turns into this sexy, blond, curvy goddess who's rockin' life."

"It's not like that," I protested.

"Don't undermine yourself. You did this. And *this* is not a place the average person would be rocking life. It looks more like the kind of place you go to hit rock bottom."

"Wow. Thanks a lot."

"You know what I mean. I would be miserable here. But you're clearly thriving. Every time we talk, you're excited about something happening at school or about another hike you finished."

Sylvie rolled her eyes and patted my hand. "What Maeve is trying to say is that you've found the best version of yourself here. You seem fulfilled and happy, and you look smoking hot. Not that looks are important."

"So spill." Maeve leaned forward. "What's the secret? The mountain air or the creek water or the outhouse or the moose burgers? What kind of magic do the locals keep hidden up here?"

I sat back on the couch and enjoyed the warmth of the fire. "I chopped that wood," I said, gesturing to neat a stack next to the fire.

"Sorry, what?"

"Some of it. I chopped some of it."

"Damn, girl."

I shrugged. They were right. I did feel different. "I walked into this town so desperate to impress people, and no one really cared that I was here. Every single person made me prove myself. And so I get up every day and do what I want to do the way I want to do it. And I wear the clothes I want."

"Good for you. That's amazing."

"And I dyed my hair because why the fuck not? I take my mental health walks in the mountains. And work my butt off at this school that, oh my God," I lean forward and rest my elbows on my knees, "you guys, this school needs so much help."

"They need you, Alice. And you're already making big improvements."

I smiled. Sylvie always knew what I needed to hear. "The school needs, like, fifteen of me, but one will have to do for now. Plus my very pushy pro bono retiree secretary."

"This is a story I need to hear." Sylvie grinned. "Let me get more wine." She jumped up and made a beeline for the kitchen area but stopped short when a loud knock on the door startled us all.

"I'll get it," she said.

"No need." I was off the couch and in front of the door in a flash, steeling myself when I heard a telltale bark on the other side.

Doorknob in hand, I cracked the door open a few inches, but the two dogs pushed themselves inside, immediately darting for the kitchen, where they would help themselves to any leftovers they could reach.

"Brawny," I said, eyeing Henri. He was wearing a dark coat and a navy wool beanie. And he looked nervous.

"I brought you these," he said, holding a large bunch of colorful wildflowers tied with twine.

Before I could reach out to take them or thank him for his kind gesture, Maeve was behind me, pulling the door open wider.

"Hello. Who is this?"

"The landlord," he said, holding out his hand. "Henri Gagnon."

She took his hand, no doubt crushing his bones with her signature handshake. "Maeve Watson, I'm Alice's older sister. Come in and join us."

"No need," I said, nudging her out of the doorway. There was no way I was letting my sisters interrogate Henri. They would ask too many questions, and I didn't yet have the words to describe what had happened between us. I had woken up in his bed this morning, for fuck's sake. He'd walked me home and kissed me and then gone to work.

Maeve hip-checked me out of the way and welcomed him inside with a sweep of her arm. Sylvie was on the couch, petting both dogs, who were panting at her feet, already hopelessly in love with her.

"You should put those in water," Maeve chided. "And get Henri a glass of wine."

"I'm so sorry," Henri said, following Maeve. "I don't want to intrude."

"Don't be silly. We came up for a visit since it's a holiday weekend. We wanted to check on Alice."

She patted the couch. "Tell us about yourself, Henri." Shit. There was a telltale gleam in her eye. Nothing got by Maeve. It was why she was such a good accountant. If she found out about the previous night, there would be no hearing the end of it.

I wasn't ashamed. Just confused.

I'd had sex with Henri. Several rounds of hot, dirty, intense, multi-orgasm sex, followed by hours of cuddling and an awkward goodbye. My feelings were all over the place, and I was struggling not to romanticize our time together. Doing my best not to fall hopelessly in love with the man after one night.

Instead, I was trying desperately to channel my inner cool chick, who could compartmentalize and enjoy casual sex. But then the bastard showed up with flowers, looking delicious, and here I was, back to square one.

After a thorough interrogation and dinner, Henri left. As I shut the door, I braced myself for what was coming.

"So," Maeve said, "are we doing this the easy way or the hard way?"

Sylvie refilled our wineglasses with a smirk, clearly in anticipation of extracting every detail out of me.

Maeve threw her legs over the arm of the chair. "She's definitely sleeping with him. The question"—she paused to take a sip—"is when did it start?"

The two of them watched me silently, waiting me out. Sylvie with her sweet, concerned face, and Maeve with a look that would force a confession from even the most hardened criminal.

I threw my hands up. "Since yesterday." I huffed, plopping onto the couch and burying my head in a frilly throw pillow.

"Oh, *now* it's getting good."

WOOD You Be Mine?

"For Christ's sake, I'm not even sure I like him. He's grumpy and irritable and communicates in grunts." I squeezed my eyes shut, trying desperately to make sense of the last twenty-four hours. We had spent more than a month flirting, and I hadn't hidden my interest, but things had gotten real fast.

"But?" Maeve drummed her fingers on the coffee table.

I groaned into the pillow. "But he's also kind and considerate."

"And has dogs," Sylvie added.

Maeve chuckled. "And chops wood."

"Oh, he doesn't just chop it. He's a champion lumberjack." I finally uncovered my face and sat up, describing the competition yesterday and how insanely hot it was.

Maeve fanned herself. "You had no choice. You had to fuck him." She shrugged. "A lumberjack competition? That sexy man was swinging an axe around to impress you?"

"I think that counts as a marriage proposal in the state of Maine," Sylvie joked. "We should check the bylaws."

"Shut up." I chucked the pillow at her face.

"God, we've been so worried about you. We thought we'd have to come up here and bring you back to Havenport. But you're positively thriving."

"Crushing it," Sylvie agreed.

"To Alice." Maeve raised her wineglass, and Sylvie followed suit. "She moved to the sticks and got her dream job. She looks gorgeous doing it and is fucking a hot lumberjack. All hail the queen!"

Chapter 25
Henri

I hadn't seen Alice since I crashed her dinner with her sisters on Sunday night. Work was kicking my ass this week, and it was only Wednesday. I was still slowly making my way through all of Dad's notes and paperwork. The boxes sat in my home office, staring at me every time I walked by the door.

There were so many unanswered questions and cryptic notes. It made me simultaneously frustrated and despondent. Some days, the regret sat on my chest like a heavy weight, making it increasingly harder for me to breathe. He had been one of the most important people in my life, and I never fucking told him that. It had always been hard for me to understand my feelings and talk about them. So we'd worked side by side for years, and I never stopped to thank him for all he'd taught me or to tell him that I loved him.

It wasn't our way. We grunted and back-slapped and never talked about feelings. But now that he was gone, I cursed myself every time I couldn't find the words to express my emotions. And I used work as an excuse to pull away from my family when I should have been drawing them even closer.

When I walked through the door, I was greeted by my insane dogs. I let them out quickly but planned to take them on a long walk later, in hopes of running into Alice on the trails. I was desperate to see her. And I wasn't afraid to admit it.

We hadn't yet talked about what happened last weekend. She'd implied she wanted casual, and I'd agreed to it, but that was before three rounds and a snuggle sleepover.

If she still wasn't interested in anything serious, my cock would have to deal with it. That horny fucker wanted to wife her up immediately. But it was best to take things slow. I just needed to convince her to give me a chance.

So when I'd seen the unfamiliar car in front of the cabin on Sunday, I'd panicked and run down there like a jealous, lovesick lunatic. And, idiot that I was, the only thing I accomplished was interrupting her visit with her sisters and clueing them into the idea that something was going on between Alice and me.

The one with the dark hair—Maeve—was clearly sizing me up and sniffing me out to determine whether I was good enough for her little sister.

The answer was no, obviously. She didn't need to work so hard to come to that conclusion.

But now I was even more desperate to see Alice. To get her alone, to look into her beautiful eyes and kiss her soft, delicious mouth and figure out what the fuck was happening because my mind and body were at war.

Alice made me think about the future. A future where I wasn't a lonely workaholic who sat and drank scotch with no company but my dogs every weekend. For so many years, I had shut out even the possibility of meeting someone. I was too focused, too driven to succeed. Especially after Dad died.

But now things were different. My mind was opening up to the possibility of a life shared with someone. Specifically Alice. A life with love and laughs and potentially a family someday. Once these ideas started floating around in my brain, I couldn't make them go away. And right now, I didn't even want to. I wanted to see her and talk to her and be with her.

So I just happened to be reading a book on my porch when she came home from school. And my dogs had conveniently run down the hill to greet her. I hurried after them, mentally promising them extra treats tonight for being such excellent wingmen.

"Alice," I said, my heart suddenly pounding. "You look nice."

She removed a giant tote bag from the back seat and gave me a weary smile. "Thanks."

I took it from her and shut the door. "Long day?"

She tipped forward to give the dogs some love. "The longest. I usually leave at four thirty, but I had to give some of my students a ride home."

I followed her inside, holding her tote while she took off her coat and shoes and immediately pulled her hair up into a messy bun. My fingers ached to unravel it.

"How are you?" she asked, taking the bag from me and pulling out folders and files.

I swallowed thickly, frozen to the spot. I had no clue what to do or what to say. What was I even doing with my hands? I quickly shoved them into my pockets and rocked back on my heels, searching the recesses of my mind for something to talk about.

"Henri?" She quirked one eyebrow.

At that, I lost it. I closed the distance between us in two strides, pushed her back up against the table, and kissed her.

She melted into me, wrapping her arms around my neck as I deepened the kiss.

She pulled back after a moment, her face flushed. "You're going to make me do it, aren't you?"

"What?"

"Talk about this?"

"We could keep kissing." I dove in again, biting her bottom lip. I was mad for this woman. My hands roved all over her, slowly unbuttoning the buttons on the blue shirtdress she wore. It was demure yet sexy and would look even better on the floor.

She pushed my hands away gently and stepped back. "Let's sit and talk."

I followed her to the couch. The dogs were sprawled out, waiting for more belly scratches, so I stepped over them and obliged, keeping my attention fixed on them while she settled on the couch. I had the sinking feeling she was going to shoot me down.

When I finally looked up, she gave me a kind smile. Not a sexy, I-want-you-naked smile, but the kind reserved for elderly people and children. It made me want to vomit.

"I want to take you out," I blurted, trying to beat her to the punch. "Last weekend was intense. And I can't stop thinking about you."

She bit her lip. "It was intense. And fun. But we agreed to just one night."

"It doesn't have to be."

"We barely know each other."

"I can think of a few ways to fix that." I gave her my best flirty smile, which was probably more of a grimace. Flirting with unbearably sexy women wasn't something I spent much time practicing.

My relationship history was a shitshow. Mostly casual relationships, and some one-nighters, interspersed with one toxic long-term relationship that fucked me up so thoroughly I had sworn off dating for years after.

A man like me had no business being with a woman like Alice. But I couldn't stay away. I couldn't let this kind of attraction slip through my fingers without at least trying. Because beautiful, smart, funny women who drove me fucking crazy did not walk into town every day. And they definitely did not move into the rental cabin next door.

"Let's spend time together. Get to know one another. I find you fascinating, buttercup. Fascinating and beautiful and infuriating all at the same time."

She blushed, and I knew I was making progress. "I don't know how to do this," she said softly.

I tucked a loose strand of hair behind her ear. "Me neither. But I'd like to try."

She looked down at her hands. I wanted to take all of her doubts and throw them right into the wood stove. Was it just me? Was I the only one feeling this?

"If you're not interested, no hard feelings," I said.

She shifted in her seat and tilted her head, studying my face for a moment. Her brow was furrowed, and there were dark circles under her eyes. She was under so much pressure at school, and I wished I could do something to make it better.

"I'm interested," she said slowly, and my heart clenched. "Trust me. I'm just not sure."

I nodded, searching for a suitable response and coming up empty.

"For me, sex involves feelings..." She trailed off.

I turned her slightly and massaged her shoulders. "So you have feelings for me?"

She sighed and leaned into my touch as I tried to unwind the tension in her neck. Her muscles were so tense. When I hit a particularly difficult knot near her shoulder blade, she arched her back, making my cock harden.

"Maybe? I don't know. But if we kept going, I would. And that's not fair to either of us. I'm trying to accomplish a lot here. I don't want a relationship. And I'm not sure I'm cut out for casual. So it's probably best to move on."

Working down her shoulders, I watched her body relax.

Clearing my throat, I assured her, "I would never get in the way of your goals, Alice. Never. But I would love to spend time with you. Think about it. This weekend. You and me. We'll go somewhere fun, get out of Lovewell and cut loose."

I gently tugged the elastic out of her hair, letting the honey waves tumble down over her shoulders, then got to work massaging her scalp, starting over her ears and working up toward the crown of her head.

She said nothing, but she let out a tiny moan and tipped her head back farther. I'd be thinking about that moan tonight when I was alone in my bed.

"Okay," she breathed after a few moments. "I'll give you one date."

Chapter 26
Alice

"Why did I let you talk me into this?" I shouted from the back of the plane. "I'm terrified."

Henri turned back and smiled. "You're safe. Walt's been doing this since before either of us was born."

He patted Walt on the shoulder, and the older man gave me a thumbs-up.

When Henri had suggested a date, I never imagined it would include a small aircraft. But here I was, squeezed into the back of a tiny floatplane, wearing a headset and terrified for my life.

Tall and wiry and wearing an old-school flight suit, Walt was at least seventy-five years old. His wife Irma had helped him prep the plane while we waited on the dock. It was bright yellow, with large pontoons and looked like a relic from the World War II movies my grandpa used to love.

My gut was telling me to run, that the FAA had probably not inspected this thing in a few decades. I would rather not plummet to my death, but it was a beautiful, clear day, and the lake was gorgeous. Henri was naturally an anxious, overprotective type, and yet he was totally at ease.

He reached over the seat and squeezed my hand.

"Don't worry, darlin'," Walt said, steering the plane toward the middle of the lake. "I've been doing this a long time. Started flying in middle school, then for the Army in Vietnam, and then back up through these woods for the last forty years or so."

Henri smiled. "We're in good hands, buttercup."

"Prepare for takeoff," Walt said, working the controls of the plane.

We picked up speed, the pontoons cutting cleanly through the water. And then Walt jerked the nose of the plane upward, and we were taking off, soaring up over the lake and into the air.

My heart was in my throat, but I was consumed by excitement and in awe of the scenery. Slowly, we climbed, the plane feeling even smaller as we left the ground. After circling around the lake for a few minutes, we headed northwest, gliding over the town and the forest.

The forest was formidable, even from this vantage point, and dotted between the thick pine groves was the most breathtaking fall foliage. Thousands of trees turned every shade of yellow, orange, and red, creating a vibrant carpet leading up to the mountains.

After a few minutes, my heart rate steadied, and a smile crept onto my face. Soaring up above the forests in such a tiny plane meant we could feel every bump, but my nerves adjusted, and I could finally take in the beauty below us.

I pressed my face to the tiny window, marveling at all I could see.

We passed small towns and followed the river, watching as the wilderness stretched out endlessly toward the horizon.

"Look down," Henri instructed.

We were cruising over what was probably a large pond, but from the sky, it looked like a puddle. There were at least a dozen moose on the banks, munching on nearby leaves and twigs and drinking water. They looked like mice from our height.

"Holy shit."

"You'll see lots of moose from up here," Walt explained. "Maybe a few bears too, but they're harder to spot."

Walt brought the plane around, pointing out the mountains that made up the end of the Appalachian Trail and taking us lower to admire another glistening blue lake. The plane was loud, but our headsets allowed us to talk. Henri calmly explained what we were seeing and reassured me often that we were safe.

"What's that?" I asked, pointing to a spot in the distance where the carpet of pines seemed to stop.

"Wanna take a look?" Walt asked, steering the plane in that direction.

"That's the fire site," Henri explained. "There was a huge forest fire in the 1970s. They're rare in Maine, but this one took out thousands of acres. This used to be logging land in the old days. Back before the road was built."

Walt pulled the plane around, and I saw the most amazing thing. A small valley surrounded by towering pines that was filled with scrub and plants and what looked like long grasses.

"That's fireweed," Walt explained. "It takes decades for a forest to recover from a big fire, and most of it did. But this one spot—it's just clear."

"In the summer, it's filled with wildflowers. I'll bring you back here to see it," Henri said. "It's called a super bloom when that happens. The fire releases all these wildflower seeds that grow and flourish in the soil, even when the pine trees don't come back."

"Fascinating." The valley looked lush, even in the late fall, but still slightly barren, insulated from the world by tall trees and giant mountains. I admired its stark beauty as Walt circled around and headed back toward the mountains.

But just as my poor heart finally calmed, we were descending fast, cutting through the sky as the trees got closer and closer. I squeezed my eyes shut, telling myself that Walt's reflexes had to be exceptional if he still had his pilot's license. We landed with a small splash on another large lake. But unlike our takeoff point, this area was completely remote. No houses, roads, or boats to be seen. Just a long wooden dock.

He circled around twice, reducing his speed before taxiing toward the dock.

"Couple hours?" he asked, giving Henri a nod and a wink.

"Yes."

Henri helped me out, gently lifting me onto the dock and steading me as I got my land legs back. My heart was racing, and I had never felt more alive.

He took the large basket and a bag from the seat next to where I had been sitting and gave Walt a salute. We watched as he started the engine, did a lap around the lake to gain speed, and then took off, disappearing into the forest.

"Where are we?"

"Big Eagle Lake."

"And there are no people here?"

"No, buttercup. We're on Gagnon land. This is part of our logging claim. There are no homes up here. No roads, either. We built the dock and shed a few years ago for supplies and gas for the crews who work the camps."

He wandered toward the shed at the end of the dock. "At some point, we'll extend the roads up here to the lake, but right now, it's purely a drop-off point. Come on." He held out a hand, and I took it.

Once he guided me off the dock, we stepped carefully over a rocky area and headed for a small, secluded spot lined with a few trees for shade at the water's edge. Henri pulled a few pieces of firewood out of the bag he'd carried over and arranged it inside a small rock circle carefully before getting the flames going. I watched him, zipping my coat up against the October chill and enjoying the care with which he approached this simple task.

Once the fire was burning, he crouched low and produced a thick blanket from the bag. Once he'd laid it down, he rummaged around the bag once more.

"Sit," he said, producing a small kettle and another blanket.

"Did you pack a picnic?"

He peered up at me, a small blush creeping up his cheeks. "Maybe."

"You don't seem like the kind of guy who enjoys a picnic."

"That's where you're wrong. I love a good picnic. Now sit so I can spoil you."

In minutes, the fire was roaring, putting off lots of heat and warming my cheeks, and he had unpacked fancy cheese and bread and nuts and what looked like expensive chocolates.

"Hot toddy?" he asked, squeezing a lemon wedge into a stainless-steel mug.

"Yes, please!"

No one had ever done anything so unique and thoughtful for me before. We were miles from civilization, and that should probably terrify me, but with Henri, I felt relaxed and safe.

"What are we toasting to?" I asked.

"Your first floatplane ride," he said, leaning down and pressing his lips to mine before clinking our mugs together.

I took a sip of the delicious hot whiskey. "That was something I never thought I would do."

"It's how we get around up here. There aren't always roads,

and even where there are, they aren't always reliable. And with so much wilderness, we need a means to keep an eye on things."

"Do you fly around a lot?"

He shook his head. "No, not anymore. We used to have planes. Walt flew for my dad and granddad for years. But that was in the seventies and eighties, when the trees were plentiful and business was booming." He shifted, pulling me closer. Despite the cold air, the fire and his proximity kept me perfectly warm.

"Things have been a lot harder in the last decade or so. Global competition for wood drives down prices and floods the market. And the paper mill closed about ten years ago, further hurting the demand. A lot of lumber companies have sold out and gone corporate, making things even harder for little guys like us to compete. So we sold the planes a while ago. We do some air work, surveying, photos, and that sort of thing. But we mostly hire bush pilots or use drones."

I craned my neck to look at him. "Did you love coming out here when you were a kid?"

"Of course." He nodded. "I loved everything about the forest. Still do. Places like this, totally pristine and untouched, are so rare and so perfect. A lot of people think we just cut down trees, but it's so much more. We plan and strategize and plant to create sustainable forests that can keep providing for future generations."

His face was animated, and his eyes were shining. Henri was a man of few words, so hearing the passion in his voice and understanding the commitment he had to his work was inspiring. His face lit up when he explained the different species of trees around us and how important the moss was in helping generate regrowth and fertile soil.

"Did you always want to be a lumberjack?"

He snorted. "Yes and no. It's complicated."

I nibbled a piece of cheese and inspected him. "I've got the time, Brawny. Tell me everything."

"Timber's in my blood. It's the foundation of our town, this region. It's part of my family history. And it's always felt, I don't know, important. Like continuing the business my great grandfather started was more significant than becoming an accountant or a chef or something."

"I can see that. It's part of your story."

"Exactly. I was raised in the woods, drove my first dump truck at thirteen. Somewhere along the way, I fell in love with the idea of working hard and producing something every day. My grandfather always bragged that Maine timber built Boston and New York. That those big cities, and the houses in the suburbs, all exist because of people like us, up here in the mountains, working hard every day. Libraries and hospitals and small businesses. These trees built those communities just like they built ours."

Something clicked into place with his exposition. The picture of Henri in my head was becoming more rich and complete. There was so much depth under the beard and the flannel and the surly attitude.

"That's kind of beautiful."

"I wanted to get to work full time the day I graduated from high school, but my parents insisted I go to college. So I went to U Maine and graduated with a degree in forest science."

"That's useful." I smiled.

"Some days." He sipped his whiskey. "I like science, enjoyed the research, and was eager to put it to use. I worked with outside consultants and the state regulators to put together our sustainability plan. It was adopted by all the logging companies in the state. My dad was so proud."

"I'm sure he was."

"And I worked on even more projects to make us sustainable. Went to conferences, read papers. Dad was even pushing me to think about grad school. And then he died suddenly, and I was in charge. The CEO."

"I'm so sorry, Henri." I squeezed his arm. "That must have been so difficult."

He shrugged. "So now I'm the boss."

I snuggled closer to him. "For what it's worth," I buried my face in his flannel, "you're doing an amazing job. I'm sure your dad is so proud of you. So many people could never have stepped up like that. But your love for this town, your employees, and the forest? It's so clear."

"Thanks." He cleared his throat. "Want to try the chocolates I brought?"

"Yes, please."

After cheese, chocolate, and another hot toddy, I was warm and comfy. I was snuggled up with Henri, watching the fire, and feeling truly relaxed for the first time since I'd moved up here.

"I answered your questions," Henri hedged.

"Mmm," I replied, still snuggled up in his warmth.

"Time for you to answer mine." He rubbed a hand down my arm and squeezed. "Why don't you want a relationship?"

I sighed and sat up, wishing we could continue to soak in the peace of the moment. "Do we have to do this now?" I gave him my best impression of a petulant stare.

But he didn't budge. He just sat quietly, waiting for me to talk.

"I don't have the best history," I explained.

"Who hurt you?" he growled.

"No. Not like that." I ducked my head and tugged on my sleeves, covering my fingers. "Me. I hurt me."

With two fingers under my chin, he forced me to meet his gaze. "You're going to need to explain this to me, buttercup."

"The guys I dated were fine. They weren't the problem. I didn't value myself. Didn't put my needs first. Fell into relationships with people who were wrong for me. Or even worse, one-sided relationships."

He pulled me closer, nipping my ear and kissing my neck. "I assure you—this is not one sided."

"I placed such low value on myself that I managed to only connect with guys who also didn't value me. I didn't know how to speak up for myself, assert my needs, or demand respect in relationships. So I'm working to unlearn decades of bad habits."

"I think you're doing a damn good job," he whispered just below my ear.

"Thank you." I gave him a small smile. "But that's why I can't pursue a relationship. It's not you. It's me. And I actually mean that."

He stopped kissing and pulled away. *Damn.*

"Bullshit," he whispered.

"Excuse me?"

"I'm calling bullshit. You're scared. And that's fine. I'm scared too. But I've known you for a couple of months now. You're no wilting flower, and you're no pushover. You've had no trouble asserting your needs with me."

He gently stroked my jaw, pushing my chin up until we were eye to eye. "When I look at you, I see a badass. You showed up in a new town, a new state, and jumped right into the deep end. Look at all you've done at school. You've made friends. You're part of the community now. Hell, even Bernice likes you."

"She doesn't like me."

"She gives you pie. For Bernice, that's a huge step. Stop

selling yourself short. Don't deny what you want because of the arbitrary rules you've made up in your head."

"Hey." I gently batted his hand away. Henri was too observant for his own good.

He grabbed my hand and pulled it to his lips, gently kissing my palm. "Because I think we're dating, and I'm pretty happy about it."

"Oh really?" I smirked.

"Yup." He pulled me into his lap. "We've slept together. Multiple times. And we're on a date."

"A first date."

"Technically. But everyone in town already thinks we're dating, and your sisters approve of me."

"What makes you think that?"

"Please." He laughed. "Maeve would have castrated me in my sleep if she didn't." He wasn't wrong about that.

I moved my legs to fully straddle him as he ran his hands down my sides teasingly and gripped my hips.

"So let's give it a try." He gripped my ass over my jeans and ground his thickening erection into my center.

"You are impossible." I groaned, desperate for friction.

"I know. But you like it."

"Fuck. I do like it."

"And you drive me insane. But all it does is make me want you more." He thrust up gently, showing me exactly what I did to him. "Do you understand, buttercup? This isn't one sided. I'm in this all the way, and I'll follow your lead."

"Okay," I breathed, dizzy with lust as he snaked one hand beneath my coat. "We can try. But casual."

"As long as you're mine, I'll take it."

Chapter 27
Henri

Lust fogged my brain as I kissed her, my body on high alert. The adrenaline from the day surged through me, and I needed her. Now.

God damn this Maine weather. We each had on so many layers. I pawed at her coat, trying to get it unzipped. My fingers itched to feel her curves, and my cock ached in my pants. Thank God I had the good sense to pack several blankets, in addition to a box of condoms.

Within seconds, I had her on her back with her coat unzipped as I tasted her neck and let myself fall into the sensations of Alice.

"It never goes away," I said, pulling her hair back to give myself better access to that sweet spot behind her ear.

She arched for me, always ready to give me what I wanted. "What?"

"Wanting you. Craving you. I thought I could do it. I thought we could have a night of fun together to blow off steam. But you're under my skin now, buttercup. I need to taste you and touch you and possess you."

I captured her mouth in a kiss while I roughly pulled down her leggings, exposing her creamy thighs. My primal instincts roared inside me as there was only a tiny scrap of panties separating me from what my body craved.

"I want it too. I've been thinking about you so much." She moaned as I tugged her panties to the side, exploring with my fingers.

"Good. Because we're in the middle of nowhere; you can scream as loud as you want," I said as I thrust one finger inside her.

"God, you're already soaked." I circled her clit with my thumb while adding a second finger. Her back arched off the blanket, and her inner muscles squeezed my pumping fingers.

"Henri." She wiggled beneath me as I pinned her to the blanket. "I need—"

"Tell me," I said, biting her nipple through her sweater and loving how her thighs quivered. "What do you need?"

"I need you inside me." She gasped as I sped up, reveling in how wet and ready she was.

"Maybe. If you ask nicely."

"Please." She gasped as I continued to tease her. "Please."

I reached into my bag and pulled out a box of condoms. She pushed up onto her elbows. "A full box?"

I shrugged. "You're rubbing off on me, buttercup. I'm optimistic. Now get on your knees. I want you to look at the forest while I make you come."

She blushed, clearly not used to taking orders, but complied, treating me to the most gorgeous view I had ever seen. It took every ounce of my willpower not to thrust inside her like a wild animal. My balls ached and my cock twitched at the promise of being inside her.

I slowly stroked myself, taking a moment to breathe before

easing myself inside her. She gasped, a sound I'd never get tired of, as she adjusted to my size.

"Please," she begged again, and I could tell she needed this as much as I did. Slowly, I moved, anchoring my hands on her luscious hips and trying to stay in control. I'd start counting the pine needles on the trees if it meant I could make her come. Because there was no way in hell I wasn't going to make this amazing for her.

"Faster," she cried.

"No." I said, giving her a gentle spank. "I'm taking my time and enjoying the feel of your delicious pussy wrapped around me."

She moaned, and I spanked her again. "You like that, don't you?"

She nodded, pushing back and meeting my thrusts, arching her back and making it harder and harder for me to remain in control. This woman challenged me on every level, and I reveled in it.

"Don't go slow," she panted between gasps. "I need you rough."

My peripheral vision blurred as my body surged into hers. Fuck, I needed her.

"Touch yourself," I said, my voice shaking slightly. "I want to feel you clench around me when you come on my cock."

She brought her hand to her center, tightening immediately when she rubbed furiously at her clit.

I sped up, reveling in the feel of her and the sounds she was making as I grabbed her hair with one hand. She needed this as badly as I did, and that knowledge, that we craved one another, kept me going while she fell apart around me.

She screamed and bucked against me, shouting my name into the forest. I could only hold on for a few seconds after she finished, shuddering deeply as my vision narrowed and my brain shut off.

We collapsed in a heap on the blanket, and I immediately wrapped my arms around her for warmth. I inhaled deeply, loving the smell of the forest mixed with her natural scent. The sky was clear, and the air was crisp, and my heart was dancing around in my chest. It had been a risk, flying her out here, but the way she was curled up in my arms, sated and almost purring, made it worth it.

By the time Walt came back to pick us up, Alice could not stop smiling. We did our best to clean up and not look like we hadn't been fucking in the woods, but I don't think we were fooling anyone. Especially as we both had pine needles in our hair. But she didn't seem to mind, kissing me and giggling as we climbed back into the plane. All her hesitation from earlier had vanished, and I felt like I was on top of the world.

"I want an invitation to the wedding," Walt grumbled as we took off, the plane flying gracefully into the air and into the clouds.

Chapter 28
Henri

I was in a daze, an Alice-induced stupor. We had spent
every night together since our picnic the previous weekend, yet I couldn't get enough of her.

With Alice, I felt exhilarated and comfortable all at the
same time. I wasn't worried about saying the wrong thing or
coming off like an asshole. Rather than seeking solace in the
solitude and silence I used to crave after a long day at work, I
surrounded myself with the sound of Alice's laughter and the
feel of her body snuggled against mine on my couch. She was
so different from anyone I'd ever known. Headstrong and independent but warm and loving too. I'd seen her with the
students, with my siblings. Hell, with this entire town, and I
knew she was special. Our time together only solidified that
observation.

I found myself in town Friday afternoon, seeking the
largest, strongest coffee I could find. Spending so much time
with Alice managed to make me sleep deprived while somehow
less grumpy.

Nothing got by my siblings, of course. Paz teased me about

my coffee consumption and asked how my neighbor was doing, where Adele was far more obvious. Telling me daily how much she liked Alice and how I better not scare her away with my repulsive personality.

I ignored them. Trying to juggle nonstop work crises didn't give me a lot of time to chat.

The holiday season was coming, and the Main Street shops were decking the halls. Things were less ornate than when I was a kid, but Lovewell still brought out the cheer. On my way to the diner, I stumbled across the new salon. I'd been so busy with work and Alice that I hadn't taken the time to scope it out since I'd learned of its existence.

I had never been a salon kind of guy, but Alice had mentioned that her friend Becca owned it. Alice had me feeling inspired. If she could get up every day and work hard for all of Lovewell, I could at least patronize a new small business.

Plus, I hadn't had a trim in a while, and if there was one thing that could make me put a little thought into my appearance, I supposed it was having a woman in my life. A woman. *My woman.*

It had been a long time coming, but maybe I was finally ready for something real and lasting and forever.

Becca, the tattooed proprietress, was friendly and efficient and didn't ask me too many questions. Both were excellent qualities in a hair stylist. "You know," she said, scissors poised as she studied my head, "I can give your beard a trim too. Clean it up and moisturize."

"Um...sure."

"Just in case you have any other hot dates planned for the weekend." She winked at me.

"You know?"

"Of course I know. The entire town knows Walt flew you two out to a remote lake for a sexy picnic. I may be new in town, but I've got ears." She threw her head back and laughed. "Plus his wife Irma is in the knitting group with my mother-in-law. The old ladies talk a lot."

"We're just dating casually," I said, swallowing thickly. Things between Alice and me were new, and although I was beginning to think long term, that didn't mean I wanted the entire town butting in.

Becca laughed. "Sure, you are. You know, since you're in town, you should stop by. School's out in an hour, and I'm sure she'd like to see you."

"She does like coffee," I mused.

"Yes. Especially a cinnamon latte with almond milk."

As I was leaving, Becca gave my hand a firm shake. "She's special. I hope you realize that."

I nodded. I most certainly did.

I took Becca's advice and headed over to the school. Along the way, I grabbed coffees, my mother's favorite green tea with honey, and a box of tasty looking cookies.

The Lovewell Community School had changed drastically since I was a kid. It was clean and bright, and kids were playing on the playground while teachers supervised the pickup line.

I knocked on the glass of the main office, and my mom looked up and smiled, giving me a wave.

I made my way in, only to be stopped by a tiny person with a scowl on her face.

"Can I help you?" She had blond ringlets and couldn't have been more than six.

"I'm here for a visit," I said, standing up straighter and trying to look like an adult rather than the lovesick teen I felt like on the inside.

"Are those cookies?" Her little eyes grew wider.

"Yes. Would you like some?"

She smiled and nodded eagerly, bringing her clasped hands to her chest. My heart clenched. I didn't have a lot of experience with kids, but if they were all this sweet and adorable, I couldn't imagine how Alice got any work done.

When I flipped opened the box, she squealed with delight. "These are fancy ones! Tucker, come here."

A moment later, a scrawny tween emerged from the back room, looking nonplussed.

He had shaggy hair and wore a Pokémon hoodie that was several sizes too large. But his eyes softened when the little girl handed him a cookie. *Tucker*. Alice had been talking about the kid nonstop. And his little sister. She worried about them endlessly and was trying to communicate with their foster parents, who sounded less than helpful.

"Tucker," my mom said in the most gentle voice I'd ever heard her use to scold a child. From the love that shone in her eyes, it was clear she was completely charmed by these kids. She certainly never spoke that way when admonishing me.

"Thank you," he said, his mouth full. He took another cookie, then turned and headed to the back room again.

"I'm Goldie, and that's my brother Tucker," the little one explained, helping herself to another cookie. "What's your name?" Her blue eyes were bright and curious.

"Henri Gagnon," I replied.

"Are you here to visit Principal Watson?"

I paused. Technically, yes, but I wouldn't admit that to this child. "I'm here to see my mom," I said, leaning down so my mom could kiss my cheek.

"Ooh, I'm so flattered. To what do I owe the pleasure?" she asked.

"You always come to my office bearing food. I wanted to return the favor."

I loved my mom, but her bullshit detector was well honed after having raised four hooligan children. "Sure, sweetie. I'm with my friend Goldie on this one. I think you came to see the lovely Principal Watson."

Goldie laughed. "Do you want to marry Miss Watson? Ugh." She made a gagging face.

I rolled my eyes. Kids were brutal.

"She's in her office," my mother said, grasping my arm and turning me in the direction of the closed door. "Try smiling. That might work."

I knocked softly on the door and opened it a crack. Alice was sitting in her chair, staring at the wall next to her desk. It was covered in neat rows of Post-it notes, all in different colors.

"Hi," I said, letting myself in and shutting the door behind me.

She turned and looked at me, her face breaking into a wide smile that made my stomach flip. That smile turned me inside out and made everything foggy every time she directed it my way. It made me want things. Things I had no business wanting.

"I brought you a present." I held up the cup.

She jumped out of her chair and snatched the cup from my hand, throwing her free arm around my neck. When she pulled back and took a sip, she made a satisfied moaning sound, and then she pulled me down for a truly indecent kiss.

"I'm so happy to see you."

"I'll swing by more often. That was quite a greeting."

She shrugged and arched a brow, then took another sip. "You brought me coffee." She gestured to a large fuzzy beanbag chair in the corner. "Have a seat."

"I'll stand," I said, putting my free hand in my pocket and

surveying her office. "You have quite the operation out there. The pint-sized greeter is a nice touch."

She smiled. "We're finding our way. Tucker and Goldie are great kids who don't have a lot of positive adult role models. I pay Tucker to work here after school fixing things, and Goldie usually colors or plays with your mom, then I drive them back to their foster home."

"The kid likes to fix things? When he runs out of stuff here, Adele can put him to work. We have more than enough broken stuff in our shop. She was building engines when she was his age."

Alice's face broke out into a big, beautiful smile. She threw her arms around my neck and pulled me down for another kiss. "Oh, Brawny, you put up a good front, but beneath the grumpy exterior, you're a big softie."

I scoffed, but I wrapped my free arm around Alice and enjoyed the feel of her pressed against me. "I think you like it," I whispered in her ear.

She kissed me again, gently biting my lip. "Oh, I like it, Brawny. I like it a lot."

Chapter 29
Alice

This was too much, too soon, and too fast. Logically, I knew it wasn't a good plan. Relationships didn't move at this speed, and partnerships weren't built on a foundation of orgasms and wilderness adventures.

But being with Henri for the last few weeks had me throwing out all my old ideas about relationships and partnerships and what I wanted. That white picket fence and the "perfect" husband? Those dreams felt like silly delusions now. Especially with him sleeping beside me, his strong arm thrown across me possessively.

Because Henri was real. And my attraction to him grew by the day. There was no way in hell this would be more than a fling, but I found that I was totally on board with that.

Without the pressure of trying to make him like me, I was free to be myself. I wasn't worried about convincing him to become my boyfriend or my husband. I didn't fret about whether I was good enough.

With Henri, I didn't feel self-conscious or less-than.

I felt his desire, his reverence, his respect every minute we were together.

And day by day, bit by bit, being here was healing me. I was sanding down the sharp edges of my insecurities and embracing my true self even more.

Lovewell was pushing me to be a better version of myself, to step into my light. The days weren't easy, but I was doing things my way.

And after a lifetime of waiting for my turn, this felt like a revelation. I was a principal, I was making positive changes in this community, and I had the company of a good, kind, and devastatingly sexy man.

From an early age, I was taught to wait until I was worthy. While Maeve was playing sports and Sylvie was taking music lessons after school, I was going to step aerobics classes and attending Weight Watchers meetings.

God forbid I'd done something fun. My mother made it clear that I didn't deserve fun, at least until I solved this fundamental flaw in my existence.

My mom would say things like: "When you're thin, you can go to the beach/sleepover/school trip/summer camp." Like thinness was a special state of being that would change my life. And like the good, gullible idiot I was, I believed that my life was terrible and would magically change when I was skinny.

So I waited. Patiently. I waited through all the workouts and the diets and the vitamins. While I watched my sisters and friends take risks and try things and grow.

And then one day, I was out for a walk through Havenport with my sisters, and I realized that I was happy. I was worthy. Granted, these revelations took several months of therapy, but I got there.

I'd wasted decades waiting instead of living. So I had a lot of missed time to make up for.

I gazed at Henri, his bare chest warm and inviting, and figured why wait? And then I kissed my way down his chest and stomach. Because fuck sleeping. This was so much better.

I was getting a bit too comfortable in Henri's house. It was incredible and cozy and luxurious all at once. Everything about the house was huge. The ceilings, the windows, and his bed. Even the bathtub was almost the size of a small swimming pool. I had ordered a silly amount of bath products online and had even convinced him to join me a few times.

So after a Sunday spent mostly in bed, I soaked in that glorious tub, reveling in the delicious soreness of my muscles after a weekend with Henri.

Between all the orgasms, we cooked, read, and played chess. We were having the kind of fun I hadn't thought I could ever have with a man.

Henri might have been on the quiet side, but he had never-ending lists of questions about me and the work I did at school. He grinned when I told him about the partnership I'd set up with the university to provide art and music workshops for my students. When I told him I was also talking to the education department about bringing in student teachers to help out in some of our understaffed classrooms, I was bursting with pride.

"You're exactly what this school needed," he told me, making my heart sing. "You've got ideas and you're out there pounding the pavement, making things happen."

I blushed, uncomfortable with his praise.

One of the things I had learned during my short time in Lovewell was that this community could rally. They took care of their own, and people were willing to help if asked.

So I asked. It was terrifying at first. Especially for a recovering people pleaser who believed she should never inconvenience anyone.

It was difficult, but I'd do anything for my students. Because their needs went so far beyond academics. They needed a school where they were supported wholly, where they had the necessary resources. Where they were fed and loved and encouraged every day. And I couldn't do it alone.

So I started small, first with a local electronics store, to see if they could help me source a used but reliable commercial printer. They couldn't, but since the owner's grandkids went to my school, he offered to donate a washer and dryer for our gym. Now kids without access to laundry facilities would have a place to discretely wash their clothes after school when they needed it.

From there, things grew. Becca came by the first Friday of every month and offered haircuts, Loraine and I pushed through the paperwork to qualify many of our students for the state's free lunch program and had even received conditional approval for a breakfast program for all of our students.

Our bake sale had raised funds that would allow us to start an after-school program, and we had formed a fundraising committee of parents and staff to come up with more ideas. My inbox was overflowing with emails from people who were excited about the school and wanted to help.

We still had a long way to go, but we were making progress.

I wandered through the house, dressed in one of Henri's T-shirts and a pair of panties, and found him in his home office. It was a small room on the first floor outfitted with a large desk that was currently covered with paper. Scraps littered the floor, as well, and binders were stacked up in one corner. It was a far cry from the rest of his exceptionally orderly house.

I stepped around a small stack of boxes and approached him. His brow was furrowed, and his shoulders were drawn up with tension.

"Can I help?"

He scratched his beard, looking me up and down. "I wish. You don't happen to read Acadian French, do you?"

"Sorry. Just basic Spanish over here."

He leaned back in his chair, pulling me into his lap. "Fuck, you're not wearing a bra." His hand was already up my shirt, pinching one nipple hard. I shifted farther onto his lap, feeling the erection straining his jeans.

I raised one eyebrow. "Really?"

He tilted my chin up and gave me a stern look. "What did you expect to happen? You're prancing around my house in my shirt and no bra looking like a wet goddamn dream. I want to bend you over the desk right now and fuck that tight pussy while you scream my name."

He twisted my nipple harder, and I arched back, enjoying it. I had never been with a man so direct before. Henri told me what he wanted and was not ashamed to be as dirty as he liked. It was liberating and invigorating to be the source of his lust and his pleasure.

I leaned in and kissed him. "I'd like that very much," I said, "but first, there's one thing I need to take care of."

I slid off the chair and onto my knees, settling myself between his legs. His eyes bulged as he looked down at where I kneeled in front of him.

I slowly lifted the hem of his T-shirt over my head and threw it across the room.

"Pants off," I ordered, massaging my breasts.

He stumbled getting up, but had his jeans unzipped in record time.

"Now sit."

I gripped his throbbing cock with my left hand and slowly lowered my mouth, licking just the tip and enjoying his resulting groan.

I had never been one for blow jobs. In my experience, guys rarely reciprocated, and it was never much fun. Sure, I had given them halfheartedly to ex-boyfriends, but never had I reveled in the experience, wanted it as much as I did at that moment.

I slowly took him in my mouth, taking my time and exploring every single inch of him. His thighs quivered as I licked and sucked, enjoying every second.

Eventually, I took him to the back of my throat, and he moaned.

"Buttercup. Fuck. Your mouth is just as amazing as your pussy. But you gotta stop, or I'll come."

I shook my head, smiling as I sped up. "Please," I said, pulling back and looking up at him. "I want this." My pussy throbbed with need. But I ignored it. I needed to focus on him. On his pleasure.

He groaned again, reaching down to cup my tits.

I squirmed as he pinched my nipples, but I couldn't get distracted. I was going to give him this. Letting my hands work him in tandem with my mouth, I took him deep, rejoicing in the way his leg muscles clenched as I did.

"Look at me," he growled, gently grabbing a fistful of my hair. I peered up and held eye contact while continuing to work his cock thoroughly. I loved it. I felt so sexy and so desired, and the taste of him drove me wild.

And then he was coming in my mouth, never breaking eye contact as I swallowed every drop. I sat back, very pleased with myself as Henri collapsed farther into his desk chair.

"Fuck, Alice," he said, panting. "That was...You are..."

I smiled. "Speechless, Brawny?"

"As soon as I recover from whatever you just did to me, I'll be spanking that sassy attitude right out of you. And then I'll eat your pussy all night long."

Are those maps?" I asked. We had finally made it back downstairs after Henri insisted on going down on me until I came three times. He really was persistent, my Brawny Man.

He nodded, getting up and spreading a couple out on the desk. "These boxes were in my parents' house at the time of Dad's death. Mom said he obsessed over them. He was constantly reviewing them in the garage, which makes no sense. We have updated maps and satellite images and GPS coordinates at our disposal, so why would he fixate on these?"

"How old are they?"

"From my great-grandfather's time. Before the Golden Road was built and we went into partnership with the other families. In those days, they did all their business in Acadian French to keep others from learning their secrets."

"Crafty."

"And confusing. We have administrative assistants and digital files at the office. So why were these old boxes in his house and why the hell was he looking at them so obsessively?"

"Maybe it was a hobby or a curiosity," I offered.

"My dad was all about the business, all the time. He wouldn't have wasted his time unless this had something to do with our business and making things better. I think he was looking for something specific. And I keep finding notes and scribbles with random French phrases on them. *Sinistre nord* and *l' épanouissement*. I have no earthly clue what he was talking about."

He paced around the small room, stepping around the

boxes gracefully. "What the hell, Dad?" At the window, he stopped and gazed out at the mountains with his hands on his hips. I had never been close to my dad, but I could see how much Henri loved and admired his father. To lose him so tragically and then to have to take on the burden of keeping the family business going would be too much for most people. But Henri Gagnon was far from average.

The more time we spent together, the more Henri's grouchy demeanor faded. He was a proud man, plagued by anxiety over doing the right thing and living up to the example set by his father. But under the flannel shirts and the beard and the axe-throwing was a kind, gentle heart.

"You're doing a great job," I murmured, wrapping my arms around his waist and resting my cheek on his back. "He would be proud of you."

He stood still for a moment, then spun and returned the hug, burying his face in my hair. "It's like he's trying to tell me something, but I don't understand." He confessed into my neck. "Did you know my family thinks it wasn't an accident? His death?"

I froze and squeezed him tighter. Talk about terrifying. Was this what had been weighing on him?

"We've all had trouble accepting it. Some more than others. And all along, I've tried not to fall into the blame game."

All I could do was hold him and hope my physical presence would give him the comfort that words couldn't achieve.

"But how the hell can I be rational about all this when I'm sorting through cryptic files and notes?"

"Take a break. I'll make dinner. Then I can help you sort through it. Maybe a fresh set of eyes will help."

He nodded. Still holding me. "Thank you, Alice."

"For what?"

"For being here and being you."

Old Alice would have laughed and shrugged off the praise. She would have been uncomfortable with his vulnerability and honesty. She didn't know how to accept a compliment.

But I wasn't Old Alice anymore. So I held him tight and let his words fill me up as I worked on believing them.

Chapter 30
Alice

Tucker and Goldie's foster father, Eric, had barely even looked at us when we picked the kids up earlier that morning. He was a thin, older man with small, mean eyes. He didn't even speak to the kids, just opened the door and slammed it shut behind them. Every interaction we'd had was unpleasant, and I worried about Tucker and Goldie in his care.

We started the day with a trip to Bangor to the Maine Discovery Museum, where we dug for dinosaur bones and learned about the human body. Even Tucker got into it, chasing Goldie through the two-story indoor treehouse while she screamed with glee.

My mind spun with all the possible opportunities for school field trips and on-site learning programs. I got the director's business card and planned to call on Monday. I took notes on my phone while I chatted with some of the employees about the science experiments and low-cost STEM projects I thought we could implement at school.

The past few months had been filled with nothing but

administrative work. Just the thought of hands-on learning with my students was filling me with excitement.

"You really love it, don't you?" Henri asked. "Being an educator."

I threaded my arm through his as Goldie and Tucker made spherical bubbles in an exhibit. "Yes. I do. I enjoyed being a classroom teacher, but I love setting the tone for the school, analyzing curriculum, and putting big ideas into action."

He gazed down at me, a smile teasing his lips. "I can tell."

"I want so much more for the kids in Lovewell." I sighed. Our little school needed so much help. The to-do lists were endless, the budgets too meager, and we were understaffed. But I wanted it badly. A safe space where each child received what they needed to grow and thrive. But that dream felt so far away.

"You'll get it. I believe in you."

Back in town, we walked around Main Street, stopping to say hi to Becca and Kali at the salon and then heading toward the diner.

"Who wants pie?" Henri asked as Tucker and Goldie ran ahead.

"Blueberry?" Goldie asked. "With vanilla ice cream?"

Henri nodded.

"Me, me, me!" She jumped up and down on the sidewalk, curls bouncing.

Henri gave me a smile. I felt guilty loading them up with sugar before dropping them back off at their foster home, but there was no way I could resist the pure joy radiating from that girl.

We squeezed into a booth at the diner. Tucker and I sat on one side, with Goldie next to Henri on the other. After we'd ordered coffee, milkshakes, and slices of pie, Goldie's little shoulders shook as tears rolled down her cheeks.

"What wrong?" I asked, squeezing her hand across the table, the sight of her tugging at my heart.

She sniffled loudly. "This is the best day ever, and I don't want it to end."

Henri watched me, pain etched in the rugged lines of his face.

"Miss Alice, you're my best friend. And now Henri is too."

"Hey," Tucker exclaimed, "I thought I was your best friend."

She shook her head. "You're my best brother. That's a very important job too."

I took a deep breath, searching for a way to delicately soothe her, but before I could, Henri jumped in.

"You know, I have trouble making friends. People usually think I'm too grumpy."

"You're not grumpy."

"Thanks. So your friendship means a lot to me. And we need to check with Miss Alice, but how about we do this again? Another weekend?"

"Really? We can have another playdate?"

Henri laughed. "Yes. And how about you pick where we go?"

She spent a few minutes contemplating this, her lips pursed and her arms crossed, before shouting out, "I wanna go to Disney World."

Henri pretended to consider it, scratching his chin. "Hmm...That's a great suggestion, but a little far away. How about someplace in Maine to start?"

We were brainstorming places to visit when Bernice arrived with our food.

I was handing napkins to the kids when Goldie proudly proclaimed, "Miss Bernice has the best pie in the world."

And then the strangest thing happened. Bernice smiled. I

had assumed her facial muscles had atrophied after years of scowling, but the woman was clearly delighted. "And you are the sweetest girl in all of Maine. I think you need a second slice."

"Yes, ma'am." Goldie nodded so forcefully, her whole body bobbed.

"And maybe some chocolate chip cookies to take home?"

Goldie clapped her hands. "Ooh, yes. Miss Bernice, do you wanna be our best friend too?"

"I'd be honored, sweetie."

After stuffing ourselves silly, we headed back to Mountain Meadows to drop the kids off. I was already feeling queasy. I had spent months trying to communicate with their foster parents, who were ambivalent at best and combative at worst. They couldn't be bothered to show up for parent-teacher conferences or to fill out necessary paperwork. And they weren't remotely concerned about sending them off with Henri and me for the day.

I actively worked to check my judgment as we drove into the trailer park and pulled up to their home. Tucker jumped out, his silly smile gone, then helped Goldie out of her booster.

"Thank you," he said, giving me a hug and Henri a manly handshake. "This was fun. And you made Goldie really happy."

I leaned close and put a hand on his shoulder. "You have my phone number, yes? Never hesitate to call me if you need anything."

He nodded. "Thanks, Miss Alice."

We drove silently back through town and up the mountain to my cabin, the highs of the day replaced by the low of having to say goodbye. Of leaving them in an environment that I wasn't sure was best for them. But they weren't my children, and as long as they weren't in danger, there was nothing I could do.

Henri turned off the ignition in front of my cabin and turned to me. "Do you want kids?" he asked after a long moment of silence.

This was a complex and loaded question. Not the kind one asked the person they were casually dating. But I didn't have the energy to play coy or dance around the issue.

"Yes," I said softly. "I do."

He nodded, still staring out the windshield at the mountains in front of us.

"What about you?"

He shrugged. "Not sure. Never really saw that for myself."

"You could have fooled me. You're a natural."

"They're really special kids."

"They are."

We lapsed into silence again, neither of us moving from our seats. Something was happening that I didn't have the energy to unpack or analyze. But I didn't hate it.

"Biological? Or would you be willing to adopt?"

My eyes filled with tears. This was a lot, especially after the day we'd had. I wanted to brush him off, make a joke, and be alone. I didn't want to confront the growing intimacy between us and the heartbreak of having to leave Tucker and Goldie.

For a few moments, I said nothing. Just let the tears run down my cheeks. Henri put his arm around me.

"Adopt," I said after composing myself. "I definitely want to adopt."

Chapter 31
Henri

Falling for Alice Watson was never my intention. In fact, I had studiously tried to avoid it. But she had slowly unraveled me, picking apart all my defenses bit by bit. And here I was: raw, exposed, vulnerable. But it didn't hurt. Instead, it felt like a new beginning.

We were building something significant, and I wasn't sure how we'd even gotten here.

I could say the word casual until I was blue in the face, but what we were doing was anything but.

We woke up together most days.

Every night, we cooked together and talked through each day's challenges.

We spent time with Tucker and Goldie, went to Sunday dinner at my mom's, and slowly became essential parts of each other's lives.

November brought with it relentless cold and the start of our busy season. I was working around the clock, running numbers with Paz, fighting with Adele over equipment, and setting schedules with Richard. Remy had been unreliable, blowing off meetings and forcing me to pick up some of his slack. He was up at camp now, getting crews organized and supervising the cranes, but I had a nagging feeling that something was really wrong. Thank God for Richard. He had been my dad's right-hand man for decades, and I prayed he wasn't ready to retire anytime soon. Remy had always been slated to learn the ropes from him and take over that side of the business, but that wasn't looking likely this year.

I came straight from the office to Alice's cozy cabin and let myself in a little after eight. She was curled up on the couch with a book and both of my dogs, who spent as much time here as they did at my place.

It started when I found them eating out of custom dog bowls with their names on them. And then one of those fancy memory foam dog beds appeared at her place, and I officially lost the battle. Not that I blamed them. I'd much rather sleep here with Alice every night than in my house alone too.

She looked so peaceful and beautiful snuggled up on the couch. I strode right over and kissed her, taking her ponytail out so I could run my fingers through her hair.

Without words, I pulled her up to standing, deepening our kiss and letting my hands roam.

"You okay?" she asked while I kissed her neck.

"Mm-hmm." I grunted, untying the belt of her silky robe.

"I missed you. We've barely talked these last few days."

I nodded as her robe fell to the floor, revealing her flimsy tank top. All I could think about was the feel of her skin, the little noises she made when I drove her wild.

"Henri," she said, gently pushing at my arms. "We need to talk about some things. I don't want to be a booty call."

Her words hit me like a slap across the face, and I reared back. "Alice," I urged, "you are so much more than a booty call."

"Am I? Because things between us have been intense these past few weeks, and yet you haven't said anything. We've never talked about what this is or where it's going, and I'm starting to worry."

I took a step back and ran my hands through my hair. I was making a mess out of this. Of course I was.

She backed away from me, picking up her robe and clasping it to her chest, sadness and vulnerability clear in her confused eyes and her frown.

My chest ached. Did she really have no idea how much she meant to me?

"I know this has been fast—" she said.

"Please," I interrupted.

She held up a hand. "And I'm probably not your usual type."

What the hell was happening? "What are you talking about?"

Her face flushed pink, and she backed up a few more steps, putting more distance between us. "I guess. I don't know. I'm sure the other women you've been with are different."

"My brain isn't even hearing you right now. Other women? I can't even conceive that other women exist anymore. All I think about is you."

Her eyes widened. Good. I wanted her to understand where I was in this relationship.

"I just mean, I don't know. What's your usual type?"

"My type is Alice Watson."

She put her hands on her hips. "I'm being serious, Henri. You can't expect me to believe that."

I stalked across the room and pulled her into my arms. She was trembling, and her eyes were watery. I'd never been good with words, but I had to get this right. "I've never had a type. But then I took one look at you and thought, 'that's it. That's what I want.' You're the one I want. My type is you. That's it for me."

I tipped her chin up and ducked down, hoping she could see the truth in my eyes.

She started to protest. "But—"

I shut her up with a kiss. A deep, hungry, desperate kiss. The kind that said things my words simply could not.

I pushed her back on the couch. "I want you. I want this. I want it all."

She moaned as I pulled down her yoga pants, kissing and nipping at her inner thighs. How could she not understand? A booty call? I was head over heels for her and planned to wife her up as soon as she would allow it. Clearly, we had a lot to talk about. But first, I had a job to do.

"No panties," I observed, kissing closer and closer to her sweet pussy. "Good girl."

Her back arched off the couch as I tasted her, taking my time to savor just how wet she was for me. "I care about you, buttercup," I said, easing one finger inside her. "And I've clearly done a shit job of showing you that."

I lapped at her with abandon, relishing the way she writhed beneath me. Her thighs trembled and her pussy was soaked. She tasted so fucking good. "And yes, we need to talk." I added a second finger, ignoring my aching cock and focusing all my attention on her pleasure. Her flushed skin, racing heart, and hard nipples. I nipped at her clit and worked her over until her inner muscles clenched around my fingers. "But first, I'm going to make you come so hard you forget all these insecurities and remember you're mine."

Chapter 32
Alice

I liked when a guy went down on me as much as the next girl, but it had never been something I needed, something I reveled in. It was an infrequent yet pleasant surprise that I enjoyed and didn't think much more about.

But while screaming through my first orgasm, I realized that maybe I had been wrong. Because the way Henri devoured me was quickly becoming an addiction. He used his hands and his lips and his glorious tongue. There was nothing half-hearted or tentative about the way he approached my body. Instead, he dove in, making his enthusiasm for my pleasure clear.

And I loved it. The feel of his beard between my thighs and his thick fingers inside me. He never hid the way he felt about my body, and slowly, the cracks in my self-esteem were healing. I had spent decades convinced that I was undesirable. Trying to contort and squeeze myself into fitting into society's mold for how a woman should be. But Henri clearly communicated his desire. Not verbally; he wasn't much for pretty words, but in the way he looked at me, touched me, devoted himself to my pleasure.

Heart pounding, I lay on my back, recovering from the things Henri had done to me with his tongue. I reached for him, needing to feel the heat of his skin, but found that he had already rolled off the couch.

He was padding through the living room in his boxer briefs, his erection standing proud.

"What are you doing?" I yawned, watching him step into the bathroom.

"Just grabbing some tools," he called over his shoulder. When he came back to the open living space, he was carrying the pink box where I kept my special toys.

I sat up, my contented haze clearing. "What? Why?" My pulse raced and my cheeks warmed. The last thing I needed right now was a deep dive into my vibrator collection.

He placed the box on the end table and bent low, giving me a quick kiss on the lips.

"Because I'm curious. I want to know everything about you." He flipped open the lid. "Plus, it'll be fun to try some out. What do you think?"

"You don't have to..."

"Hmm." He bit his lip as he studied each one. "You have quite a few options."

"That is a very normal, healthy amount," I protested.

He chuckled softly and held up my favorite vibrator. "What's this one?" It was a rose gold colored one that worked with just the right amount of pressure. He studied it as if it were an alien life form, tilting his head one way and then the other.

"It's called a Satisfyer," I said, bringing a palm to my heated cheek.

With a massive hand wrapped around the device, he turned it on. "Show me," he said, his voice husky. "Show me how you use it."

I froze. I'd never used a toy in front of another person. But the raw need in his eyes made me brave. It made me feel like trying something new and showing him a different side of me.

Taking it from him, I slowly lowered it, lingering between my thighs. "It's just air pressure," I said, finding the perfect spot on my clit.

His eyes were hooded with lust, and he slowly stroked himself over his boxers. "This is so fucking hot," he grunted. His chest rose and fell as his eyes locked on my hand and the way I was controlling the toy and teasing myself.

It took a moment to get into position, but the second I did, pressure built inside me. It was embarrassing how quickly I could make myself come after years of solo practice. I wiggled my hips to get a better angle and groaned loudly.

"May I?" He splayed his hand over mine, closing his eyes. It felt so naughty, lying here while he watched. His hand covered mine while I rode the Satisfyer, letting it take me over the edge and right into the abyss. His warm hand over mine only made the feelings of vulnerability intensify.

Suddenly, it wasn't enough. With my free arm, I pulled him on top of me, kissing him and letting the vibrator drop to the floor.

"I need you," I said, kissing down his neck. Playing with toys was fun and all, but now I craved the kind of reassurance and connection that could only be had with him on top of me, with our bodies connected.

He pushed up onto his forearms and looked into my eyes. "Tell me, Alice. Tell me exactly what you need."

I arched my back as he kissed his way down my chest, giving each breast ample attention.

"I want you." I gasped as he bit one roughly.

"Really."

"Yes. I want you. Your soft heart, your grumpy attitude, and your big cock. All of it."

He peered up at me, and a slow smile spread across his face. "Good girl. Because I'm going to give you all of that and more."

Chapter 33
Alice

Something big was coming, and I could feel it. I bit my lip and studied Henri while he stared back at me from the other side of my bed, where we'd migrated to after a round with the Satisfyer. *Could I handle this?* Finally put my feelings into words and lay it all out in the open?

His heart beat against my abdomen, strong and steady. And that was Henri. Strong and steady. A man who kept his word, who gave with his whole heart, and who protected the people he loved.

And I was in love with him. It would be foolish to think otherwise. And I was terrified. I'd never been in love before.

But maybe Henri was right. Maybe we could figure it out along the way.

But before I could open my mouth to tell him that, the phone rang.

I picked it up, ready to silence it, when I saw the number for the police station on the screen.

"Hello?"

"Principal Watson, this is Chief Souza calling. I've got a bit of a situation here that I could use your help with."

I sat up and looked at Henri. What on earth was going on? And why would the chief of police be calling me so late?

"We've got a young man here. Tucker Fournier."

A wave of nausea swept over me, and I sucked in a deep breath to quell the feeling.

"He had a little dust-up tonight with his foster father. A neighbor called 911, and we intervened."

"Jesus, is he okay?"

"He is. His sister is here too." I swung my legs over the edge of the bed, holding up one finger to Henri when he grabbed my arm and furrowed his brows in concern.

"We removed them from the home. I got some files here, and I think I'm supposed to call their caseworker down at social services, but he asked me to call you first."

"Of course. Can I see them?"

"Yes. We're holding them here until someone can take them. It'll probably be morning before we get through to anyone at social services."

"I'll be there shortly. Tell them I'm coming."

I ran into the police station fifteen minutes later, still wearing my pajamas under my winter coat, while Henri parked my car. When I hung up, he'd already pulled on his jeans and a shirt, and he was lacing up his boots. We had driven here in silence, any memory of our night together obscured by my fear for these kids.

The station was a squat stone building on Main Street. It was well-lit and clean but deeply depressing, nonetheless. I was greeted by the chief of police, an older man who had visited the

227

school a few times, and one of his deputies. They led me through the main area into a small room that was a little darker and even more dismal. The ceiling tiles were stained, and there was nothing but a small, beat-up couch. I had an immediate urge to grab both kids and flee. But first, I had to talk to them.

I kneeled in front of the couch where Goldie was huddled and pulled her into my arms. Her beautiful little face was tear-stained, and she was shaking, but she was eerily silent. Her hair was a tangled mess, and she only had on a T-shirt, even though it was November and the temperature was in the midtwenties.

"Tell me what happened." I turned to Tucker, who sat beside where his sister had been, staring at his hands.

"He was gonna hit her." He looked up at me for the first time, the bruise above his right eye glaring in the overhead light.

Goldie whimpered in my arms, and before I could ask Tucker to explain, Henri barged in.

The look of sheer rage on his face when he caught sight of Goldie in her disheveled state terrified me.

He froze, relaxed his hands where they'd been fisted at his sides, and asked, "Goldilocks, do you know if there's a vending machine here?" in an unnaturally sweet tone.

She let go of my neck and looked up at Henri with pure love in her eyes. "Can I get peanut M&M's?"

"Of course." He put a hand out to her. "As long as you promise to share with me." He led her across the station, thankfully giving me a moment to talk to Tucker.

I waited until I heard the door close and then gave him my best stern principal stare. "Full story. Right now."

He ran a hand through his shaggy locks. "Goldie was having trouble with her homework. She got frustrated and was whining. And then he started yelling at her. Called her stupid and said some mean things about my mom. So Goldie started to cry. He said he'd give her something to cry about and got up and raised his hand like he was going to hit her. I couldn't let that happen."

I swallowed down the bile that rose in my throat and squeezed Tucker's hand, encouraging him to keep going.

"So I got mad. Really mad." He broke down in tears.

I wanted so desperately to tell him everything would be fine. But Tucker had seen too much to believe empty words like that.

"So I pushed him into a wall. And then he hit me."

I grabbed his hand and held it between both of mine. "You pushed a grown man into a wall?"

"Yeah. I'm tall for my age." He sat a little straighter and wiped at his eyes. "He hit his head and started screaming all sorts of crazy stuff. One of the neighbors called the police."

My hands shook as I tried to keep my face neutral. He was in sixth grade. He should not have had to fight a grown man. Or have to protect his baby sister from abuse. My eyes welled with tears, but I vowed to figure this out for them.

"We can't stay there anymore. It's bad."

I nodded.

"Goldie thinks Mom's coming back. But she's not."

He dropped my hand and braced his arms on his knees. "She's been gone for a really long time. She doesn't want us. Mr. James, our caseworker, told me Mom signed over her rights."

What could I say to that? My heart broke for these two beautiful kids.

"If we separate," he said, dipping his chin and looking at his feet, "there's a chance Goldie could get adopted. Because people like cute little kids, but no one wants me."

"Don't say that."

"It's true. But she needs me."

I pulled his hand into mine again. "You've had to shoulder

a lot, Tucker. Far more than most eleven-year-olds. And I'm proud of you for all you've done. Let me talk to the chief and see what we can do tonight. Then tomorrow we'll contact Mr. James and make a plan together."

He nodded.

"You're not alone. There are a lot of people who care about you and are willing to help."

He peered up at me with a frown, fighting back tears. "Thanks for coming."

"There's no place I'd rather be." And it was true. This was far above and beyond my duties as principal, but over the past few months, Tucker and Goldie had become a lot more than just students to me.

For all Henri's complaints about Chief Souza, he was helpful. The foster father had been arrested and was being held overnight. The following day, charges would be filed once the Office of Child and Family Services got involved.

Souza strongly encouraged me to file a petition for emergency guardianship first thing the following morning in hopes of keeping the kids from being separated or sent to a foster home elsewhere in the state.

"You're a great candidate, and I'll make some calls."

I shook my head. There was no way in hell I was prepared to assume guardianship, but I wasn't sure there were any other good choices in the area. "Do they have extended family nearby?"

He laughed sardonically. "Not a chance." He looked up from his paperwork, pen poised over the document. "Trust me. If you met a Fournier, you'd be grateful they all left town. It's a small mercy, but the farther these kids are from their biological family, the better."

I closed my eyes and took a few deep breaths. He was asking a lot.

"We can delay the paperwork," he said, giving me a wink.

I turned back to look at the kids. Henri was letting Goldie play games on his phone, and Tucker was tinkering with a broken handheld radio while I worked things out with the chief.

"Let's see what the caseworker has to say."

"I'm not family, and I'm not a licensed foster parent."

"You're a principal. You've been fingerprinted, and your background check is already on file with the state. Let's face it, you're the best chance these kids have right now."

I let the weight of his words sink in. It was late, and emotions were running too high for me to fully process the implications. I couldn't take care of these kids in the long term, but they were coming home with me tonight.

Chapter 34
Henri

The following morning, my mom came over to my house to take care of Tucker and Goldie while Alice and I headed to Bangor. By the looks of the shopping bags she brought with her, they'd be busy and tired by the time we returned.

In the city, Alice met with their caseworker, filed an emergency petition with the court, and started the paperwork to become a temporary legal guardian. I admired how focused and calm she was. Because this was a deeply scary situation.

They were good kids who deserved a hell of a lot better than they'd gotten in life, but this was a huge step. Alice's heart was big, and it was growing by the day, so there was no doubt she would do right by them.

As for me, I was having trouble not heading over to the trailer park and beating the living shit out of that man. Putting his hands on a child like that? He should be eating through a straw for the rest of his life.

But instead, I sat with Alice, wearing a tie and waiting for a judge to review her emergency petition. We had been warned that it would take all day, but Alice was not deterred. She took careful notes, jotting down ideas and questions as we waited.

I had grown up with two loving parents in a chaotic but warm home. We didn't have much, but we were loved and cared for. It gutted me that Tucker and Goldie didn't have a safe place to land or people who loved them unconditionally. And they weren't the only ones in our area. Hard times, drugs, and shitty economic policies had taken so much from our community, and these poor kids were paying the price.

"Do you think I'm crazy?" Alice asked, smoothing her hair.

"Not at all. You saw Tucker's face. We can't let them end up in a potentially worse situation with their next placement."

"But I'm so unqualified."

I gripped her arm, pulling her onto the bench next to me. "Stop that right now." I cupped her cheeks. "You're more than qualified to help them. And you will. Right now, we deal with the temporary crisis, and then we'll work on a long-term solution."

She nodded.

"You're an incredible woman, Alice Watson. Don't forget it."

I wanted to gather her in my arms and kiss her. Hold her close and tell her I loved her and would do anything to help. That I wanted a family with her and kids and dogs and wild holidays with my loud and obnoxious siblings.

But this wasn't the time or the place. And sadly, last night had not gone as planned. I wanted this. Something more, something forever. With her.

And as impossible as it felt most days, I was ready to say the words. Just as soon as we got this mess cleaned up.

"Alice Watson?" Judge Forrester was a wrinkled man who looked annoyed to have to get up and put on his robe every day.

Alice stood behind the wooden railing and smiled. Mr. James, who'd worked so diligently to help her prepare the emergency petition, sat in the row of seats behind her.

She looked so assured and confident standing in the courtroom. Meanwhile, I was sweating through my shirt, and it felt like my tie was strangling me.

The judge took his time reading through the papers, then finally looked up. "Is this your affidavit?" he asked Mr. James.

He stood. "Yes, Your Honor. The Office of Children and Families consents to the petition for emergency custody based on the exigent circumstances described."

He spent a few more minutes flipping through the file, during which I'm not sure I drew in a full breath. The thought of letting tucker and Goldie down filled me with dread. I couldn't bear it if they were sent to another foster home, or worse, if they were separated from one another. I had grown attached to these kids.

If Alice took this on, she might not want to pursue things between us. And I would accept that. Because having a safe and bright future for the kids was more important.

I could wait. I'd found Alice, and I'd wait ten lifetimes to be with her if that's what it took.

"Motion is granted. Alice Watson is granted emergency custody of Tucker and Marigold Fournier. The full temporary custody petition must be filed within thirty days."

I let out the breath I'd been holding. When Alice turned around, she smiled, and tears of relief swam in her eyes. It made me love her more. Her selflessness and devotion to these kids filled my already too full heart, and I thought I might burst. A tear slipped down my cheek—something that hadn't happened in years.

Outside, I held her hand while she planned the next steps with Mr. James.

"I've got two kids now," she said, a bit dazed. "For the next thirty days."

"Or longer," I whispered, tucking her under my arm.

She leaned into me, letting me help support the weight of fear and concern she was carrying. I only wished I could hold it all for her. "Or longer. What do I do now, Henri?" She peered up at me, her bottom lip caught between her teeth.

I kissed the top of her head. "We go shopping. 'Cause those kids need stuff."

Our first stop was Target, where we bought a set of bunk beds for the study at the cabin.

"Will these fit?" she asked dubiously.

"Yup. I'll text Paz and have him help me move the furniture out of the study. I can put these together after. Hell, Tucker can help me. He's probably better at it than I am."

She smiled. "You don't have to do all that."

I didn't respond. Just gave her my best grumpy frown.

She laughed. "Fine. You can build the bunk beds."

"That's not all I'll be doing," I said under my breath as she made her way toward the bedding area.

Alice picked out sheets and pillows and pajamas and tooth-brushes, crossing off items on a list she'd started in the truck on the way to the store.

"You can't just get the basics," I explained, pushing the overflowing cart behind her.

"They need fun stuff too. Like this." I grabbed a giant stuffed sloth. It was soft and cuddly and the size of one of my dogs. "Goldie needs this."

Alice huffed a laugh. "Okay, Brawny. If you say so."

"And microwave popcorn, and snow boots, and this kids'

smart watch for Tucker. Hold on," I said, backing up a few steps, "let me get another shopping cart."

By the time we left, both the bed and the cab of my truck were filled with clothes and school supplies and toys and stuffed animals and kid-friendly food. Alice wasn't impressed with all my purchases, but I had to do something. These poor kids had been through hell. The least I could do was make sure they had Cinnamon Toast Crunch in the morning.

Alice mumbled that I was ridiculous and going overboard, but I just shrugged.

And the look on Goldie's face when I gave her the giant sloth made Alice's griping worth it.

"I love it," she said, hugging it so tightly I thought the head would pop off. "It's so soft and snuggly. Is it really for me?"

I kneeled down and tucked a strand of hair behind her ear. "Yup. All yours, Goldilocks. And I got you a few other treats too." I showed her the new purple backpack, books, and the fancy hairbrush I had picked out for her. It promised to detangle her hair painlessly, and after this morning's incident, I prayed it was the truth.

"Henri," she squealed, throwing her arms around my neck. "Thank you."

Her excitement and gratitude made my heart grow just like the Grinch's. The stress of the day melted away while she prattled on excitedly about the cookies they had baked with my mom. I was in this moment with her, and I loved it. These kids deserved so much more than what life had given them, and I knew in my bones that Alice would help them. And I hoped she would let me be a part of it.

It hit me like a lightning bolt. Everyone's lives were about to change. I looked up at where Alice was chatting with my mom and unpacking groceries. I was ready. Tonight, I would tell her.

WOOD You Be Mine?

Tell her I was all-in. For whatever the future held. That I wanted it all with her. I just had to find the words.

Chapter 35
Alice

Henri was building bunk beds, giving piggyback rides, and reading bedtime stories. It was disorienting. We hadn't even talked about what all this meant yet, and my brain was running at a hundred miles an hour. Kids, birthdays, holidays, graduation, sitting on the porch in retirement, talking about the good times. Jesus.

After the overwhelming events of the day, I needed sleep and a shower and time to think all of this through. I was now the legal guardian of two kids. For at least the next thirty days. It was my responsibility to keep them safe and fed and happy. I adored Tucker and Goldie, but we had a long road ahead of us.

Not that one could tell by looking at them. They'd spent the day with Henri's mom, baking cookies and doing art projects, and then they'd helped Henri build their bunk beds. As Henri predicted, Tucker jumped right in. Goldie was more of a hindrance, but she had so much fun that neither of us wanted to take that away from her. They were so thrilled with the tiny study, and Tucker had even teared up at one point.

I looked in the mirror and winced. The dark circles under

my eyes were massive, and my hair was greasy and stringy. I looked even more tired than I felt, if that was possible. Physically, I was exhausted, but my brain wouldn't shut off. There was so much to figure out. I'd need a lawyer and a plan and lots of help.

And then there was Henri. He was in the kitchen washing dishes and being the most helpful, sexy, kind man on Planet Earth. We needed to talk. I needed to know I wasn't alone with these intense feelings. Because while he was great at chopping wood and delivering orgasms, Brawny was not great with words. And right now, I needed words.

I took another look at the kids. Tucker was curled up with a book and a flashlight in his top bunk, and Goldie was fast asleep on the bottom, clutching her stuffed Sloth, which Tucker had named Speedy. Her blankets were on the floor, and her golden curls spilled all over the pillow. Rochester was standing guard next to her bed, and I gave him a scratch as I pulled the blanket over her sleeping body.

"Alice," Tucker whispered. "Can you tuck me in?"

My heart clenched, and I nodded, trying to fight back tears. I knew how much a simple gesture like this could mean to a child who'd been given such little affection. After he was settled, I turned out the light and went back to the kitchen, ready to lay things out with Henri.

When I found him, he was pacing, his face stony and his posture rigid. He had his phone clutched to his ear, holding it so tightly I thought the screen might crack.

"Is he alive?"

My breath caught. *What happened?*

"Destroyed a cold deck? A fight? I'm coming up. Give me a few hours."

He hung up the phone and looked at me, pain etched in the lines of his face, and regret clear in his eyes.

"That was Richard." He ran his hands through his hair. "Remy's a mess. He's drunk and destroying things. Crashed his truck into a pile of logs and caused a slide we'll be cleaning up for days."

I stepped in front of him and grasped his hands. "Is he hurt?"

"I don't think so." He shook his head. "But I've got to get up there. We've got guys threatening to quit, and we'll be behind schedule all week. I have to go sort things out."

"Are you okay to drive? How about I make you a cup of coffee to go?"

He nodded. "I need to grab my laptop and a few things from my house. Can you keep an eye on the dogs for me? I don't think Rochester will leave Goldie."

"Of course. He won't. He's standing guard next to her bed."

Henri smiled. "Good man."

He pulled me into his arms, resting his chin on my head. "You're doing a great job, Alice. It's been a hard couple of days, but I'm damn proud of you. And we have a lot to talk about. But first I need to deal with this disaster."

"I understand." I wanted to cling to him. My situation with the kids was daunting, and I needed his calm, steady presence. I needed his strength to help me get through tomorrow and every day after.

"Everything will be fine. They're in great hands. There's no cell reception up there. If you need to reach me, text Paz. He's got the radios and the sat phone. I'll reach out in a couple of days."

I nodded into his chest, soaking up his warmth while I still could.

With two fingers, he tipped my chin up and pressed his lips to mine. But it wasn't enough. I pulled him closer and kissed him deeply, letting myself get lost in the feel of his lips and his hands on my body.

"It's so hard to leave you," he murmured, kissing my forehead.

"But you're coming back." I wanted to say more. Tell him I loved him. That I wanted to do this for real. Ask him if he'd be willing to take on Tucker and Goldie too, as I was planning to fight like hell to keep them.

But the words died on my lips. He was worried about his brother and his employees and his business. I couldn't lay all this on him too.

"As fast as I can, buttercup."

Chapter 36
Henri

With one more kiss to Alice's cheek, I was gone. I had a lot of driving ahead of me. She had packed a thermos of hot coffee and snacks while I grabbed my laptop and chargers and a few changes of clothes. By the time I hit the road, it was after ten. The drive was less than two hours, but the road conditions were terrible. Even though every muscle in my body ached, I pressed on, refusing to wait until morning to make my way there. Remy needed me, and so did the crew.

I spent the ride up to camp kicking myself. I should have seen this coming. I should have kept better tabs on my baby brother.

As the oldest, I'd taken it upon myself to keep my siblings in line. Be there for them when they needed something. Remy had been spiraling for a while, but I hadn't been able to get him to open up about it. And that was the problem. I should have already known. I should have been helping him work through it.

Instead, I ignored the warnings. Even though I knew the

risks. I'd spent the last fifteen years in this business, one of the deadliest professions in the world. Safety, precision, and careful decision-making kept people alive and fed, and that was not a responsibility I took lightly. It was also something my little brother knew in his bones. So the reasons for his behavior were anyone's guess.

Instead, I'd diverted too much of my attention to Alice. I was being selfish, letting myself get wrapped up in her and ignoring my responsibilities.

Growing up, Remy had always been the wild one. He struggled in school and got himself into trouble constantly.

The kid was always climbing trees, adopting pet squirrels, and building forts.

He was a forest child, through and through.

That's what made him a perfect fit for this business. He wasn't a businessman like Paz or a manager like me. Instead, he belonged out in the forest. He had instincts the rest of us could only dream about.

And the potential Stihl sponsorship? That would be a game changer for him. He was on the path to become a professional athlete. And if he was fucking it up, I would kick his ass. He was made for more than this business. He had charisma and talent and vision.

The pain in my gut intensified. I'd taken my eye off the ball. This was why I had shied away from relationships for the last several years. Because my business and my family demanded too much of me. And if I didn't keep a close watch, everything went to shit.

But now? Alice was too important. And the kids too. I'd make it all work, no matter how far I had to stretch myself.

An hour into the drive, my phone rang.

"Paz," I said after I hit the Answer button on the steering wheel.

"What the fuck is going on?" His voice echoed through the truck speakers.

"No idea. I'm on my way. Richard has him under control, but we're behind schedule and everything is going to shit."

"He totaled a truck and destroyed a cold deck?"

I groaned.

Paz growled. "He could have killed someone."

"Or himself." I swallowed thickly.

"What the fuck? He's been drinking more than usual, but I had no idea it had become such a problem."

"You could have told me that."

"Figured you'd noticed. He's been acting weird, and I've caught him drinking during the day a few times."

I resisted the urge to pull out my hair. Why were my siblings keeping key information from me?

"I'm on my way. You coming?"

"I have to meet with the feds and the lawyers tomorrow morning."

I groaned. Of course. The fucking feds. As if I didn't have enough problems. "Can we reschedule?"

"You don't reschedule with the feds, dumbass. It's fine. The lawyers do all the talking anyway. I'll be there to take notes and make sure the Heberts don't fuck anything up."

"Radio me after the meeting."

"I will. I'll email over the notes too."

I squeezed the steering wheel a little tighter. "Thank you."

"You couldn't do this without me."

"I'm aware."

This was the problem with family businesses. Our employees were actually related, or people like Richard, who were close enough to be considered family.

The boundaries were blurred, and there was virtually no objectivity.

I had to constantly balance my responsibilities as a brother and a son with those of a CEO. Our employees depended on me so they could feed and house their families, so it was essential that I kept the trucks running. But my siblings needed my guidance. They needed a role model and a surrogate father when necessary. And lately, I had been slacking on that job.

"You call Adele?" I asked.

"Not yet. I think she's with her professor."

"Call her. We've got to get the truck towed out of there, and there may be damaged equipment she'll need to get started on."

"On it. She'll be pissed."

"That's why you're calling her. I'm driving through the woods in the middle of the fucking night. It's the least you can do, little brother."

"Be safe," he said, his voice low and serious.

"Always."

"And if he needs a good ass kicking, verbal or physical, don't be afraid to give it to him. Messes like this can cost lives. He knows better."

"Don't I know it."

The sense of dread at camp was palpable. The flood lights we rigged so we could work in the dark on winter mornings were on, and trucks were parked haphazardly. The road was blocked by a mess of massive logs. Fuck, that was a major hazard. We'd have to get a crane in here tomorrow to clean this up.

I parked and hustled to the main dormitory building, one of six buildings at Gagnon camp. This was our main outpost in the north woods. We had dorms, houses, an office, and a small shop for repairs set up here, along with pole barns and other structures for storing materials and fuel.

But the dorm my grandfather had built in the sixties was the heart of camp. It was a squat, ugly-ass building that had absolutely no charm but was always filled with music and laughter. When a couple dozen guys lived up here for weeks at a time, working around the clock, someone was always cooking while someone else played a guitar, and flag football games took place out front almost daily.

But tonight it was eerily quiet, despite all the lights being on and the random equipment strewn about.

I found Remy in the showers, fully clothed. He was slumped against the tile wall, soaking wet and still wearing his work boots.

He looked like shit. His beard was untrimmed, and his eyes were hollow and rimmed with dark circles.

"What the fuck?" I muttered, standing over him. "Are you drunk?"

He didn't even look up at me. "Not anymore," he grumbled. "Those motherfuckers locked me in here. I've probably caught pneumonia. Richard turned the water main off a while ago. Said I was 'wasting natural resources.' Asshole."

Richard wasn't wrong. The last thing we needed was an issue with our well.

"Fuck. I don't have the time or the patience for your shit right now." I paced in front of him. "You're a leader here. You have responsibilities. If you're drunk and reckless, people could die. What were you thinking? You crashed your truck? After what happened to Dad?"

He slumped even lower, if possible, staring at the floor tile, but he said nothing.

"Fucking say something before I punch you!"

"I'm a fuck-up. Fire me. Send me to jail. I don't care." He clenched his fists. "I don't deserve this job or this family or this life."

I stopped my pacing and turned to him. "Jesus, dude, what is going on?"

He hung his head. "Crystal."

"Where is she?"

"No clue." Remy shrugged. "Probably off fucking the dude she left me for." He buried his head in his hands.

I watched him silently for a long moment, not knowing what to say. Then I cleared my throat. "Do you want to talk about it?"

"Fuck no, I don't want to talk about how my fiancée was fucking another man behind my back," he bellowed. "The woman I've been with for years. My past, my present, and my future, all fucking gone and destroyed."

I slid down the wall next to him until we were sitting shoulder to shoulder.

"I'm sorry," I said simply, because nothing I could come up with would take his pain away.

"She's been seeing him for more than a year. While we were planning *our wedding*. I knew, man. I knew something was wrong. She was always with friends, making excuses to go to away on weekends. She's been gone for months. But it wasn't until yesterday that I knew why."

I slumped against the wall next to him. Fuck. He was in so much pain, and there was nothing I could do to fix it. When we were kids, I'd clean up his cuts and scrapes and cover them with Band-Aids or buy candy from the drugstore for him when things got hard. But this kind of betrayal was beyond my skill set.

"You're still going to kick my ass." It was a statement, not a question.

I nodded. "Fuck, yes. I have to kick your ass. You recklessly endangered our business and our employees, as well as your own life."

He sniffed, but he didn't argue.

"I'm fucking devastated for you, and I care about you. This

family is my first priority every day. And I'll help you get through this. But for now, go upstairs, get changed into dry clothes, and go to bed. I've got to check with the crews and make a plan to clean up your mess."

"Thank you."

"I'll be here for a few days. Tomorrow, you'll be up before the crew. You'll scrub every inch of this dormitory and cook a big breakfast for our teams. You will apologize to each person individually and take responsibility for your shitty behavior.

"Once we get things straightened out, I'm taking you to Mom's. You will be suspended indefinitely while you get help dealing with this."

He looked at me for the first time, anger simmering in his eyes. "Are you shitting me?"

God, he looked skinny and tired. He'd clearly been on a downward spiral for a while. How had I not noticed? The guilt washed over me, but I pushed it away. I'd stew over it later.

"We've been through a lot over the past year. I want to know about what happened with Crystal, and I want to talk through this more when we're both well-rested. But right now, I've got work to do, and you need some sleep."

Remy studied my face for a few moments, his jaw tight, but a look of resignation formed on his face. "You sound so much like Dad right now."

"Is that an insult?"

"Nope. Just an observation."

He hauled himself up off the cold floor and shuffled for the door. "Watch out, Henri," he said, turning just before the threshold. "Wouldn't want you turning into him too."

Chapter 37
Alice

I hadn't heard from Henri since he left late Monday night. The kids and I returned to school on Tuesday and were working on getting ourselves into a routine.

There was no cell reception where Henri was, and I didn't have one of the fancy radios they used. He was bound to be busy, but that didn't make waiting for word from him any easier.

Without him here, my thoughts and feelings had nowhere to go, so I channeled them into being the best emergency guardian I could be.

After school, Tucker and Goldie came to my office, as they always did, while I finished up the workday. When we got home, we took the dogs for a long walk, and then Goldie and I worked on the *Frozen* puzzle Henri had bought while Tucker finished his homework.

"Can we live here forever?" Goldie asked, trying to find the right spot for Olaf's nose.

A bolt of panic shot through me. Was I cut out for this?

How could I help these kids heal and grow and thrive? I was barely holding it together most days.

"Do you want to?"

She grinned. "Oh yes. This is the best house ever. We have our own room and bunk beds and dogs. I've always wanted dogs. And Henri. I love Henri."

I looked at her smiling face. *You and me both, kid*, I thought to myself. As if my relationship with him wasn't complicated enough, now I had a six-year-old who was attached to him. Not that it was hard to get attached. He tended to grow on people. *Grumpy bastard.*

"Henri doesn't live here," Tucker said from the kitchen table, where he was definitely not working on multiplying fractions. "And we only get to live here for thirty days, remember? We're lucky to even get that."

Goldie's face fell.

"Tucker, come here." I waved him over to where we sat on the floor near the wood stove. When he settled next to me, I took each of their hands. "I'm so happy that you're here. Both of you. I care about you so much."

Tucker rolled his eyes. "But—"

"No buts, mister. I don't know what the future holds. I'll work as hard as I can to make sure you're safe and happy and have a wonderful home. It might be with me, or it might be with someone else. That's not for me to decide."

"Why not?"

"Because that's not how the system works. But I promise you're not getting rid of me, okay? I'll always be part of your lives. I'm the lucky one here. Got it?"

I pulled them both close, tears streaming down my face. I had only been in Lovewell for a few months, but I had already gotten so much more than I bargained for.

The call came in the middle of the day on Friday. Loraine's scream had me racing out of my office.

I found her standing next to her desk, sobbing. The phone was in her shaking hand at her side, and when she held it out to me, I put my arm around her and grabbed it.

"Hello?"

"Alice, it's Paz. There's been an accident. It's Henri."

I grabbed on to the desk when my knees buckled. "What happened?"

"I don't know all the details yet. He was driving a load to the mill, and the brakes failed. He jumped out of the cab before the truck ran off the road. He's being airlifted to the hospital in Bangor."

The room spun. I slumped against the desk, pulling Loraine with me.

"I'm headed there now. Adele is coming to get my mom at school. Can you help her?"

"Of course. What else do you need?"

"Nothing. I'll text you when I know more. Just take care of my mom, okay?"

I helped Loraine up and got her coat and purse. I walked her outside and waited until Adele pulled up in front of the school, her face pale and tear-stained.

"Mom," she said gently when she rounded the hood. "It'll be okay. He's conscious. We'll go see him right now."

"Your father," Loraine sobbed, her words almost incoherent. Adele and I herded her to the passenger door.

Adele gently helped her into the seat, buckling her seat belt and stroking her hair. "It's not like Dad, Mom. He'll be okay."

The waiting room at the trauma unit was cheerful and bright but totally silent. Goldie and Tucker played and read, while Paz paced, Adele swore, and Remy brooded in silence. The moment Adele and Loraine pulled out of the school parking lot, I collected the kids from their classrooms and headed to Bangor, where we had been waiting for hours. Henri was in emergency surgery to repair a ruptured spleen, but we hadn't heard much else.

I needed to see him. To touch him, to verify with my own eyes that he was okay. Because the alternative was too horrific to bear.

A few hours later, Goldie was asleep on my lap, clutching Speedy, while Tucker played video games on my laptop with headphones. I stroked Goldie's hair, studying Tucker's face and noting how the bruise was already fading. I pulled Goldie closer; time did heal. These kids were proof of that. And I could only hope the same would be true for Henri.

Loraine stepped into the room with fresh coffee and news. "Surgery went well. He's in recovery now." She gave us a watery smile. "Doctor says no other organ damage; just a few broken ribs."

Relief washed over me at the hope in Loraine's eyes.

And then, for the first time in hours, Remy spoke. He gently took Loraine's hand and, with tears running down his cheeks, said, "It's my fault, Mom. I'm so sorry."

The room fell silent again.

"What are you talking about?" she asked.

"He wouldn't have been driving if it hadn't been for me." His tears fell one after the other down his face now, and his hands shook. "It's all my fault. I'm the fuck-up. I'm the loser. My own fiancée doesn't want me, and then I almost kill my big brother."

"Stop that right now," Loraine said firmly, pulling him into a hug. "You know I don't allow self-pity. This is not your fault." She pulled back. "But I do want to know what's going on. Start talking."

I made a move to pick up Goldie. "I'll step out," I said, waving for Tucker to follow me, uncomfortable with listening in on their private conversation.

"Stay," Loraine said. "Henri needs you here."

I nodded, unsure of how to respond, and sat again, holding Goldie in my lap. Remy explained. First about his fiancée and then about his drinking, and finally about how he had been neglecting his duties at work.

Adele and Paz were visibly angry, both wearing frowns and clenching their fists as Remy continued, but Loraine listened carefully, holding his hand and letting him speak.

When Remy finished, Paz shot off question after question, quizzing him about the events of the last few days.

"Why was he driving in the first place?"

"Lenny quit because of me. Said he wasn't going to die because I couldn't get my shit together. We were so far behind and had to make our quota for the week, so Henri insisted he'd drive a load down to the mill. He wanted to get some face time with the owners as well, to smooth things over. Said it wasn't a big deal."

"Did he inspect the truck before he left?" Adele asked, her brows furrowed.

"Of course he did. We went through the full process. Richard tracks everything on his computer and signs off before drivers leave camp. Call him."

"Were you on the radio? Did he send word that he was having brake issues?"

"No. I was talking to another driver who was ahead of him at the time. Last I'd heard from Henri, things were going smoothly, and he was headed down Baxter pass."

"He knows how to drive that road," Loraine added. "Been doing it since he was a kid."

"Then the radio lit up that the brakes had failed, and he was jumping out. We sent the other driver out to find him, and I called search and rescue."

Loraine put her arm around his slumping shoulders. "You did the right thing, Remy."

"You saved his life by responding so quickly," Paz added.

Adele, however, was not satisfied by his version of events. "How the fuck did this happen? This is my fault. I'm responsible for the maintenance of that truck."

"Brakes fail all the time, Adele," Paz said softly. "You know that better than anyone. We have protocols and training specifically for this situation because it happens. We've got old trucks on unpaved roads hauling hundreds of thousands of pounds."

"My brakes don't fail," Adele said, her voice steely. She crossed her arms over her chest and glared.

"The trucks come in, what, every three days?" Remy asked. "But this truck didn't. Because of me. We missed its schedule maintenance because we're so behind."

Adele gritted her teeth and lunged at him. "What the fuck, Remy?"

Paz grabbed her shoulders. "Get it together. Whatever happened, we'll figure that out. Henri's okay, and that's the most important thing right now."

"I've got to make some calls," Adele said, already pulling her phone from her pocket. "I'll send someone out to look at the truck and see if we can get it hauled out. I want to inspect these brakes myself, or what's left of them. And you," she eyed Remy with disgust, "don't even talk to me right now."

She paced just outside the waiting room door, phone pressed to her ear. Remy was slumped in his chair again, head hung and looking dejected. I was torn between wanting to hug him and wanting to slap him. The anger was winning at the moment; it welled up within me, and my blood went hot. He had caused so much hurt and suffering, not to mention the ulti-mate cost to the business. But I swallowed back the fury, remembering how heartbroken and lost he was.

Paz padded over to me and opened his mouth to speak, but then the door to the waiting room opened.

The doctor, a friendly woman in her fifties, stepped inside. She looked briefly at the chart in her hands before giving us a warm smile. "He's awake."

Chapter 38
Henri

Everything hurt. From my toenails to my beard hairs, every inch of me ached. And I wasn't sure where I was or what had caused all this pain.

Things were blurry, but I must have been okay since my mother was alternating between crying beside my bed and yelling at me for not being more careful. Thankfully, the doctor had the good sense to give me plenty of pain meds so I could block out some of it.

Paz had been in to see me, and Adele, and my mother never left my side, but there was one person I was aching for, one person I wished could be here too.

I sat up and sipped from the water on the bedside tray. Moving hurt like a motherfucker, but I was lucky. Just a few broken ribs and a ruptured spleen. I probably looked like shit, but I'd recover.

"Does Alice know?" I asked, steeling myself for her answer.

"Of course. She was here for the entire first day, but I sent her home with the kids because the doctors kept your visitors to a minimum that first day after your surgery. She stops in with supplies and food every day. And she's being very kind to Remy. He hasn't left the waiting room since Friday."

I got a surge of energy at the thought of her being nearby. "Is she here? Can I see her?"

My mom grinned and raised an eyebrow. "Of course. She's in love with you, Henri. That much is obvious. So you better not fuck it up. She's one in a million."

"I know, Mom."

"I mean it. She and those kids, you'd be stupid not to hold on to them."

"I plan on it." I cleared my throat. "Can you get her, please? And give us some privacy?"

"Fine, fine." She gathered up her knitting and her purse and tsked all the way to the door. I swore she was more concerned with my relationship with Alice than my injuries.

When footsteps sounded outside the door, I wished I'd at least taken a minute to look in a mirror. The second she stepped across the threshold, my breath caught. Even in the fluorescent hospital lighting, she was beautiful.

"Henri." Tears were running down her cheeks as she perched on the edge of the bed and squeezed my hand gently. "I don't want to hurt you, but I want to hug the shit out of you."

I laughed. "Just be careful." I beckoned her with my arms outstretched. "Got a couple broken ribs."

More tears fell, and she scooted closer, sitting next to my hip. "I'm sorry, Henri. I'm sorry I didn't say anything before you left. I wanted to."

I wiped a tear from her cheek. "I should have been clear from the start. In that truck, I had to make a split-second decision. And when I did it, all I thought about was you. Getting back to you and telling you all the things I've been holding in."

"Like what?"

I kissed her hand. "Like how I'm batshit crazy, head over heels in love with you."

She leaned forward and pressed her lips to mine. "The feeling's mutual. We've got a lot to talk about, but I'm not leaving this hospital room until you know this: You're mine. I'm yours. It's real. End of story."

"I like it." I smiled. "It may be a while before I can chop wood for you again, though."

She shifted closer to me on the bed, a hand resting delicately on my arm. "Don't worry. My sexy lumberjack neighbor taught me how to do it myself."

She kissed me again, the feel of her lips on mine making my heart soar. Even broken and bruised, just having her close made me feel like the luckiest man on the planet. "I think we should move in together," I said into her hair, soaking in the familiar scent. "And get married. And adopt Goldie and Tucker."

She pulled away, eyes teary. "Whoa there, Brawny. That's probably the painkillers talking. Slow it down. "

"Nope. I'm not slowing down. I want you forever."

One tear crested her lower lashes, followed by another and another, until she stopped trying to fight them and let them spill down her cheeks.

I held her hand, knowing I had to do this right. "I'm a grumpy bastard who loves the forest, silence, and you, Alice Watson. I'm not easy to live with, but I won't let you go. You are too beautiful and smart and mouthy for your own damn good, but I love the shit out of you."

"I love the shit out of you too."

I growled through the pain, pulling her closer and kissing her with everything I had. I explored her with my lips and my hands, mapping all the familiar curves I'd missed. It had only been a few days, but I was starved for her touch.

She pulled away, gently patting my chest. "Before this goes

beyond PG, there are two little people outside who are desperate to see you."

I sucked in a breath. "Really?"

"Oh yes. Goldie has made about eighty-six drawings for you. We could probably wallpaper this room with them. But the doctors said you can't have too many visitors at once."

"I don't care," I argued, shaking my head. "Let them in."

"I figured you'd say that."

She shuffled across the room and cracked the door open, and soon Tucker and Goldie were pushing their way inside.

"Henri," Goldie screamed, throwing herself onto my bed. I winced but wrapped my arms around her tiny body. "I missed you," she cried. "We were so scared."

I kissed the top of her head. "I'm sorry."

"You have to promise never to do this again," she scolded, giving me the most adorable admonishing look.

"I promise." I told her, biting back a smile.

"Here." She plopped her stuffed sloth next to me. "I brought Speedy so you have someone to snuggle with while you get better."

I cupped her sweet face. "Goldilocks, you are the best girl in the world. Do you know that?"

She shrugged. "Just promise you'll get better."

"I will. I'll be better really soon."

"We were scared, Tucker and me. He said you could have died, and you could have broken all your bones."

I smiled at her and turned to Tucker, who looked sheepish. "It's okay to have questions," I said. "And I can tell you all about what happened to me later. But right now, I want to hear about you. Do you like the bunk beds at Alice's house?"

"We love them! And I use the new backpack you got me every day."

She chatted happily for a while, showing me some of her

drawings and even getting Tucker to talk a little. They were happy with Alice, and I prayed they would get to stay.

Because I loved Alice, and I was growing to love these kids too. Before Alice, I'd grown accustomed to the numbness that accompanied my isolation, but now my feelings had returned full force, and I wasn't going to screw it up.

I'd survived. And now it was time to really start living. Just as soon as I could get my ass out of his hospital room.

Chapter 39
Henri

I had just closed my eyes, finally getting comfortable in my recliner, when Heathcliff ran to the door and barked. Rochester, of course, followed suit, and the two of them fed off each other, barking up a storm. Adele had texted a few minutes ago. She needed to meet with all of us as soon as possible, so she and my brothers were on their way over. I had been discharged from the hospital with strict orders to rest, and I'd been stuck at home most of the week, taking phone calls between sleeping and eating all the amazing meals Alice was force-feeding me.

I hated being laid up. I hated not being in the office, or better yet, in the woods, during such a critical time for our business. Paz was stepping up, and Richard was running things at camp, but I would have to return soon. Too many people depended on me.

Paz let himself in, with Remy right behind him. He had been staying at Mom's and was attending Alcoholics Anonymous meetings every day. He still looked like shit, though. I wanted so badly to help, but he had pushed us all away, revealing very little and spending all his time apologizing or doing chores around Mom's house. He came over every afternoon and took my dogs out, throwing sticks for them for hours. But he never stuck around after, and he certainly never opened up.

They raided my fridge, then sat on the couch, talking about yesterday's Patriots game while I kept my eyes closed and ignored them, waiting for Adele.

She arrived shortly after, still wearing coveralls streaked with grease and dirt. Her ponytail was sagging to one side, and she looked pale and exhausted.

"What's going on?" Paz asked, a look of concern crossing his face at her appearance.

She paced for a moment, tugging at her ponytail and looking between us. "Dad," she finally said, pausing and turning to look at us. "Something went wrong. With the brakes and—"

Paz interrupted. "We've been over this. The occupational safety inspector said it was weather and road conditions."

Adele's face morphed from exhaustion to anger. Her eyes narrowed, and her jaw clenched. "No shit, Paz. You wouldn't even know how to read that report. I explained it to you in the first place." She huffed and put her hands on her hips.

"Listen to me. Dad knew his trucks and he knew the roads. There was a reason he got off the main road. He didn't want to go down the pass. It was too steep and too wet, so he tried to go around." A tear rolled down her cheek, and she took a deep breath.

Before she could go on, Remy stood and put an arm around her shoulders. "It's not your fault," he said gently. "He went off the main road, and the mud and rain became too much. Those old roads aren't maintained anymore."

She pulled away. "No. Dad could sense that something was

wrong with the brakes. That's why he went around the pass. Maybe he felt brake fade, I don't know. But he knew something was wrong."

"He didn't radio in any brake issues," Paz argued.

She took a step back and paused for a moment, wiping the tears from her face. "I had his truck hauled into the shop. I took it apart yesterday and worked on it all night."

I sat up in my chair, wincing as my broken ribs burned. "What? We put it in the scrap yard for a reason, Adele. It's too much for you." This was why we had begged her to let it go. Dad made a bad call that night. The weather didn't cooperate, and he may have been tired. She would torture herself forever, and none of this was her fault.

"It's not too much. You don't get to tell me what I can handle, Henri. After what happened to you, I couldn't take any chances. Something isn't right."

She walked to the door, where she had dropped her coat and reached into her backpack. Then she pulled out a small metal mechanism the size of a water bottle.

"What's that?" Paz asked.

She handed it to him. He lifted and lowered his hand a few times, as if weighing the device, and inspected it.

"That's an automatic slack adjuster. I took it off one of the rear right brakes on the truck Henri was driving." She pointed to faint scratches in a circular pattern around the top bolt. "See those? They're from manual adjustment, which by law, is illegal."

Paz passed the slack adjuster to Remy. "I'm not following."

"I removed them from every other brake. They were all pristine. Only one was tampered with."

"Keep explaining," Remy said, studying it in his hands.

"The other brakes would have worked properly, adjusting

the brake slack and applying the brakes evenly. Except this one." She pointed at the slack adjuster in question.

"So you've got an unstable truck on the road. One that's more likely to roll, skid, or flip. But the brake system won't register an issue because everything looks fine on the surface. When the state inspectors checked, they looked good. The drums were fine, and the fluid levels were appropriate."

"It's not possible," I murmured. *Right?* The likelihood of that happening was almost zero. No. I shook my head. She was grieving and grasping. That was it. We had put this behind us. We were moving on. I was getting up every day to continue Dad's legacy. This wasn't possible.

Then Adele produced something similar. "This was from Dad's truck. See those same scratches?" She pointed to marks of a similar size and in the same location as the previous one. "Scratches like this happen when you use a wrench on these. We calibrate using a computer system and sophisticated tools. Only an idiot would take a wrench to a delicate mechanism like this."

"What are you trying to say?" Paz insisted.

"These weren't accidents. Someone messed with the trucks."

My lungs seized. We ran an ethical, fair business and treated our employees well. Messing with brakes got people killed, or close to it. So who would do something like that? It didn't make sense.

"You can't be serious," Paz argued. "Are we going to just take this slack adjuster to the police station and expect them to be able to pinpoint the person who may have tampered with them? How would that work?"

"I don't give a shit about the police. They're too useless to do anything. Listen to me," Adele pleaded, walking the length of the room again. "Dad's death was not an accident. Someone set him up, knowing the odds of something going wrong. They only wanted to make it look like an accident."

Remy looked confused, holding the slack adjuster in his hands. "And someone did that to Henri too?"

She nodded. "Looks like it."

"Probably those Hebert fuckers," Paz shouted, joining Adele in pacing around my living room.

Remy agreed. "I wouldn't put it past them. Everyone loved Dad. The Heberts are the only people who've ever had issue with him. Because he refused to sell to them all those years ago."

"Guys," I cautioned, the pounding in my head coupled with my exhaustion making me woozy. "We have to think carefully about all of this. We can't throw around accusations and half-baked theories."

Adele stopped in front of me. "We have to do something."

"And we will. First, we stop and think." I ran my hands through my hair as my mind raced. "We need to gather the evidence and document everything carefully. In the meantime, Adele, you need to go up north to check every truck. No truck leaves camp until it's been inspected by Adele herself or someone she trusts."

She nodded.

"I'll go with her," Remy said. "I can help."

"Good." I nodded. Remy could use the work to keep himself busy. "Paz and I will review security footage and maintenance records."

I stood, every cell in my body screaming in pain. I waved my siblings in and pulled them into a giant hug.

"Those are our trucks on our roads, and they're being driven by our people. We can't take any chances. No one dies on our watch," I vowed.

After they left, I slumped in my desk chair, begging my dad

for help. A sign, a clue, anything to help me make sense of this mess and keep my family and employees safe.

I looked down at the jumble of papers. I hadn't made my progress, especially since I'd been in the hospital. I studied the pages again, reading the broken French scribbled in the margins. *Sinistre Nord*. Where had I seen that before? What the hell was Dad trying to tell me?

I leaned back and thought about Alice and the kids, about the future I wanted with them, a future that was bright and happy and, most of all, safe. It was time to step up and figure this out once and for all.

So I picked up the phone. "Mom," I said after she answered. "My French is rusty. Sinistre," I said, my accent shitty after years without practice. "Means evil, ominous, that sort of thing, right?"

She sighed deeply. Paz was the only one of us who regularly still spoke French, and I knew it plagued her that we had let so much of our heritage decline. "Yes. But it can also be used as a noun to mean a disaster, an incident, or a blaze."

"Like a fire?"

"Uh-huh. Like a bad thing that happened. That sort of thing."

I sat there, my mouth open, flipping through the old maps Dad had insisted on keeping, until I found one from the 1970s. There were notes scribbled everywhere, and the boundaries and roads were different. I took a moment to orient myself and stared.

Past the northern corner of our land, the area outside the boundaries of the logging claims near the Canadian border, there was a large circle in which someone had scrawled *incendie de forêt 1973*. The fire. The Northern Forest Fire.

There were no roads up there. Not anymore. But there

used to be. I flipped through the maps, looking for any signs of work, development, or outposts in that area, but found nothing.

I looked up at the sky. "Thanks Dad," I grumbled. It wasn't much, but it was a start. There had to be something I was missing. And I wasn't giving up until I figured it out.

Chapter 40
Alice

After recuperating at home for a week, Henri was getting back on his feet just in time for Thanksgiving. We packed up the kids and the dogs and headed to Loraine's house, where the four of us, Paz, Remy, Adele, Becca, Kali, Dylan, and Dylan's little sister Hazel, all crowded around the table. The relaxed atmosphere was a far cry from the Thanksgivings of my past.

The original thirty-day emergency custody order was set to expire in a week, and I had already applied for temporary guardianship of Tucker and Goldie. I had also started the licensing process to become a foster parent in hopes that it would help with the custody ruling. I now knew in my bones that I wanted to adopt them. The past few weeks had only confirmed what I already knew. I loved them. And I would fight like hell for the privilege of becoming their mom.

It had not been easy. We were all adjusting, and the future was filled with uncertainty. I was getting the hang of being a guardian, and I loved them more every day.

And I wasn't the only one. The entire Gagnon family had

embraced Tucker and Goldie. Loraine spoiled them rotten and watched them anytime I asked, and Adele welcomed Tucker into her shop, where she let him play with engines and all sorts of power tools. And even the normally serious Paz kept a secret sugar stash for Goldie in his office.

Unsurprisingly, Loraine didn't let me lift a finger in the kitchen. Instead, I sat next to Henri and watched as Tucker helped Goldie build a Lego set that Paz just happened to have in his car. Despite his assurances that his ribs were healed, I was still afraid to hurt Henri. He was lucky to be alive. His body had sustained a lot of trauma. I sat next to him, gingerly holding his hand, but he was having none of it. Instead, he wrapped an arm around me and pulled me so close I was almost in his lap.

I laid my head on his chest and let his heartbeat soothe me. We had a long road ahead of us. His world had been turned upside down by his accident and revelations about his father's death. The entire Gagnon Lumber team was working nonstop to check and recheck every piece of equipment, and they were cooperating with law enforcement and state regulators. Henri had vowed that there would never be another accident on his watch. I worried that the weight of this pressure would keep him from recovering. I worried it would swallow him whole.

I sat as he and his siblings talked and made plans. Adele ranted while Paz paced. Henri had filled me in on how his sister struggled with the weight of her recent discovery. He had also assured me that he wasn't in danger. That they were working with the authorities to reopen the investigation into his father's death.

It still scared the hell out of me. I wanted Henri happy and safe and whole. I wanted to wrap him up in my arms and keep him safe forever.

But I closed my eyes and knew in my bones that things

would be okay. Maybe it was just my naïve optimism, but I knew that Henri and I could face these challenges together. I would be by his side through it all.

And so we feasted and laughed for hours and ate our weight in pie. I was happy to learn that Mainers made an exception on Thanksgiving, welcoming pumpkin and apple to the table along with the usual blueberry. The kids played and ran around with the dogs in the freezing cold. Adele showed Tucker photos of engines on her phone and promised him a set of wrenches for Christmas, while Goldie drew an elaborate family portrait with the new set of crayons Loraine had bought her.

After the dishes had been dealt with and some of the guests had left, I found myself curled up with Henri again while we chatted with Paz. Remy had already left for the evening. He had been lying low, working with Henri to help get things back on track. The family didn't say much else about it, but I felt for him. Remy carried so much weight on his shoulders, and I hated that he was pulling away.

The kids were asleep on the couch, Goldie's head on my lap. It had been a long day, but one filled with fun and family and laughter.

"Have you decided?" Henri asked the same question he'd asked me each day since we were reunited in the hospital. He couldn't wait for the kids and me to move in with him. His house was much bigger than the little cabin I shared with Tucker and Goldie now and had plenty of room for toys and books and privacy for adult time.

The cabin *was* getting crowded, and I missed waking up next to Henri every day. But the kids were barely settled, and I didn't want to uproot them or confuse them. Not to mention the delicacy of the legal process to become their guardian.

And Henri was up to his eyeballs with the crisis at work.

The last thing he needed was us invading his space and distracting him from getting to the bottom of his father's death and saving the family business.

I nuzzled against him. "You know I want to, but I should wait until we get the temporary guardianship decision, at the very least. I'm walking a tightrope right now and don't want to do anything that could delay the process."

He murmured an "okay." He understood. We'd had the same conversation several times, but I couldn't blame him for being frustrated.

"And you have so much going on..."

He shifted, pulling me closer. "I do. But I'm not letting that get in the way of what's important. What if"—he tucked my hair behind my ear and kissed my temple—"I proposed? How about that? Then we can start being a family now."

My heart leaped. But it was too soon. We couldn't. Maybe someday...My inner optimist started running wild with the possibilities.

I chided him. "Henri Gagnon, stop that right now. Do not upstage your mother's Thanksgiving feast."

He waggled his eyebrows. "She wouldn't mind."

I narrowed my eyes and poked him in the chest with one finger. "Don't even think about it."

"Fine." He nuzzled my neck. "I have a better plan anyway. But I will ask, and soon. So you better be ready to say yes."

Daphne Elliot

Want more Henri & Alice?

Scan below to download the bonus epilogue
Warning: it will make you laugh, cry and swoon!

Need more Lumberjacks in your life?
The next book in the series, Wood You Marry Me, is coming
April 20, 2023.
Preorder available on Amazon.

Also by Daphne Elliot

HAVENPORT

The Quinn Brothers Series

Trusting You

Finding You

Keeping You

The Rossi Family Series

Resisting You

Holding You

Embracing You

Novellas

Rediscovering Us

Dad Bod Bartender

A Touch of Wrath

LOVEWELL

The Lovewell Lumberjacks Series

Wood You Be Mine?

Wood You Marry Me?

Wood You Rather

Wood Riddance

Acknowledgments

Thank you for taking this trip to Lovewell with me! This book would not have been possible without the help of so many talented and dedicated people. I can't believe this is my tenth book in two years.

This book would not exist without Erica Connors. Thank you for being my friend, my cheerleader, and the best PA ever. You read every single word I write, constantly giving feedback and pushing me to do better. I appreciate your honesty and support. We have cried and laughed and yelled together over the past two years and I am a better person and writer because of you.

My legal sister Brittanee Nicole, thank you for your love and support throughout this process. You are one of the busiest, yet most positive people I have had the pleasure of knowing. Your hustle is legendary and I'm rooting for you every single day.

To my author squad, Jenni Bara, Elyse Kelly, A.J. Ranney, and Swati M.H., I love you all and am so lucky to have met you. This can be such a lonely journey, but your friendship is such a gift.

To my beta readers, Amaryllis, Amy, Hayley and Jenni, thank you all for helping me work through Alice & Henri's journey and giving me helpful notes.

Amaryllis, Cady, Meagan, Randi, and Paige, thank you for

your love, support, and constant cheerleading. I am so lucky to have you on my team.

Sarah Sentz, thank you for the gorgeous cover.

Beth, thank you for your thorough editing. I am amazed by your patience, professionalism, and kindness. I'm sorry I'm such a lazy writer and never put my quotation marks in the right place.

Jane, thank you for the gorgeous photos. Taking photos of shirtless men is a hard job, and I'm grateful you do it.

Cody and Jordan, thank you for the amazing cover photo. You are beautiful people, inside and out, and I am honored to have you on my book.

Thank you to my mother, who always pushed me to do my best and believed in me even when I did not. I am the kind of person who decides to write books in my nonexistent free time because of you.

Thank you to my family for being hilarious and loving and silly.

And finally, thank you to my patient and devastatingly handsome husband. You are my original Alpha Roll.

About the Author

In High School, Daphne Elliot was voted "most likely to become a romance novelist." After spending the last decade as a corporate lawyer, she has finally embraced her destiny. Her steamy novels are filled with flirty banter, sexy hijinks, and lots and lots of heart.

Daphne is a coffee-drinking, hot-sauce loving introvert who spends her free time gardening and practicing yoga. She lives in Massachusetts with her husband, two kids, two dogs, two fish, and twelve backyard chickens.

Find Daphne At:

daphneelliotauthor@gmail.com

Stay in touch with Daphne:
Subscribe to Daphne's Newsletter
Join Daphne's Reader Group
Follow Daphne on TikTok
Like Daphne on Facebook
Follow Daphne on Instagram
Hang with Daphne on GoodReads
Follow Daphne on Amazon

Printed in Great Britain
by Amazon

18704412R00163